Ci

Cinnamon Girl

Lawrence Kessenich

To Michael
you lived through this time,
and I hope you enjoy
my take on it.)
Thanks for your support!

Laurence

NORTH STAR PRESS OF ST. CLOUD, INC.
St. Cloud, Minnesota

Published by
North Star Press of St. Cloud, Inc
PO Box 451
St. Cloud, MN 56302
www.northstarpress.com

*For my friends from UWM and UW in the late '60s,
especially Chris, Tom, Carmen, Peter, Kathy, Paulette, Mike, and Fran.
We always hoped we would change the world for the better,
and in some big and small ways, we have.*

~ 1 ~

TELEVISION LIGHTS FLARED on behind the police line, blinding us. For a few seconds, it was eerily quiet. I heard a siren in the distance. Then they charged.

Time seemed to stand still. I saw their clubs waving over their heads, but in the penumbra of TV lights it all seemed unreal, like a war movie in slow motion with the sound track cut out.

Then one of the TV riggers stumbled and fell, dousing his lights, and I snapped back to reality. It was only thirty or forty policemen against 200 or so of us, but we were bareheaded and wearing jeans and sneakers and they had helmets and billy clubs and jackboots, and they meant business. We all realized simultaneously what was happening. Somebody yelled, "Let's get the hell out of here!" and everybody ran for it.

A couple of people fell, and for all I know got trampled, if not by their brothers and sisters, then by the cops. Some of the cops were yelling and had their clubs up high, ready to bring them down—happily—on a hippie head. Someone near me was foolish enough to taunt them, but I just kept running.

I headed for the bluff that overlooked Lake Michigan, where the underbrush was thick around the trees. I reached the verge as a smaller guy slipped through an opening in the brush just ahead of me. We crashed down the hillside together, barely keeping our feet, branches whipping our face. At the bottom of the hill, we emerged from the vegetation at a gallop and, exhilarated by the chase, continued through the lit park and across Lincoln Drive and out onto the broad beach, collapsing on the damp sand at the water's edge.

As we lay there on our backs, panting, unable to speak, I gave my confederate a closer inspection. He was lean and wiry and wore a black t-shirt and black jeans. He had a high forehead and a shock of black hair, pulled back in a ponytail, a roman nose, and a thick goatee. His deep-set brown eyes brimmed with mirth, even as he struggled to get his breath. Laugh lines etched their corners, although he was clearly no older than I was.

When he'd caught his breath, laughter overtook him, the goatee jumping as he howled into the darkness. I stroked the anemic blonde hair on my own chin and smiled.

"Goddam cops," he finally said. "When it comes down to it, you just can't argue with 'em."

He turned on his side and extended his hand.

"Tony Russo," he said.

"John Meyer," I replied.

We shook, joining palms and grasping the heels of one another's hands.

"Most people just call me Russo," he added, running his fingernails through his scalp, maybe combing out sand.

"Want to smoke a 'j'?" he asked. He dug into his jeans pocket and pulled out a crushed cigarette pack.

I looked around warily, and then felt embarrassed by my caution.

"Why not," I said. "The cops are all busy cleaning up the park."

Tony extracted a joint from the pack, but it was broken in two places.

"Shit, this is no good," he said. "Let's get a few hits off of these pieces. Then we'll go back to my place and do up a decent one."

"You live nearby?"

"Brady Street. Above Headroom."

"Is that your shop?"

"Nah. I couldn't run a business if I tried."

He struck a match and lit a piece of the joint, taking a long, deep hit as he did. He handed the joint to me, and I took a good hit myself. It was smooth and sweet.

"Nice stuff," I croaked, holding in the smoke.

"Yaaaah," said Tony, breathing out luxuriously, like the Cheshire Cat in *Alice in Wonderland* with his hookah. "I got it from my friend Jimmy. He knows some South American dudes who get the stuff from home."

The piece was nearly burned up after two hits. Tony told me to toss it or eat it. I popped in into my mouth, putting out the live coal with saliva, and swallowed it. Tony was already lighting the second piece.

"You have roommates on Brady?" I asked.

He smiled but couldn't answer right away, because he was holding in a hit. He held out the piece of joint to me. I took another hit, too, drawing some of the sweet smoke up my nostrils. Tony exhaled and laughed.

"You might say I have roommates," he said. "A wife and a kid."

I blew out my hit. "No shit? A wife and a kid already?"

"Claire and I have been married almost two years, now, and Jonah's six months old."

The dope was beginning to make me feel everything in an exaggerated way. My chest ballooned with every breath of fresh lake air. My eyes were wide, taking in the sparkling lights across the bay in South Milwaukee. The sound of lapping waves was captivating.

"It freaks me out, sometimes," said Tony. "Hey, man, watch yourself."

I looked down at my hand, which seemed as if it was detached from my body. Then I felt the heat of the coal on my fingertips.

"You want to eat it?" I said.

"Pop it into my mouth."

I did as he asked. It sizzled on his tongue. He chewed it up as he set about lighting the last piece of the joint.

"You meet Claire at UWM?"

"Uh-huh. You go there, too?"

"I'm an education major . . . I guess."

"Hey, me, too. But you don't sound too sure about it."

"Are *you* sure?"

"I guess not. Seems right for now, though."

"How about Claire?"

"Pre-med."

"That's ambitious."

Tony nodded agreement as he toked on the freshly lit joint, and then handed it to me. I sucked in a small hit, then snorted a few more to fill my head with the lovely aroma. I was getting good and stoned. I handed it back to Tony.

"Let's split," he said.

We started walking along the beach, not saying much, just enjoying our buzz with the soft breath of a breeze off the lake and the whoosh of cars on Lincoln Drive. It was perfectly clear, stars shining through the glow of city lights. Out on the horizon, where the sky darkened above the water, stars massed like fireflies. We walked right by the Brady Street footbridge, which would have taken us more directly to Tony's apartment, and continued on past the floodlit marina, past the old Coast Guard station with its tall white mast, devoid of flag for the night, past the duck pond lined with willows swaying sensuously.

We followed Lincoln Drive as it curved up toward downtown, then turned onto Prospect Avenue and headed back toward Brady Street. Prospect was a busy street lined with shops, apartment buildings, gas stations, and the occasional private home. It followed the bluff above the lake, but the roar of traffic shattered our meditative mood.

"That was nice stuff, Tony. Thanks for getting me high."

"Not bad, is it? It's a perfect night for it, too. I could get used to this kind of weather."

We passed an old church with a half-timbered parish house attached to it. On the wall beside the house's entrance was a carefully lettered wooden sign that said "DRAFT COUNSELING CENTER." We noticed it simultaneously.

"Bummer," said Tony.

We walked in silence for a minute under the garish yellow glow of the streetlights. Tony tugged his beard thoughtfully.

"What would you do if they drafted you?" he finally asked.

"God, I don't know. There's no way I'd join the army with that dumb-ass war going on, and I sure couldn't deal with prison, so I guess I'd have to go to Canada. But that scares the shit out of me, too, running off someplace where I don't know anybody, not being able to come back and see my family. I can't see faking insanity or pretending to be a conscientious objector, the way some guys do—there are wars I'd fight in. What about you?"

"Pretty much the same. I'd try hiding out in this country before I'd run off to Canada—maybe somewhere out West. There's a lot of open space out there. Like the song says, 'Any way you look at it, you lose.'"

A pall hung over us for the next few blocks. Then we turned onto Brady Street and walked silently past 1812 Overture Records, Age of Man, The Silver Shop, B.J.'s Antiques and other storefront businesses until we came to the Headroom head shop below Tony's apartment. We peered in the window at paraphernalia, ranging from tiny alligator roach clips on beaded leather thongs to a huge, freestanding glass bong. Our mood brightened immediately.

"Maybe you should get to know this guy, Tony."

"I should. Maybe he'd give me that bong for my birthday."

He unlocked the electric pink door next to the storefront and we entered a dark stairwell.

"The light's busted, so watch your step."

My moods are vulnerable to my environment, especially when I'm high, so I felt like my whole world had gone dark as we climbed the steep steps. I kept a hand on the wall, which was covered with peeling paint. At the top, Tony slipped his key into the door, and while I wondered how he managed to find the keyhole, he jiggled it until it turned, then pushed open the door.

Maybe it was just a function of standing out in the narrow, dark stair, looking into the bright expanse of the room, but the place seemed like a shining refuge in an ominous realm. In truth, it wasn't all that bright, just a couple of lamps casting pools of yellow warmth on the shabby rug and furniture. In the far pool was a ratty green couch with a woman perched on its arm, her long bare legs crossed. She wore a short, lacey white dress, and a magazine rested on her lap. She held a cigarette in her hand and the smoke from it caught the light of a standing lamp beside her, obscuring her face. She looked like a *Vogue* magazine version of an impatient bride waiting for her groom.

As we entered, she swung her head toward us, her long, straight, strawberry blonde hair sweeping away the smoke to reveal a lovely, pale face with green eyes and a few freckles sprinkled like cinnamon across her nose.

"What are you doing home so soon?" Tony asked her.

"The shower was cancelled at the last minute," she replied. "Rosie got sick. So Katie and I just sat around here and drank beers."

"Bummer. How's Jonah?"

"Fast asleep, thank God."

"Oh, hey," said Tony, "this is John. We met at the park. John, Claire."

She focused those green eyes on me. They caught the light and glowed like cat's eyes.

"Hi," I managed to croak, my throat suddenly dry. I swallowed to wet it. "Tony and I just happened to choose the same hill to run down. We almost got our heads bashed.

"Bashed?" she said, concern in her voice. "Did it get that bad?"

"We didn't let it. We all scattered like leaves to the wind, huh, Tony?"

He was already reaching into a small rosewood box on the mantel for more weed.

"It wasn't worth getting our heads busted for that pissy little park. This'll blow over, and we'll be sitting at the fountain smoking joints in no time."

He sat down on the couch, spread out some of the marijuana on an album cover and began to clean it, picking out seeds and stems. I just stood there staring at Claire, who had finished her cigarette and was stubbing it out in a big green glass ashtray on the sofa. She leaned over and started rummaging around in her fringed leather purse on the floor.

"Hey," Tony said to me, "sit down and make yourself at home, will you. You're making me nervous."

Claire sat back up, a fresh cigarette and a pack of matches in her hand.

"Do you want a beer?" she asked.

"Sounds good."

"Tony?"

"Absolutely."

She lit her cigarette before getting up. As she held the match to it, I noted the contrast between her delicate wrist and her full breasts, revealed by the scooped neck of dress. It was an extraordinarily sexy combination. When she rose and went toward the kitchen, I had to stop myself from following her.

"Hey," Tony said to me, "if you're not going to sit down, why don't you put on an album. Anything you want."

"I was listening to Neil Young," called Claire from the kitchen. She pronounced it "Yun." "Would you mind playing 'Cinnamon Girl' once more?"

"Happy to," I called back.

I went to the stereo, which sat beneath a screenless window that looked out onto Brady Street. In an apartment across the way, illuminated by a blacklight, a strobe flashed in time to a Rolling Stones tune. I fixed on the throbbing light and sound, completely spacing out for a few minutes.

"Hey, man," said Tony, "are you going to turn that thing on, or what?"

"Huh? Oh, ya. Sure."

I found "Cinnamon Girl" on the record label, clicked on the turntable and poised the needle over the cut. Then I clicked the arm release and watched the arm descend, ever so slowly, it seemed, toward the record. Just as the song began, I turned to see Claire re-enter the room, pale as an angel, a can of Old Style beer in each hand.

"I want to live with a cinnamon girl," Neil Young sang, "I could be happy for the rest of my life with a cinnamon girl."

Claire handed my beer to me and smiled, then set Tony's on an end table and went back out to the kitchen for her own.

I sat on the floor, across from Tony, who had rolled several thin joints. He lit up the first one and passed it to me. I took a long, languid hit. When Claire came back into the room, I handed it to her, my fingertips grazing hers as I did. She took a couple quick hits and announced that she was going to change her clothes. Tony suggested that she take the joint along, which she was happy to do. He handed me another and put a match to it.

"You live on the East Side?" he asked as I toked on the fresh joint.

I held up a finger to indicate it would take me a moment to answer, and passed him the joint. Then I blew out the smoke, feeling the gentle collapse of my lungs as I did.

"I still live with my folks up in Whitefish Bay. It's not ideal, but it's free, and they mostly leave me alone."

"I can dig it."

"You both work?"

"Claire's an aide at a nursing home near UWM and I work at the docks—when they'll take me, that is. You've got to go down there every morning, take a number, and wait around to see if they call it, unless they're so busy that everybody works. The longer you work there, the lower your number gets, because guys are always quitting, but you've got to go every morning."

"Must be tough work."

"It's either really tough or no work at all. And it's all day, too, so I have to take night classes. Sometimes I think I'm crazy to try to—"

A pair of motorcycles roared by on the street below, drowning out his words.

"—but the money is so damn good, I hate to give it up, especially with the kid."

We smoked in silence for a few minutes. Neil Young was singing about a man needing a maid. Claire came back into the room wearing a bright red tube top that outlined her breasts and ragged, cut-off jeans that displayed her slim, tanned legs. Her feet were bare. I paused in mid-hit, my eyes wide. The jeans were cut off so high that the white pockets peeked out below. Her long, golden hair was pulled forward over her right shoulder. She sat down beside me on the floor, smelling of sweat and herbal shampoo. I felt the vibrations from Neil Young's guitar go right into my chest and down through my body.

"Should I light another 'j'?" asked Tony.

"Not for me," I said. "I'm buzzed."

"Claire?"

"Not right now."

We sipped our beers for a while without speaking. The album ended, and there was a break in the traffic below, so, for moment, it was almost quiet. Then a sudden breeze sprung up, rattling the Venetian blinds, and the traffic noise resumed.

"You live around here?" asked Claire.

"In Whitefish Bay, with my folks. But I work part-time at Siegel's Liquor Store, over on Oakland, delivering booze and stocking shelves. It doesn't pay much, but the hours are flexible, so it's good for school. I hear you work at a nursing home."

She was pulling another cigarette from her pack of Kool 100's.

"Colonial Manor—just up the hill from Siegel's, as a matter of fact."

"I've noticed that place. Do you like it?"

She lit her cigarette, shook out the match, and tossed it into the green ashtray, which sat on the floor in front of her.

"It's a living," she said.

Tony took a cigarette for himself and offered the pack to me. I didn't smoke much, but it seemed like the thing to do at the moment, kind of like Indians passing the pipe to a new friend. I took one. Tony struck a match and lit mine before lighting his own.

"I can't imagine working in a nursing home," I said. "You must have to deal with a lot of disgusting stuff. I admire you."

"I'm not sure I can deal with it, either."

"You should see her when she gets home from work sometimes," said Tony. "She's so wasted and bummed out she can hardly move."

"But at least you're trying," I said. "That's more than I could do."

Just then, the doorbell rang. In my stoned condition, it took me a moment to comprehend what the sound was.

"Who could that be?" Claire asked Tony.

"Who else? Kolvacik. He must have had to take Mina home early tonight—probably to avoid getting his legs broken by her old man."

Tony went to the window, leaned out, and called down, "Kolvacik, you thoughtless slob, go away. We're in bed."

"So what?" Kolvacik called back. "We'll just make it a threesome, like always."

Claire smiled at me and took a sip of beer.

"In your dreams, Kolvacik," Tony shot back.

"Come on, Russo, let me in. I promise to keep my hands off Claire, okay?"

Claire laughed.

"Come on, Tony," she said, "let him in before he wakes up Mrs. Rosetti. She'll call the landlord again."

Tony turned back to us.

"Ah, she's deaf as a post," he said. "She only calls if she *sees* something she doesn't like. But I'll let him in."

He put his head out the window again.

"Sit tight, Kolvacik. I'll be right down."

He went out the door to the stairwell, leaving it open behind him.

"Tim's an old friend of Tony's," said Claire. "They've known each other since they were kids—and that's just about how old they act, sometimes. Tim is fun, though. You'll like him."

"Holy shit," Tony exclaimed from the bottom of the stairs. "What the hell is that thing?"

"It's a conga drum, dipshit," said Kolvacik. "Imported from Darkest Africa."

"What do you plan to do with it?"

"Eat breakfast off of it, what else? Come on, Tony, take the chain off, will ya. You're stoned, aren't you?"

"Me? Nah."

"Well, in that case, I've got an even better surprise for you."

Kolvacik's voice dropped to such a quiet level we couldn't understand what he was saying.

Then Tony said, "Well, why didn't you say so? You can throw that ugly drum into the dumpster next door, but bring that shit up here."

"No way," said Kolvacik, as they started up the stairs. "Love my hash, love my drum. This stuff's going to help us make beautiful music together."

My first impression of Kolvacik as he came through the door was that he wasn't much taller than the drum he carried in front of him, chest high. Thin, short legs in jeans appeared below it, and a small head with wild, frizzy black hair and dark, beady eyes peered over the top. The drum was made of dark wood carved with African figures and had an animal skin with the fur still on it stretched over the top. Kolvacik plopped it down on the carpet and gave it a few loud, quick raps.

"Remember, kemosabe," he intoned, "I'm leaving the safari at Nairobi."

Then he looked at me.

"Who the hell are you? Whoever you are, if you're thinking about getting into Claire's pants, forget it. She's already promised if she ever has an affair, it'll be with me. Right Claire-bear?"

I blushed, but Claire just laughed. "Right, Tim," she said.

Tony closed the door and shook a finger at Kolvacik.

"You touch my woman and I'll cut you up in little pieces and bury you inside that ugly drum, you hear me, boy?"

Kolvacik put on a look of horrified innocence.

"But, Tony, baby, I thought we were friends. Friends share and share alike, right? Come on . . ."

"You 'come on' enough for both of us," said Tony, then turned to me. "John, this is Tim Kolvacik—a certified maniac, in case you haven't noticed. Tim, John Meyer. We met at the demonstration tonight."

"Oh, man," said Kolvacik, "don't tell me you actually fought the cops over that dippy little park? What a waste of time. I, on the other hand—" He reached into his pocket and extracted a small foil package. "—was using my time wisely, scoring a gram of pure Indian hash."

He set the foil on the drumhead and pulled it open.

"Look at how dark this shit is."

We gathered around to admire the hash. As much as I was put off by Kolvacik's big mouth, I had to admit he wasn't exaggerating about this stuff. It was dark and rich, smelling of wild flowers and earth.

"Care to sample it?" he asked.

"Of course," said Tony. "That weak weed we've been smoking is already wearing off."

"Then, let's party!" cried Kolvacik. "But, hey, where's the music? What is this, a morgue? We need sounds. Russo, I want Santana full blast, or you aren't touching this stuff. I'm not sharing it with a bunch of nuns. I came here to break in this drum and, by God, I'm going to break it in!"

We snorted a few small pieces of the hash by sticking them on a pin and lighting them. It was exhilarating stuff—not too hard on the head, but plenty of body rushes. Before long, we were following Santana's beat, Kolvacik on his conga, me on Tony's bongos, and Tony on an end table. We beat our hands raw while Claire danced around and around the room, hypnotized by dope and sound.

Why the neighbors didn't call the police, I'll never know. I'd have thought even deaf Mrs. Rosetti could have heard us. And we kept it up well past midnight. It was Jonah who finally stopped us. We paused between albums and heard him crying pitifully from his bedroom. Claire went to him immediately. Tony decided it was a good time to cut the music and go help her, and even Kolvacik had the good sense not to protest.

"The natives are restless, man," he said to me after they'd left the room, a small-toothed grin splitting his hairy face.

I smiled weakly. He began tapping his conga lightly with two fingers, glancing up at me occasionally, though he avoided eye contact. I sensed that he was studying me.

"These are good people, don't you think?" he finally said.

"They seem to be."

"They are—you can take that from me. You plan to be friends with them?"

"Maybe. How the hell do I know? I just met them tonight."

"You know. It's bullshit to say you don't know. Do you or don't you?"

I reached for Claire's cigarettes and fumbled the pack as I tried to pull one out. The hash and the drumming had made me speedy, and Kolvacik's questioning wasn't helping any.

"What do you want from me, man? Sure, I'd like to be friends with them. Is that okay with you?"

He drummed all ten fingers on the conga, making a sound like the drum roll before a firing squad execution. He looked right through me with those beady black eyes. I had to look away. He ended the drum roll with one good thump of his palm.

"Just don't fuck with them, you hear? They're the best people I know."

I still hadn't succeeded in freeing a cigarette. I stood up, the cigarette pack still in my hand, then threw it down.

"Hey, man, get off my case, will you? I don't know what your problem is, but I don't like being threatened. You take care of your business, and I'll take care of mine."

I was trembling a little. I went into the kitchen for a glass of water and found Claire walking Jonah back and forth along its narrow length. Only the dim light on the stove was on. If possible, she looked even more beautiful in that light. Tony was nowhere in sight.

"Is Jonah okay?" I asked quietly.

"Fine. I like to walk him in here when the refrigerator is humming. It seems to calm him down."

Jonah was a fine-boned, brown-haired doll in baby blue Dr. Denton's. I suddenly had an overwhelming desire to take him in my arms.

"May I hold him?"

Claire looked a little surprised, and then pleased.

"Sure."

She handed Jonah to me carefully. His big brown eyes fluttered open for a few seconds, but he stayed asleep. He felt warm and vulnerable against me. He smelled of milk and baby shampoo. It was so cool, holding a baby. The whole damn person, right there, practically in the palm of my hand. I knew I'd been held like that, too, but who can remember that far back? For a minute I spaced out on how big a person would have to be in order to hold me like I was holding Jonah. Seems like that was what I needed most, to be held. Then I flashed on holding my little brother, Steven, who'd been born when I was a freshman in high school. Steven always smelled that way, too.

Mingled with those familiar baby smells were others. Maybe I was hallucinating, but I thought I could identify my own sweaty odor, the green smell of the underbrush Tony and I had run through, the sandy smell of the beach, and all of them overlaid with the pungent perfume of the hashish. But there was another, far more exhilarating one. It took me a few minutes to figure out that it was the musky scent of the body that had given birth to the baby in my arms, the smell of a woman, Claire's smell. I took a deep breath, savoring it.

~2~

KOLVACIK LEFT SHORTLY AFTER our little confrontation—eyeing me suspiciously for staying, it seemed to me, but not offering to give me a ride home. The buses to Whitefish Bay had stopped running long before and Tony was too tired to take me, so he offered me the couch. I didn't sleep well. I rarely do the first night in a new place. The old apartment and the street below were full of unfamiliar sounds, and I was still buzzed from all the dope. I finally nodded off, just before dawn.

When I woke up, sun was streaming in the window. Keeping my eyes closed against it, I turned toward the back of the couch, hoping to go back to sleep. Then I heard a strange mewling sound. My eyes snapped open, and I looked over my shoulder. There, in an overstuffed red chair on the other side of the room, sat Claire in a thin summer nightgown unbuttoned to the waist. Jonah sucked at her breast. She was attending to him and didn't see me watching her. She pulled him off her breast, exposing a large, wet nipple, covered it, then exposed her other breast and moved Jonah onto it. I felt a stirring between my legs.

Claire looked up and saw me staring, but she seemed unabashed.

"Good morning," she said. "Did we wake you?"

I yawned deeply and rolled over onto my back, being careful to keep my knees up.

"No, I think the sun did."

"This is the brightest room in the apartment. That's why I like to feed Jonah in here."

"Tony up, yet?"

14

"He's been down at the docks since five-thirty."

"You're kidding! After last night, he's going to work at the docks all day?"

"He does it all the time. If he doesn't show up, he loses his number. He's working toward joining the union."

"Does he like the job that much?"

"He likes the pay."

"I wish I could do that, bust my butt and make a lot of money. My brother does it every summer. Then he doesn't have to work during the school year and he can concentrate on studying. I work part-time, year-round. I can only stand shit jobs in small doses."

"Me, too."

She shifted Jonah back to the other breast. I couldn't help watching. Her breasts were white as vanilla ice cream, her nipples reddened from Jonah's sucking.

"Hey," I said, "what's the story with this Kolvacik guy? He got all serious on me last night, while you and Tony were in the other room. He asked me if I thought I was going to be friends with you guys, then warned me to be nice to you because you're the best people he knows."

"Tim said that?"

"It was pretty strange."

"He's a strange guy. Most of the time, he acts like a flake, but all of a sudden he'll get serious like that. It always surprises me, too. I wouldn't worry about it."

"I won't. I was just curious. What's his story?"

"He's from Mequon, and I guess he always felt out of place up there— like a blue-collar guy in a white-collar suburb is what he told me. He moved down to the East Side right after high school, and now he works at the Harley-Davidson plant in Wauwatosa. He goes to school nights, like Tony does. He's got his own Harley, and he treats it better than he treats Mina, his fiancé. I like Mina a lot. She's a little Italian girl who grew up here on the East Side."

"Nasty to women, huh? I don't like that."

"Actually, that's not fair to Tim. Mina gives as good as she gets. She's quite a flirt. Tim pretends not to care, but he does."

She began to shift Jonah again. This time I glanced away, out the window. The sky was deep blue, with little puffy clouds scattered about. It looked to be a perfect summer day.

"Tim just doesn't want anybody to get too close to him. Tony's a bit like that."

I looked back at Claire.

"Tony? I can't believe that. He seems so open and friendly."

"I don't mean he gets nasty, the way Tim can, but he'll only open up so far. Then he starts making jokes and you can't get anything out of him. Believe me, I know."

"I believe you. I'm just surprised."

"So was I . . ."

She pulled Jonah off her breast and put him over her shoulder to burp him.

"The little guy looks pretty tired," I said.

"He always wants to crawl right back into bed in the morning—just like your mother, right Jonah?"

He let out a resonant belch, and Claire and I laughed. She laid him down on her lap, buttoned up her nightgown, then took him in her arms again and stood up.

"I'm going to change him, then have some coffee. You want some?"

"Sure. But why don't you let me change him. I've got lots of experience."

"From where?"

"I'm the second oldest in a family of seven. I was fourteen when my brother Steven was born. I took care of him all the time. We had a good time together."

"I'm impressed."

"That's just the way it was. I didn't do anything special."

"But it sounds like you enjoyed taking care of a baby. Not every boy would feel that way."

"I suppose not. Anyway, can I take him off your hands?"

"Be my guest."

She held Jonah out to me.

"Uh, why don't you set him down on the carpet, for now. I've got to get some clothes on. I'm nekid under here."

She laid him on the floor on his belly. He immediately turned himself over onto his back.

"Hey," I said, "neat trick."

"He just started doing that a few days ago. But that's as far as he can go, so don't worry about him getting away."

She left the room and I lay there watching Jonah flail around on his back. The sun had made a puddle of light on the rug beside him, and he kept reaching his hand into it, watching the hand light up. He had big, round, dark-brown eyes—definitely Tony's—that glowed with wonder each time he did this. Occasionally, he would look up at me and smile. I could have watched him all day.

Before I knew it, Claire was at the kitchen door, telling me that the coffee was ready. She seemed amused and pleased I was so fascinated with Jonah but reminded me that he still needed to be changed.

I slipped into my jeans and shirt and took Jonah into his room. The changing table consisted of a piece of foam rubber on top of a low black dresser. The only other furniture in the room was a beat-up red crib with a worn teddy bear decal on the headboard and a nice old wooden rocking chair. The room was so small it looked as if there was barely room to rock.

Having shot off my mouth about my expertise, I was surprised at how awkward I felt changing a baby again. But the little tricks came back to me as I did it, and Jonah seemed content with my technique. When I was done, I took him out to Claire in the kitchen.

"Thanks. Why don't you pour yourself some coffee while I put him down to sleep. With any luck, I'll only be a minute."

"Is it all right if I use your phone. I should call my folks and tell them where I am."

She pointed to the wall phone, beside the living room door. I dialed and got my mother on the first ring.

"Mom, this is John."

"Where have you been all night, young man?"

"With some friends over on the East Side. Tony and Claire. You don't know them. They have a six-month-old baby named Jonah."

"Jonah? That's an unusual name. Why didn't you call us last night?"

"I didn't decide to stay until real late. I didn't want to wake you up."

"How many times have we told you, we'd rather be woken up at night and know where you are than wake up in the morning and wonder."

"Why do you have to know where I am all the time? I'm nineteen years old, for Christ's sake! If I was living on my own, you'd never know where I was, so what's the difference?"

"The difference is, you're not living on your own, and as long as you live in this house, you'll follow our rules. And don't swear at me, young man! I don't appreciate your filthy mouth!"

"Filthy mouth? Jesus . . ."

"There you go again!"

"If that's the story, maybe it's time for me to get out of your house. You don't seem to like anything I do."

"You do whatever you want, but as long as you live in this house, you'll—"

"Follow your rules. You already said that, okay?"

"Don't 'okay' me, young man. I'm your mother. Now, will you be home for supper tonight, or not?"

"No. I have to work."

"Will you be home afterward?"

"Maybe. I don't know, yet. Probably."

"Well, don't forget to call us if you're not coming home. I lay awake wondering if you're alive or dead."

"Okay. I'll call."

I hung up, poured some of the coffee Claire had made and returned to the living room couch. I was agitated, as always after that kind of conversation with my mother. And they were getting more frequent. I knew I would have to move out before long. Between her dissatisfaction with my personal habits, Dad's dissatisfaction with my politics, and their mutual dissatisfaction with my religious beliefs—or lack thereof—things were getting ugly. And, yet, I was afraid of going off on my own for the first time. I wasn't confident about my ability to deal with the real world of paying rent and utility bills and tuition and buying food.

As I sat there, deep in thought, Claire came in, coffee and cigarettes in hand, and sat down on the couch, opposite me. She had put on some shorts and a red tube top.

"You have an argument with your mom?"

"Just the usual bullshit."

"What's that?"

"Oh, you know, she wants me to call in at night, she doesn't like the way I talk—that kind of stuff."

"Must be tough still living at home. I couldn't do it. You'll get along with them better once you're out on your own."

"I wish I could do it, now. I don't know, though . . . I'm a little freaked out by the idea of supporting myself. Did you feel that way when you first moved out?"

She chuckled. "I still feel that way, and so does Tony. It's scary."

"It must be even scarier when you've got a kid to support, huh? How do you manage to deal with him, along with all the other stuff in your life?"

Claire took a long drag on her cigarette, blew out the smoke, then shaped the ash on the edge of the green glass ashtray, which she'd balanced on the back of the couch.

"I can't tell you how easy it is to do things for him. It's hard work, but you don't even think about it, you just do it. It must be in our genes, or something. As far as jobs go, you do worry a little more about having one, but you also have a reason to go to work, and that makes it easier to face the jobs. You planning to have kids, someday?"

"When I find the right person. Right now, I have enough trouble handling myself."

"I can relate to that. Having a kid doesn't make that any easier."

I took a sip of my coffee, which I'd neglected. It was lukewarm. I set the mug on the floor.

"Don't you worry about your problems fucking up Jonah?"

"All the time. But what can I do about it? He's here and he's stuck with me. I do the best I can."

"I wish I could be so accepting of life."

"Have a kid."

We both laughed.

"No thanks," I said. "Not just yet. I have enough on my mind. Which reminds me—shit!—I've got to read a novel for American Lit. this morning! I completely forgot about it!"

I stood up, abruptly. "You don't happen to have *The Red Pony* by Stein-beck, do you?"

"I'm afraid not. We don't have a lot of books."

"What time is it?"

"About eight. There's a clock on the back of the stove."

I zipped in there, saw it was ten after eight, and zipped back out.

"Look, Claire, I hate to run off like this, but I've got to go. We're sup-posed to write an essay on the book in class, and it's a teacher I really like. I looked for it at the library, yesterday, but all the reserve copies were checked out. Then I forgot to go to the bookstore for it. It's short, so I still have time to read it, if I can get it right away."

Claire tamped out her cigarette calmly and rose to say goodbye.

"I'm sure you'll do fine," she said. "You seem like a pretty smart guy."

"Thanks, but I won't look too smart if I haven't even cracked the book. I'll give you and Tony a call, soon, okay?"

"I hope you do. We just moved in, so we're not in the book, yet, but you can get our number from information."

I promised I would and scurried down the steps and out onto Brady Street. I knew if I double-timed it over to Prospect and stuck out my thumb, I'd get a quick ride to UWM. The day was already sticky, so by the time I hit Prospect, I was sweaty and uncomfortable—probably as much from nerves as heat. I was picked up almost immediately by a guy in a beat up black Volks-wagen bug with a white peace symbol painted on the side. He dropped me right behind the bookstore, so I hurried in, found *The Red Pony*, and headed for the checkout counter. As I did, I reached into my jeans pocket for money. Two quarters. That was it. The sum total of cash I had on hand.

I swore out loud to myself. There was no other bookstore nearby, the library copies were gone, and I didn't know anybody in the class who might have finished the novel and could lend it to me. In short, I was out of luck. Unless . . . Unless I just ripped off the book. Could I justify doing some-thing like that? I thought about the ridiculous prices the store charged for textbooks and decided I could. Besides, it was a desperate situation; I didn't see any other choice.

I went behind a bookshelf, bent over as if I were looking at something on the lowest shelf, pulled my shirt out, slipped the book inside the waistband of my jeans, and pulled my shirt down over it. Then I sauntered toward the front, trying to look casual, past the checkout counters, and out the front door. Home free. Then I felt a heavy hand slap onto my shoulder. I froze.

"Hold it right there, son."

My stomach went to my throat. I whirled. It was a middle-aged security guard in uniform, with the name Schumacher on a black tag above the pocket. I don't know how I could have missed seeing him on the way out.

"I know you've got a book under your shirt. Let's have it."

People were walking by as we stood there, but Schumacher's posture was so unthreatening that no one seemed to notice what was going down. I saw a trash barrel not far away and fantasized about running to it and dropping the book in before Schumacher could actually see it on me. Then I realized it was hopeless scheme. I pulled the book out of my pants and handed it to him. He looked at it closely and shook his head.

"This is it? For a ninety-five cent paperback you risk getting arrested? I'll never understand you kids."

"I have to read it for a class this morning, and I didn't have enough cash on me. I know it was stupid."

"You can say that again."

He looked at the book again and shook his head.

"Come with me. I'll see what I can do for you."

Meekly, I followed him into the store and all the way to the back. He kept slapping the book against his thigh as he walked along in front of me. A few people looked at us curiously, but most didn't even notice us, since Schumacher was thoughtful enough not to lead me by the wrist and make it obvious what was going on. Still, my face was burning with humiliation.

The security "office" was a tiny bookstore file room, full of three-drawer filing cabinets, with a gray metal desk and two thick wooden chairs crammed into the back. The desk contained a torn blotter, an old black rotary telephone, a pad of paper, and a few manila file folders.

Schumacher directed me to the chair beside the desk, sat down himself, tossed the offending book onto the blotter and picked up the phone receiver. He dialed a few numbers and waited, picking up the book and shaking his head as he did.

"One lousy buck," he mumbled.

I felt like an idiot. But, most of all, I was scared. I'd never been arrested. The worst thing I'd ever faced was a speeding ticket. I had little doubt that the consequences for theft—even petty theft—were more serious.

"George? This is Art Schumacher. I caught a kid lifting a ninety-five cent paperback here. He says he was supposed to read it for a class and didn't have enough cash on him to buy it. He looks pretty scared, so I doubt he's ever pulled anything like this before. How about we let him off the hook this time?"

He listened for a moment and got a disgusted look on his face.

"Aw, come on, George. He can't mean anybody. Let's give the kid a break."

He listened again. His face didn't change.

"Okay, okay. But I think it's stupid. See you later."

He hung up the receiver, took off his hat, and set it on the desk.

"I'm sorry, kid. The manager of the bookstore insists that we prosecute shoplifters, no matter what they take. We're going to have to book you."

My stomach dropped. How was I going to explain this one to my parents? I could only hope I wouldn't have to.

"Have you got your student ID?"

I pulled out my wallet. My hand was shaking, but I managed to get out the ID and hand it to him. He took a cheap ballpoint pen from his pocket and started writing on the little pad in front of him.

"Okay, John," he said, "I'm going to write down your name and student number, then send you over to the campus police office. They'll take your fingerprints and a couple of photos and check you for priors."

I felt like I was on a TV police procedural. It seemed unreal. Schumacher handed the card back to me.

"Now, don't get any funny ideas about skipping out, instead of going over there. With this information, we'll just come and find you. You know where the campus police office is located?"

"It's just up the street on Maryland, isn't it?"

"That's correct. You go ahead, now."

"One more thing, Mr. Schumacher. Do my parents have to find out about this?"

"How old are you, son?"

"Nineteen."

"Then it's up to you. But, if you want my advice, tell 'em. They'll probably find out, sooner or later, and then they'll be twice as mad."

I appreciated his candor, but I was willing to take my chances. I didn't relish the confrontation if my dad found out I'd been arrested. I thanked Schumacher for trying to get me off, and then headed for the campus police office. It was one in a row of bungalows the university had bought for office space. It looked disturbingly like my family's house. The guy who dealt with me inside was not as considerate as Schumacher had been. He didn't use my name once, and he practically broke my fingers as he rolled them on the inkpad and fingerprint card. But being photographed was the most humiliating part. He hung a small placard with a number on it around my neck and flashed away without saying a word, except for, "Turn sideways." By the time he gave me the paper with the date and place of my arraignment, I was dying to get out of there.

When I hit the street, I found I was hungry. I'd never eaten breakfast. I went over to the student union cafeteria and, with my last fifty cents, bought a bagel and carton of yogurt. I took it out onto the lawn beside the union. A couple of skinny, bare-chested freaks were tossing a Frisbee from one side of the lawn to the other, while a big black Labrador with a red bandana around his neck chased it back and forth between them, panting in the heat. I sat down under a tree, wolfed down my food, then pulled out the arraignment slip. It said I was to appear at the county courthouse, downtown, on Friday, September 10, at 10:00 a.m. A terrific way to celebrate the first week of fall classes, I thought. I crammed the offending slip of paper back into my pocket.

I cut the English class that had led to my troubles—there didn't seem much point in showing up. Instead, I hung out in the library reading room perusing a couple of new magazines, *Rolling Stone* and *Psychology Today*, and some literary magazines until it was time to go to work at Siegel's. I went early, so I could collect my paycheck, cash it with Mrs. Siegel, and eat a decent lunch before I started working.

It was a hot day to be tossing around cases of beer and wine and liquor, and most of the customers were grumpy from the heat, too, so the tips, when I got them at all, were pitiful. The only bright spot in the afternoon was when I drove down Brady Street and spotted Claire walking Jonah in a stroller. She was pretty hard to miss with her strawberry blonde hair and red tube top.

I honked and pulled over in front of India Imports, where we chatted through the window of the van for a few minutes, until Jonah got impatient with sitting still in his stroller. She told me Tony had called on his lunch break and said how much he'd enjoyed hanging out with me. She invited me for homemade pizza the following night. I accepted enthusiastically, promising to bring along a six-pack. I was flattered that they seemed as interested in me as I was in them.

I arrived home at ten o'clock that night, thoroughly exhausted. My parents were sitting on our open front porch in lawn chairs, the porch light off to keep bugs away, so all I could see as I walked up the driveway were their silhouettes.

"The prodigal son returns," said Dad, as I came up the steps.

I laughed weakly. "That's me," I said.

Even on the porch, standing right in front of them, I could barely make out their faces.

"Are you home for the night," asked Mom, "or are you off gallivanting around 'til all hours, like last night?"

I didn't rise to the bait. "I'm in for the night. I'm beat."

I remained standing, instead of perching on the railing, as I did when I was feeling more sociable. I was just about to go in when my father spoke up. "Say," he began—and even from that single word I could sense there was trouble coming—"you don't know anything about this Water Tower Park foolishness, down by the hospital, do you? I saw on the news that the police had to chase a bunch of kids out of there last night."

My dad was a bureaucrat with the county water department and a "weekend warrior" with the National Guard. He took civic pride and patriotism quite seriously. We'd been engaged in a running political battle ever since my junior year in high school, which was when I'd come to the conclusion that Milwaukee was a racist city and the Vietnam War a stupid, and probably immoral, war. I should have ignored his leading question, but I was too tired to be smart.

"Yeah, I know something about it. I was one of the people who got chased out."

"You what?!" he exclaimed, rising a little from his chair, then sitting back down, scraping the aluminum frame on the concrete. He was so surprised by my response that Mom beat him to the punch with the first sarcastic question. "And what was so important in that park that you kids had to gather there and disturb the patients in the hospital?"

"We weren't disturbing anyone."

"That's not what they said on the news."

"Don't believe everything you hear on TV. The loudest thing there was an acoustic guitar. That's the way it always is, just a bunch of people hanging out. The cars that go by the hospital, day in and day out, are louder than we were, and nobody tries to keep them away."

Dad cleared his throat.

"You didn't answer your mother's question, son. Why do you have to gather there? This city has one of the best park systems in the world. Why do you have to go to that one, when the city doesn't want you there?"

"The question isn't why, Dad, it's why not? The city built the damn park, presumably for people to use, but as soon as kids with long hair and beards started showing up, they slapped a stupid ten o'clock curfew on it. Why should we go someplace else? It was still a free country, the last time I looked."

I could sense my dad was getting agitated. He was swatting at imaginary mosquitoes. "It's a free country, but it's also a country that believes in law and order. If the city has decided you shouldn't be there, then there must be a good reason. It's your duty as a citizen to obey the law, even if you don't like it."

I was getting pretty agitated, myself. It had been an exhausting twenty-four hours, what with the park incident, meeting new people, smoking too much dope, being arrested for shoplifting, and tossing around liquor boxes for hours. My fuse was short, and the duty to obey line blew it.

"God damn it, don't you see that that's exactly what people said in Germany under Hitler?! Everybody just—"

"Don't you swear at us, young man!" my mother cut in.

I ignored her.

"Everybody just did what they were told and went on with their petty little lives, while the Nazis hauled away Jews and Gypsies and socialists and homosexuals and anybody else they didn't like. They made laws to cover themselves and people obeyed the laws—good little citizens doing their duty."

I was talking loudly and vehemently enough for our neighbors in the tightly spaced houses to hear me.

"I saw this great thing at a guy's apartment, a couple weeks ago. He had a picture of Hitler in a gold frame on his desk and down at the bottom of the picture he'd taped a strip of paper with the words, 'Before you obey, think!' That's what I think of laws, that they're something you'd better think about before obeying, not something you just assume are right and blindly obey."

My dad leaped from his chair and put his face into mine, close enough that I could see his eyes flashing, even in the dim light.

"You listen to me, John Meyer. Don't you ever compare this country to Nazi Germany. I was there. I fought the Nazis. I know what they did to their country. There has never been anything like that here, and there never will be, if I have anything to say about it. We're talking about good laws in this country, fair laws. You have no right to disobey those."

Out of the corner of my eye, I saw my sister Marion's face in the window of my room, above the porch. Our arguing must have woken her up.

"Only good laws and fair laws, huh? What about segregation? I suppose it was good and fair to discriminate against blacks for hundreds of years? Or to put Japanese-Americans into concentration camps during World War II?"

"What do you know about World War II? Those camps were necessary, then. And we've passed laws against segregation, now."

"No thanks to you."

"I voted for Eisenhower, Kennedy, and Johnson. Those are the presidents responsible for enforcing civil rights laws."

"You only voted for them because they were pro-union. You always said black people shouldn't be allowed to move into this neighborhood."

"They don't want to live here—except for a few trouble-makers. They want to live with their own people. And don't change the subject. I'm talking about being a good citizen, about obeying the laws, something you don't seem to know anything about."

"Oh, yeah? In case you've forgotten, I won an American Legion essay contest on citizenship when I was in high school."

God knows where that statement came from, but its utter irrelevance left all of us speechless for a moment. I looked up to see Marion still at the window.

"Look," I finally said, "I don't want to argue anymore. I'm dead tired. I'm going to bed." I put my hand on the door handle.

"Sure," said Dad, "run off, now that the argument is getting tough for you."

"Frank," said Mom, exasperated, "let him go. You two could argue all night, and you've already woken up half the neighborhood."

He sat down and waved his hand at me, looking away. "All right, go—get out of here."

I went. When I got up to my room, Marion was nowhere in sight, but my brother George, who was a year younger than I was and as conservative as they came, was sitting on my bed. He was all I needed on top of Dad.

"Gee, John," he said, pushing his thick glasses back up his nose with one finger pointed right between his eyes, "why did you come home and get Dad all riled up? You know his heart has been bad."

"I don't do it on purpose, George, okay? Now get out of here and leave me alone, will you. I'm going to sleep."

I started to unbutton my shirt, but George didn't move.

"I don't see how you can disagree with him so much," he went on. "He's been through so much more than you have. He knows so much more about life."

I stopped dead, my shirt half-off, hanging from one shoulder.

"I can't believe you just said that. He doesn't know more about *my* life, George. I'm the one who has to live it, not him. Now, get out of here and let me do it."

I finished taking off my shirt and started on my jeans. George just shook his head sadly.

"You two are going to kill each other one of these days. I hate having to mediate between you. I'm too young to be doing that."

I took off my pants and tossed them over my desk chair.

"Let's face it, George, you're older than you and me *combined*. You were born old. And nobody's asking you to mediate, so don't cry to me about it."

I could see I'd hurt his feelings, so I sat down next to him.

"Look, I know you're trying to keep the peace, and I appreciate it. But it's a hopeless cause. Dad and I are just too different."

"Too much alike, you mean."

"In temperament, yes. In our politics, no. Whatever causes it, we just don't get along. You can't change that."

He started tracing the squares on my old plaid bedspread with his index finger, not looking at me.

"Marion and Ruth woke up and started crying when they heard you arguing out there. Steven woke up, too, this time."

That was a guilt trip I didn't need. I was crazy about Marion and Ruth and Steven—and George knew it. All three of them were still in grade school, Marion about to start seventh grade, Ruth fifth, and Steven kindergarten. I would do anything in my power to avoid hurting them, but some things weren't under my control.

I put my face in my hands and shook my head, then flopped back on the bed, putting my hands behind my head and staring up at the ceiling.

"Maybe it's time for me to move out of here," I finally said.

"That's what I think," said George. "You're not around much, anyway. I think you and Dad would both be better off, and so would the rest of us."

"Okay. I'll think about it. I'm not sure how I'd afford it, but I'll think about it."

I sat up.

"Now, get the hell out of here, George. I've had it for one night."

George mumbled goodnight and left, closing the door behind him. He didn't seem entirely satisfied with the outcome of the conversation. Maybe he'd hoped to get a date for my departure.

Tough, I said to myself. *I can't go until the time is right. I'll know when I'm ready.*

I flipped off the overhead light, pulled down the covers, and flopped face-first onto my bed. It was too hot to put anything over me. I listened to George rustle around in the next room and finally get into bed, then I tossed and turned for another hour, until exhaustion finally brought sleep.

~3~

STEVEN WOKE ME AT EIGHT O'CLOCK the next morning by barreling into my room and jumping on top of me. He was five years old, small and wiry, and he often acted younger than his age, especially around me. I suppose it was because I had always been his big brother, Mark being long gone when he was born, and Jim having left for the service not long afterward. Also, I indulged him and acted like a little kid, myself, when I was around him. He brought it out in me.

I tossed him off onto the carpet and sat on him, being careful not to put my full weight on his body. I was wearing only my underpants, so he tried to tickle my sides, but he did it too hard, so it was easy for me to control my laughter. Finally, he got frustrated.

"C'mon, John, let me up!"

"Not until you tell me who your favorite brother is."

His eyes lit up. We'd been playing variations on this game since he'd first learned all our names.

"Is Mark your favorite brother?" I asked.

"No!" he shouted.

"Is Jim your favorite brother?"

"No!"

"Is George your favorite brother?"

"No!"

"Then who is your favorite brother?"

He got a devilish grin on his face.

"No one!"

I started tickling him unmercifully. He thrashed around, laughing hysterically and begging me to stop. Finally, I did.

"Okay, one more chance. Who is your favorite brother?"

"John is!"

"Are you sure?"

"I'm sure!"

"Will I always be?"

"Always!"

"Okay, then."

I got off of him. He leapt to his feet, ran to the door, and turned back toward me. "I had my fingers crossed!" he cried and went flying through George's room and down the hall.

I laughed, and that segued into a huge yawn. I wanted nothing more than to lay down and go back to sleep, but I had a nine-thirty psychology class, and I was determined to make that day more fruitful than the previous one. After psychology came creative writing, then a sociology lecture at one-thirty. After that, since I didn't have to work, I figured I'd study until it was time go to Claire and Tony's for supper.

Remembering the shoplifting arrest, I shivered, though the day was already warm. I was still shaken by it. I wondered if it meant I'd have a criminal record for the rest of my life, something prospective employers would uncover routinely. It was hard to believe I could be tainted for life because of stealing a ninety-five cent paperback, but it was a distinct possibility. Depressing.

I showered, put on my jeans and a fresh t-shirt, and filled my army surplus knapsack with all the textbooks and notebooks I'd need for the day. Then I lugged it downstairs with me. The kitchen smelled of coffee, fried eggs, and dishwashing soap. Only Marion was still at the table. She was finishing a powdered sugar doughnut and a glass of milk. Dad was at work. So was George, off to a high-paying summer "slave" at the Gisholt factory. Mom was in the basement doing laundry, and I could hear Ruth out in the driveway with Steven, trying to teach him how to play hopscotch.

"Hi," mumbled Marion.

I returned her greeting. She was the only shy one in the family. She hung back most of the time in family conversations and, perhaps because of that, was a keen observer for someone her age. I felt very close to her, and she to me, though our affection was rarely verbalized.

I poured myself a bowl of Cheerios, put milk on them, and sat down across the table from her. The sun was streaming in the pair of open windows at her back, surrounding her with a halo. We smiled at one another, but then she looked down at her plate, hiding her light-brown eyes. She seemed nervous around me. My argument with Dad the night before must have gotten to her.

"How's your summer going, kiddo?" I asked.

"Okay," she replied, her head still down.

"You getting ready for school to start up again?"

"Uh-huh."

"Did you get a new pencil case and a bunch of new folders?"

She looked up, offended.

"C'mon, John—only little kids get excited about stuff like that."

"Like hell! Oops. Hope Mom didn't hear that." I looked toward the basement door. "I still get excited about stuff like that, and I'm in college."

"But you're different."

"What do you mean, different?"

She thought about it for a moment.

"I guess it's that you still seem a lot like a kid. Most older people try to act so grown up. You don't seem to want to."

Out of the mouths of babes . . .

"Do you think that's good or bad?"

She thought again. "Sometimes I like it and sometimes I don't."

I smiled, which seemed to relieve her tension a bit. "Me, too," I said. I reached across table and chucked her under the chin.

"Thanks for being honest with me, kiddo."

I wolfed down the rest of my cereal, got up from the table, and put my bowl into the dishwasher. I double-checked my knapsack to make sure I had everything, slung it over my shoulder and groaned. It felt like it was full of rocks. I looked at the kitchen clock and realized I'd never make it to the bus I needed to take in order to get to class on time. I'd have to hitchhike.

"Tell Mom I left, will you, Marion?"

"Sure. Good luck with your weightlifting."

"Not funny," I said, shifting the bag higher on shoulder.

I walked the few blocks to Lake Drive as fast as I could with the heavy knapsack and got a ride pretty quickly from a guy my age in brand-new red Volvo sports car. His hair was long, but perfectly trimmed, and he wore a crisp white t-shirt and cut-off jeans that looked like they'd been trimmed by a New York designer. His manicured hands were wrapped comfortably around the leather-covered steering wheel.

"So, you're a student, huh?" he asked.

"Yeah. You?"

"Not any more. I just dropped my student deferment, so why the hell go to school? I'm working at my old man's investment firm. I don't do much–run a few errands and shit–but he pays me a bundle. It beats the hell out of studying–not that I ever did much of that."

He laughed as if this was the funniest thing he'd ever said. I waited for him to recover.

"Aren't you afraid of getting drafted?"

"Hell, no! You think I'd be doing this if I thought there was any chance I'd end up in 'Nam? No way, man! The draft counselor at school told me they definitely won't call any more numbers in the draft lottery this year. It's an off-year election or some shit like that. My old man says the same thing, and he hangs out with congressmen and senators. I dropped my student deferment the minute I heard that, and by New Year's Eve I'll be able to tell the draft board to kiss my ass. Then it's dope and pussy forever!"

He downshifted for one of the sharp curves on Lake Drive, which follows the meandering coastline of Lake Michigan, and then popped back into third and accelerated. The Volvo purred beneath us.

Definitely no more numbers called for the rest of the year? If he really knew what he was talking about, this was big news! Was it possible I'd escape fighting in that ugly little war without leaving the country or going to prison? The possibility was exhilarating.

I looked out at the huge, beautiful houses that lined both sides of Lake Drive. No doubt, this guy was from a similar house in Fox Point or Bayside, further north. It seemed unfair that kids who were already financially privileged always had the right information about how to get themselves into good situations and out of bad ones. I thought about guys I'd known

in high school, guys from working-class families who didn't have the apti-
tude for college, who took factory jobs after high school and got drafted
right away. A couple of them were already dead, while guys like the Volvo
driver concentrated on "dope and pussy," doing just enough to get by.
There was no justice in the world.

But I was one of the privileged, too. My family didn't have the wealth
and status of that guy's family, but I was educated and I had the right information and I was going to use it. I decided then and there I would visit
the UWM draft counselor that afternoon. I didn't like being in the same
class as the Volvo driver, but I consoled myself with the fact that I was
morally opposed to the war, not just out for a good time.

The bastard refused to go a couple blocks out of his way to drop me
off on Downer, so I could make my class on time. This after he'd just finished telling me how he could come and go as he pleased in his cushy job.
Why was it the people with the most are so often the least generous?

The classes were a piece of cake that day. It was the last week of the summer session, so the atmosphere was relaxed and casual. The profs and TA's
knew it was our job to get ourselves ready for exams, and they weren't about
to go too far out of their way to help us. They were too busy mentally packing
up beer and suntan lotion for their end-of-summer excursions. Early in the
afternoon, I slipped out of a rambling sociology lecture to go to the draft
counseling office in the student union. I avoided passing the bookstore. I had
no need for a visual reminder of the previous day's humiliation.

The draft counseling office was about the size of a study carrel in the library. When the counselor saw me through the glass and wire mesh door, he
stood up to move his visitor's chair, so I could open the door, which swung
inward. Once I was in, I had to step behind his chair, while the door swung
shut and he repositioned my chair beside his desk. I sat down and he offered
me his bony hand, apologizing for the cramped quarters and explaining it was
all the university would give him. I shook his hand and told him it was okay.

The counselor's name was Carl Lindstrom. He was tall and emaciated
and balding, though he was only a few years older than I was. His face was
unshaven. He was gentle and solicitous, speaking in a voice so soft that,
even in that tiny space, I had to lean forward to hear him. He confirmed
everything I'd heard from the Volvo driver, saying he was certain there

would be no more draft numbers drawn for the duration of the year. All I had to do was drop my student deferment and, by the end of the year, my eligibility would be over. I would be free from the threat of being drafted.

I couldn't quite believe my ears. Ever since high school, when my opposition to the war had crystallized, I'd agonized over what I would do if I was drafted. That threat was the whetstone on which I'd sharpened my social and political beliefs. And it was about to be taken away. My life stretched out before me, uninhibited by the threat of violent disruption through imprisonment or emigration. I'd played the lottery and I'd won. I was both relieved and bewildered.

Carl empathized with my feelings. He told me they were the normal ones, under the circumstances. He asked if I was morally opposed to the war, and I said I was.

"Then," he added, "you'll also have to deal with feelings of guilt over having been spared the hardships others will face. But I have something that might help you assuage that guilt."

A trace of a smile crossed his serious face as he pulled a mimeographed sheet from the middle drawer of his desk and handed it to me.

"This is about the Social Action Center, an organization with a staff of one—me—sponsored by the Quakers. We offer information about the war, the draft, and other social issues, and we run a soup kitchen and a house where runaway teenagers can come for advice and a place to crash. We're always looking for volunteers."

I looked over the haphazardly formatted information sheet, which had a big peace symbol at the top.

"I don't know if you're interested in any of the other things we do, but you might consider getting involved with our anti-war activities."

"I'm definitely interested," I said—and I was, in theory, though I wasn't much of joiner.

"Then, why don't you keep that information and stop in at our office, sometime. We're on the corner of Farwell and Brady, second floor."

I said I would, and rose to leave. Carl rose, too. I thanked him, then we did the dance with the chair all over again, and I left.

I walked across the huge concrete plain in the center of the campus toward the library. I was still in a daze over the news about the draft. It was as if I'd been training intensely for years to meet a tough opponent in the boxing ring, thoroughly terrified by his power, only to have him not show up for the match. It would take a while to believe I was going to win by default. It was a bit of a letdown.

I spent the rest of the afternoon engrossed in studying for my exams, only occasionally staring out the window to watch clouds rolling in from over Lake Michigan. It was easy to apply myself with the supper at Russo's to look forward to. At 4:30 sharp, I snapped shut my sociology book, packed up my knapsack, and went outside. The cloud cover had blocked the sun, reducing the heat, so I decided to walk the mile and a half to Brady Street. I went down Maryland Avenue, through the tree-lined residential area south of the university, and then took Farwell past the familiar old neighborhood bars on North Avenue, and past the storefronts, small factories, and apartment buildings further south. Traffic was steady on Farwell, but nothing, I knew, like it would be on Prospect, a block east, where commuters would be streaming home from downtown.

As I walked, I couldn't help reflecting on the change that had occurred in my life that afternoon. With the burden of facing the draft off my shoulders, my step was lighter and my pace quicker. I couldn't wait to tell Claire and Tony about my good fortune.

When I arrived at the door that led to their stairwell, I noticed that a cigarette butt had wedged itself underneath, preventing the door from closing tight. I pushed open the door, pulled out the butt so it would close tightly, and went up the steps, two at a time. Just as I was about to knock, I heard raised voices inside, from the back of the apartment.

"Well, fuck you!" I heard Tony say. "I work my ass off all day and then come home to this shit."

Claire's voice was less distinct, but still audible. "I work all day, too, you know, Tony. It's no picnic here, either."

"Taking care of Jonah is a whole lot easier than tossing crates in the hold of ship, I can guarantee you that. You can have a picnic if you want to. You can get out in the fucking sun and play. I can't do that."

"But at least you get to talk to some adults while you work. It's pretty boring hanging out with a six-month-old kid. He doesn't have a lot to say."

"Then you should be happy with the quiet. I don't get that either."

"God, you're impossible! Your problems are always worse than mine."

"Damn straight!"

"Look, Tony, we're gonna have to compromise here. We both need to get out at night. But tonight is important to me. If you give in on this one, I'll give in the next time, okay?"

"All right! All fucking right. I'll stay with Jonah. But don't pull this sudden shit on me. I hate it."

I heard a door slam, then footsteps approaching the front of the apartment. I knocked. Tony opened the door. He was naked, except for a towel wrapped around his waist, and his hair and beard were wet.

"Hey, man," he said, smiling amiably, "come on in."

"Good to see you again, Tony," I said.

We clasped hands.

"Likewise," he replied, closing the door behind me.

"I'm afraid the plans for tonight have changed. Claire's having dinner with her sister, Katie. I guess Katie called this afternoon and said she had to talk to Claire about some goddamn thing. So, it's you, me, and a home-made pizza, I guess. Jonah, too, of course, but with any luck he'll be asleep most of the night."

I was hurt Claire had invited me and was going off to do something else.

"Why don't you get yourself a cold beer while I put some clothes on."

I followed Tony into the kitchen, pulled a beer from the refrigerator, and sat down at the table to read the *Milwaukee Journal*, lying there next to a pack of Benson and Hedges 100's. One front-page story caught my eye immediately. It said that a right-wing industrialist named Benjamin Grob in Grafton, just north of Milwaukee, had initiated a boycott against William F. Schanen Jr.'s Port Publications for printing *Kaleidoscope*, Milwaukee's only alternative newspaper. The boycott had been kicked off the night before with a mud-slinging speech by Grob at a rally held at Grafton High School.

By the time I finished reading the article, I was steaming. *Kaleidoscope* had first been published almost two years before, when I was a senior in high school. Its appearance at the Focal Point bookstore in Whitefish Bay had led to a violent argument with my mother, when she joined a group of suburban mothers trying to get it banned as pornographic. *Kaleidoscope* had eventually faced prosecution for obscenity by the county D.A.'s office, due to pressure from these mothers.

One night, when my mother returned from a meeting of her group, I unloaded on her, accusing her of being a narrow-minded book burner. She, in turn, accused me of being immoral. I'd recently started attacking the hypocrisy of the Catholic Church and had brought home "obscene" books such as *Who's Afraid of Virginia Woolf?* and *Herzog.* She was convinced I was on the fast track to hell. Our encounter that night grew more and more heated, until she slapped me in the face. Not a smart thing to do to a teenager. I came close to slapping her back–which would not have been smart, either.

Ever since that night, *Kaleidoscope's* right to exist had been a bone of contention between us. The trumped-up obscenity charges had been dismissed, of course, having no basis in reality, and the publicity ultimately helped the paper establish itself. But I knew Grob's new boycott of *Kaleidoscope's* printer would have the full support of my mother and her cronies. I half-expected to find the article pinned to my pillow when I went home that night, the opening volley in a new phase of our running battle.

Disgusted, I tossed the paper aside and pulled a cigarette from the pack on the table. I went to the stove and lit it on the gas burner, then returned to my chair, where I concentrated on my beer a few minutes. Claire came out of the bathroom wearing the same lacey white dress I'd first seen her in, two nights before. Again it struck me she looked both wraithlike and earthy, like an embodied angel.

"Hi, John. I guess Tony's told you what's happening tonight. Bummer, huh? My sister really needs to get away from her husband and kids and talk over some things. I couldn't say no. I'm sorry."

I raised my hand to indicate that no apology was necessary.

"I understand. No problem. It's just . . . I'll miss seeing you is all."

"Will you stay over again? You're welcome to."

"I don't know. We'll see. Thanks."

She got a cigarette for herself and went to the stove. Before leaning over, she reached behind her head and gathered her long, straight hair in one hand, to keep it from the flame. Then she lit the cigarette and stood upright again.

"I've got to get going. I hope you'll help Tony with Jonah. He's not real happy being left with a baby tonight. I think he had a rough day at the docks."

I assured her I would. She retrieved her purse from the bedroom, called goodbye to Tony, who grunted in return, and left.

Tony came out of the bedroom in what I was beginning to think was a uniform for him: a black t-shirt and black jeans. He got a beer from the refrigerator, opened it, and sat down at the table with me.

"You hungry?" he asked.

"I'm okay."

"Good. I'd just like to sit and drink a couple of brews before we put the pizza together."

"You pissed at Claire for taking off?"

"What? Naa. It's no big deal. The kid's asleep right now, anyway. He may not wake up until after we–"

At that moment, displaying the perverse timing of small children, Jonah let out a wail.

"Oh, shit," said Tony.

I was up immediately.

"I'll go to him. I'd like to."

"You sure?"

"I'm sure."

"Okay. That's cool. Just try to calm him down and get him back to sleep. If that doesn't work, bring him out to me."

I went into Jonah's tiny bedroom. The shade was pulled and the room felt cool and humid. I smelled baby powder and a pail of diapers soaking in detergent. Jonah was on his belly, crying like a lost soul. I wanted to pick him up, but decided that it made more sense to leave him where he was if I wanted him to get back to sleep. I felt his diaper, to make sure he wasn't wet. Then I massaged his back through his thin white t-shirt, feeling each of his tiny vertebrae beneath my fingertips. What an astounding little creature he was. I envied Tony and Claire for having him, though I knew I wasn't ready to take on such a responsibility.

The massage began to take effect. Gradually, Jonah's cries became whimpers, then ceased entirely. He flopped his head back and forth a few times, his eyes still open, but glazed-looking. Then he was asleep. I pulled my hand away and he stayed still, breathing gently. I tiptoed out of the room.

Tony was on his second beer and had gotten another for me. It sat on the table, in a little pool of condensation.

"Thanks, man," he said, raising his beer to me. "You handled that like a pro. Claire tells me you've had some experience with babies."

"Some," I said, sitting down. "Jonah seems like a real trip."

Tony nodded. I drained the last couple swallows of my first beer, which was room temperature, then started in on the fresh, cold one. I noticed Tony had part of the newspaper spread out in front of him.

"You see that article about Port Publications?" I asked.

"It sucks, doesn't it? I bet Grob is a real asshole."

"No doubt. My mother will think he's a hero, though."

"No shit?"

"We've been arguing about *Kaleidoscope* for years, now, ever since they started selling it in 'Whitefolks Bay.'"

"Hard to believe you're from the Bay."

"It's not what you think. We're not rich. My dad's a bureaucrat with the county water department, and with seven kids—"

"Hey, my dad's with the county, too! He works for the park commission. But he's just a laborer."

"Nothing wrong with that," I said.

Tony's eyes flashed.

"Hey, man, I don't need you or anybody else to tell me there's nothing wrong with it. Just because your dad wears a fucking white collar!"

I was taken aback. "I didn't mean anything by it. Take it easy."

He rose abruptly and slammed his empty bottle into the big white plastic wastebasket beside the stove. Then he took a deep breath to collect himself. "Sorry, man," he said. "I used to take a lot of shit about my dad from guys in Mequon. They'd see him cutting the grass when they went golfing at Brown Deer Park or something and then razz me about his being a glorified janitor. I punched out a few of them."

"Look, I don't care what your dad does. One job's as good as another. Besides, it's you I want to be friends with, not him."

Tony smiled, picked up his beer and held it toward me. "I'll drink to that," he said. "To the new generation. Fuck the old standards."

We clinked bottles and drank.

"I'm really hungry all of a sudden," I said. "Let's down these beers and make us a pizza."

"I'll drink to that, too," said Tony. "Last one to the bottom of the bottle has to cut up the onions!" He tipped his head back and started guzzling.

"Hey, no fair! I've got a lot more beer left than you do!"

He ignored me and drained the bottle.

"Sorry, man. You lose. The onions are in the bottom of that cupboard and the knives are in the drawer above it. It's your party, so you can cry if you want to . . ."

"You bastard."

"Uh-uhhh! Don't let your mother hear you say that! I'll go put on some sounds. How about Joe Cocker?"

"Perfect."

"I thought I'd start out with 'Cry Me a River,'" he said dryly.

I snatched up a folded section of the newspaper and threw it at him as he scurried out of the room.

We spent the next half-hour constructing a magnificent pizza, drinking more beer and growling along with Joe Cocker. Tony rolled out the pre-made crust Claire had bought from Glorioso's, down the street. I cut up the onions, as well as black olives, green peppers, and mushrooms. Tony found pepperoni in the refrigerator and grated mozzarella and parmesan cheese. When we put it all together on a cookie sheet, the thing must have weighed three pounds, and we were ready to eat every ounce of it. We put it in the oven, and Tony went in to flip over the Cocker album.

We sat back down at the table and made small talk, and by the time the flip side of Cocker was over, the pizza was done. We cut it up, carried it into the living room, along with fresh beers, and put on Joni Mitchell's latest album. Then we settled onto the floor, our backs against the couch.

"Now, this," said Tony, rubbing his hand together, "is the life. Eat hearty."

The alcohol had made us ravenous, so, for a while, we just ate pizza and listened to Joni croon.

"Hey," I finally said, between slices, "I went to the draft counselor at UWM today. Nice guy. He says it's true about no higher numbers being called this year. He told if I drop my 2S I'll be home free, come the end of the year."

"You lucky bastard. I wish I didn't have such a low goddamn number. It pisses me off."

"You ever do anything to protest the war?"

"I've been to a few demonstrations. You?"

"A few. Usually on the fringes, though. I'd like to do more. This draft counselor runs something called the Social Action Center on Brady and Farwell. I'd like to stop in and see what's happening there."

"Count me in, if you do. I'm surprised I've never noticed the place, if it's that close by."

"I walked by today and saw a big peace symbol in a second floor window. I assume that's it."

In short order, we'd eaten the entire pizza. Joni was done singing and the evening traffic sounds were beginning to pick up on Brady Street.

"God, I'm stuffed," said Tony. "How about a 'j' to smooth things out?"

He retrieved the rosewood box from the mantel and pulled out a baggie of cleaned grass and some yellow wheat straw papers.

"Hey," I asked, "does that fireplace work?"

"Hell, no. The landlord would probably double the rent if it did. It would be nice in the wintertime, though, wouldn't it? This place gets cold."

Tony deftly rolled a joint for each of us, using the top of the little box as a platform. Then he took out some matches and set the box aside. He handed me a joint, lit it for me, then lit the other one for himself. We leaned back, savoring them quietly for a few minutes.

Eventually, Tony got up and, without a word, put on a Moody Blues album. Truly stoned music. We closed our eyes, drew on our joints and let our minds travel with the music. Soon, I was out among the stars. To paraphrase the Byrds, "I could see for miles and miles and miles." Unfortunately, my pizza-filled gut kept reminding me that, in reality, I was still earthbound.

After what seemed like hours, the music ended. The apartment was dead quiet. Even the street was quiet. The silence was deafening. I had to break it.

"Wow," I said.

"Far out," said Tony. "Don't you think that if everybody could hear those sounds stoned, they'd see the world a lot more clearly?"

"Definitely."

"I mean, who'd want to kill people if they knew they could experience something like that?"

"Nobody."

"Damn straight."

We were quiet again, listening to the mild whoosh of cars passing by, below the window.

"You know, something, Tony," I said, "I like you. You're an easy guy to be with. I like a guy I can be quiet with."

"Thanks. You, too, man."

"Remember what Louis says to Rick at the end of *Casablanca*?"

We said the line in unison.

"'This could be the beginning of a beautiful friendship.'"

When we realized what we'd done, we started laughing. And once we'd started, it was hard to stop. Every time we looked at one another, we'd crack up again. Tony ended up flat on his back, howling at the ceiling. It reminded me of when we lay on the beach together, earlier in the week, laughing together over the Water Tower Park incident.

Once we'd recovered, Tony put on WTOS, Milwaukee's progressive rock station. Jonah woke up, and Tony made him a bottle and brought him out to the living room to feed him. We started talking about ourselves, then, one of those new friend raps where you cover your whole life in a few hours. I noticed that Tony stuck pretty much to the facts, not revealing much about his deeper feelings. That made me wary, so I followed his lead. We had a lot in common, though. We were both proletarians who hated the greed and injustice in our culture. But we were also sensualists who wanted to enjoy some of the good things in life. We were determined to have a career we enjoyed, but also one that helped people. We both thought being committed to a woman was important, but wondered if traditional marriage was too restrictive. In short, we looked at life in pretty much the same way.

After Tony had fed Jonah, he put him on the floor on a blanket. We both stared at him for a long time, totally focused on him in that intense way that weed focuses you. It was so hard to believe he was there, alive, a tiny version of Tony created from his body and Claire's. It was awesome.

During our talk, the only place Tony and I seriously differed was over spirituality. We'd both been raised Catholic and we'd both left the Church, but I admitted I was always looking for something to fill the spiritual void that had left. For me, even experimenting with drugs had a spiritual purpose. Tony felt no such need. He was glad to be quit of the Church, and he used drugs only to deepen his enjoyment of things.

"Life as it is—that's enough for me," he said. "I like things I can see and touch and taste and smell. Looking for something more behind it is bullshit. You're born, you live, you die, and then you're gone. That's all there is to it."

I disagreed, but at that point in my life it was difficult to articulate what else I thought there was, so I only tried half-heartedly—and unconvincingly, I'm sure. I tried to explain I wasn't looking for something beyond life as it is, but something deeper that is part of life as it is, something we don't usually take into account as we go about earning our daily bread. Tony couldn't see it, but I even enjoyed disagreeing with him. Though he didn't understand my point of view, he really listened to what I had to say.

Tony and I were feeling so tight with one another by the time Claire returned that I was almost disappointed to see her. It had been too long since I'd had a good male friend, and I didn't want anything to break the spell. Jonah had fallen asleep on his blanket.

"You two look pretty mellow," she said, standing over us. "So does Jonah."

"I'd say we're pretty mellow, wouldn't you, John?"

"Pretty mellow just about sums it up."

"We gave Jonah a few hits, too," said Tony, smiling impishly, "so he's mellow, too."

"Yeah, sure," said Claire.

"How's Katie?" asked Tony.

Claire tossed her keys and purse onto the sofa and sat down on the floor, across from me. Her dress rode up onto her lap as she positioned herself, giving me a glimpse of her pale thighs and light-blue panties before she pressed the material down between her legs. Suddenly, I was not so unhappy that she had returned. Blushing, I looked down at my own lap.

"Katie's not so good," she said. "Al's been slapping her around again—in front of the kids, too, the bastard."

"Does he actually beat her up?" I asked incredulously.

"No, not really. He doesn't hurt her badly. He just humiliates her."

"Just," said Tony. "She should have left that asshole years ago."

"He's not always that way, Tony—you know that. You like him yourself, most of the time."

She addressed me. "Most of the time Al's really generous and warm, but he has these moods. Mostly when he drinks. I don't know. She loves him. And I think he loves her, too. What can I say . . . ? I'm gonna put Jonah to bed and get myself a beer. Either of you want to have one with me?"

"Not me," said Tony. "I'm going to bed. I've got the docks in the morning."

"John?"

"I should hit the road, if I'm going to go home."

"Why don't you just stay over again? C'mon, I don't want to drink alone."

"Well, if it's okay . . ."

I looked at Tony.

"It's fine with me, man," he said. "Have a beer and crash on the sofa again. It's a long way to Whitefolks Bay on the bus, and we sure as hell aren't going to drive you there tonight."

I reached behind me and patted the couch cushion. "Sold," I said.

"Good," said Claire.

She got to her feet and leaned over to pick up Jonah. The low-cut bodice of her dress revealed her full breasts. Again, I had to look away.

"Come on, Jonah," she said softly, as she lifted him. "Let's put you somewhere more comfortable."

Tony got up, too, and offered me his hand. We shook warmly.

"You're okay, Meyer," he said. "I like having you around."

"I like being here. Good night, buddy. It's been real."

When Tony and Claire left the room, I turned off the radio and put on Raw Sienna. I was still pretty stoned and the sensual music got to me immediately. I sat down on the floor again, leaned back against the couch, and closed my eyes. Waves of sensual energy flowed up and down my body. The touch of Claire's foot startled me.

"Are you awake?" she asked, standing over me, her hand wrapped around the neck of a beer bottle. "You don't have to do this, you know."

Her thighs were inches from my face.

"Do what? You mean stay up with you? But I want to."

"Okay. I set your beer down next to you."

She sat down and lit a cigarette, then held the pack out to me. I took one. She lit a match and leaned toward me to light it. It felt inordinately thrilling to have her do a small thing like that for me.

We talked easily together. She told me more about her sister, and we started talking about love relationships in general. I found myself relating the entire history of my relationships with women—short as it was at that point in my life. Claire seemed to soak up every word I said, which made me want to tell her more.

We were halfway through our second beer together when Jonah woke up.

"Oops," said Claire. "Feeding time at the zoo. I'll be right back."

She returned quickly, Jonah squalling in her arms. And, once again, I watched her feed him from her beautiful breasts. But this time I was stoned, and the music of Raw Sienna was reverberating in my body. Claire chatted away, and I tried desperately to hold up my end of the conversation, but all I could think about was how much I wanted to make love to her. Later, all by myself under a thin sheet on the couch, my imagination carried our encounter to an imaginary erotic conclusion.

~4~

THAT WEEKEND, NEWS ABOUT the Woodstock concert was all over the media. They were saying half a million people were there, a gathering of the counter-culture tribe from near and far. I was disappointed I'd made no effort to go. I had thought of it as just another concert, even if a mega-concert. But, hearing about it, I began to feel that I was missing a major social and cultural event of my generation.

My parents were appalled by it, of course. The newspaper accounts told of widespread marijuana smoking and some nudity in the steaming heat. We watched news footage of the swarming mass of people before supper on Saturday night. My dad muttered that there'd be "hell to pay" with that many drugged-up hippies crammed together without enough food or sanitary facilities. For once, I didn't argue with him. But I knew he was wrong. I knew there wouldn't be any trouble. Max Yasgur, the farmer who provided the land for the concert, put it best when he later said: "The important thing that you've proven to the world is that a half million young people can get together and have three days of fun and music and have nothing but fun and music, and God bless you for it!"

I had to get away that night to share the experience with people who understood it. I called Russo's right after supper, using the basement phone for privacy. Tony answered. We exchanged greetings.

"You following the news about Woodstock?" I asked.

"Yeah," he said dejectedly. "I could kick myself for not going along with Kolvacik."

"He's there?"

"Sure. Didn't he mention it the other night?"

"He made some comment about the concert in passing, but I didn't realize he was actually going."

"Hell, yes. He got tickets the minute he heard about it. He and some guys from Harley-Davidson rode their bikes out there. They offered to borrow one for me, if I wanted to go, but I didn't want to risk losing my number at the docks. What a bummer."

"I hear you. How about if we have our own little Woodstock Memorial Concert at your place? I need to share this with somebody who understands it, if you get my drift."

"The folks aren't digging it, huh? Come on over. Kolvacik's fiancé, Mina, is already here. She got left behind, too. We can all cry in our beer."

"I'll see if I can get my brother to give me a ride down. He's got the car for the night."

"Okay. But if you need a lift, give me a call."

George was agreeable enough about giving me a ride to Brady Street. He was curious about my lifestyle, being a neatly dressed, nose-to-the-grindstone economics student at Marquette, himself. My jeans and t-shirts were like dull plumage on an exotic bird to him, and he wondered if my habits were equally strange. I didn't usually tell him much about what went on in my life.

As we drove toward the East Side, I explained who the Russos were and how I knew them. George's forehead creased when I mentioned the Water Tower Park demonstration, but otherwise he didn't respond outwardly. I could see he was working up the courage to ask me something.

"You guys smoke marijuana, don't you," he finally blurted out, his eyes glued to the road in front of us.

I laughed out loud. I couldn't help it. He was so earnest about the whole thing. He looked over at me, obviously offended.

"Sorry," I said. "Of course we do. Why?"

Then he looked amazed. "Wow, you really do?"

"Plenty of people at Marquette do, too, George. I know some of them. It's not that big a deal these days."

He scratched his head as he pondered this view of reality.

"I've heard that from other kids, too. It amazes me. Isn't that stuff dangerous?"

"No more than Dad's martinis."

"But doesn't it make you want hard drugs?"

"Does Dad's drink before dinner make him want to be an alcoholic? Alcohol is a drug, too, you know. Drugs don't run you unless you let them—or unless you're wired for addiction."

He thought this over for some time.

"I suppose that could be true," he finally said, tentatively.

His overcautiousness irritated the hell out of me, sometimes.

"It's true, George. You don't have to think about it for five years to figure it out. Just take my word for it."

He let that go, and we rode in silence for the rest of the trip. But I could see he was working something over in his mind. When we pulled up in front of the Headroom, below the Russos' apartment, I mumbled a thank you, opened the door, and put one foot out. George put his hand on my arm. "Wait a second, John."

I turned back to him. "What is it, now, George?"

He glanced over his shoulder, as if worrying we'd been followed, and when he spoke his words were so soft that they were lost in the noise of a passing car.

"What?" I said irritably.

He rolled up his window to block the street noise.

"I said, I think I might want to try it, sometime."

"Try what?" I said.

"Marijuana. I'm not ready, yet, and I'm not sure I'll ever be, but if I do want to try it, will you show me how to do it?"

I couldn't help laughing again.

"You think I'm stupid, don't you?" he said.

"No. Of course not. It's just . . . we're just so different, that's all. Sure, George. If you ever decide to take the plunge, I'll be happy to introduce you. Like I said, it's really no big deal."

He looked at me seriously.

"It is for me, John. It is for me . . ."

And I could see that it was. For him it was as serious as going to a prostitute or stealing petty cash from one of his clubs at school. It was breaking the law. My friends and I never thought of it that way. We considered the law discriminatory and ridiculous and not worthy of obedience. What right did anyone have to say that alcohol was okay for some people, but grass wasn't okay for us? George was constitutionally incapable of thinking that way about established authority.

We said good night, and I watched as he drove off, shaking my head. I rang the Russos' bell. When Tony came down to let me in, I was grinning.

"What's so funny?" he asked.

"My straight little brother just asked me if I'd introduce him to dope, someday."

"Far out. Wookstock takes over the country!"

"Maybe that's it. Maybe change is in the air."

I went up ahead of Tony. When I walked through the door, Claire was in the rocking chair with Jonah on her shoulder. A woman I assumed to be Mina lay on her back on the floor with her eyes closed. She opened them. Joan Baez was warbling "Sad-Eyed Lady of the Lowlands." Claire put her finger to her lips to indicate I shouldn't talk. I went over to Claire and, spontaneously, leaned over and kissed her—a quick kiss, but on the mouth. She seemed a bit surprised, but didn't turn her cheek to ward it off. Her lips were soft and dry. She smelled faintly of mother's milk. When I turned, I thought Tony and Mina looked at me a bit strangely, but I might have been imagining it.

Claire got up and indicated without speaking that she was going to put Jonah down in his room. As soon as she left, the song ended, and Tony introduced me to Mina. She held up her hand while continuing to lie flat on her back. I shook it.

"Geez," she said, slurring her words a bit, "a handshake instead of a kiss. Could it be my deodorant?"

Tony laughed. I blushed. Mina was a beautiful olive-skinned Italian, with black hair, black brows, brown eyes so dark they were almost black, and a perfectly shaped miniature body, no more than five feet tall. She wore tight cut-off jeans and a bright paisley halter-top.

"Don't mind her," said Tony. "She's just drunk and horny because her old man's in Woodstock fucking naked hippie chicks."

"He damn well better not be," she shouted at the ceiling, her black eyes smoldering, "or I'll cut his balls off!"

She raised herself up on her elbows and looked me square in the eyes. "Or maybe I'll just fuck a tall, blonde hippie boy of my own . . . C'mon down here, big guy."

I was too horny, myself, to play such games. Without answering her, I parked myself in the easy chair on the other side of the room. Tony chuckled. "Scary, isn't she?" he said.

She turned on her side, facing me, supporting her head with one arm. Her thick, black hair cascaded down around her arm. "Aw, c'mon," she said. "Come to mama . . ."

I gulped. "I think I'd better just stay here."

"Goddamnit, a gentleman, too! Where you been hiding this one, Tony?"

He gave me a devilish look. "Just saving him for you, Mina, honey. He's all yours."

I shot him a withering glance.

"I'll go get us some fresh beers," he said. "You be nice to this boy while I'm gone, Mina."

He winked at me as he left the room. Mina crawled to her feet, adjusted her halter-top, and came toward me, a little unsteadily. Before I realized what was happening, she was nestled in my lap, her arms around my neck, her head resting on my shoulder. I felt awkward, but the sensation was hardly unpleasant. She was soft and warm and cuddly and smelled of some essential oil I couldn't quite identify. I felt her hot breath on my neck. The only thing that saved me from an embarrassing erection was that she was crushing my penis. In half-a-minute, she was fast asleep, making a tiny snoring noise.

Claire came into the room, cigarette and beer in hand, and looked at me quizzically, apparently afraid she'd startle Mina if she spoke.

"I don't think she'll wake up too easily," I said. "She's zonked."

Claire sat down on the floor and pulled the ashtray to her.

"Do you always inspire this kind of affection in women?" she asked, smiling.

"I wish."

"Poor Mina," said Claire. "She's always been a cheap drunk."

Tony came in and laughed loudly when he saw Mina on my lap. This woke her up. She looked up at me without taking her head off my shoulder.

"You're nice," she said.

"Thanks," I replied. "You're nice, too."

"Okay, Mina," said Tony as he handed a beer to her and one to me, "it's time to break out Tim's little surprise package. Where are you hiding it?"

She waved her hand in the general direction of the floor.

"It's in my purse, in a sealed envelope."

The purse was nowhere in sight. Tony finally found it around the corner of the sofa. He pulled out the envelope, tore it open, and poured four small orange tablets onto his open palm.

"Bayer aspirin for children," I said. "How thoughtful."

"Yeah," said Tony. "Tim must have left it in case Mina got a little headache worrying about him."

"Fuck you, Tony," said Mina. "It's mescaline. Tim scored some just before he left."

"Far out!" said Tony. "I've heard there was some good stuff around. Is this it?"

"Tim says it's good, for whatever that's worth," said Mina.

Claire must have noticed the concern on my face.

"Have you ever done mescaline?" she asked.

"Ah . . . no."

"It's not like acid or anything," said Tony. "It's much milder, more in the body than the head. You do see things in an interesting new way, but not all twisted up, the way it can be with acid."

"It's really nice," added Claire.

I knew immediately that, in that environment, with those people, I was ready to give it a try. I trusted them, and I was up for a new experience. It seemed in keeping with the Woodstock celebration.

"All right," I said. "I'm game."

"Far out," said Tony. "This might even wake up Mina."

She had dozed off on my shoulder again. Tony came over and shook her gently. "Come on, kid," he said. "Time to take your medicine."

She stirred, sat up, and shook her head.

"You've got to get out of working Saturdays, Mina," said Tony. "You're just not the party girl you used to be."

"Don't I know it," she replied.

"Where do you work?" I asked.

"At an answering service, out on Twenty-Fourth and Wells. You'd think there would be fewer calls on Saturday, but sometimes it's worse than a weekday. I can't figure it out. I'm dead tired."

"This will perk you up," said Tony, opening her hand and laying one of the orange tablets on it.

It looked beautiful against her olive skin.

"They always put a little speed in with it," he continued.

He gave one to me, one to Claire, kept one for himself. He held up his beer in one hand and his mescaline tablet in the other, said "Cheers," then popped the tablet into his mouth and took a swig of beer. Claire and Mina took theirs right away, too. I hesitated for a moment, then thought, "What the hell," and followed suit.

The moment I'd swallowed the tab, I thought about Jonah.

"Jesus, Claire, what about the baby?!"

"Don't worry. It's fine. This stuff really doesn't mess up your head the way acid can. I'd never do anything like that when he was around."

Nothing happened immediately, of course. It takes time for something like that to take hold. Tony put on Crosby, Still, Nash, and Young, and we just rapped for a while. Mina got off my lap and sat on the floor. We sipped our beers and waited for the gradual shift of consciousness to occur.

The first thing I noticed was that all the colorful shapes on Mina's paisley halter top seemed to be in motion, twisting sensuously in and out of one another around her breasts. Each color and shape seemed to be alive, to have a personality that manifested itself in the way it interacted with each of the other colors and shapes. It was beautiful and fascinating.

When the Crosby, Stills, Nash, and Young album ended, Tony put on Santana. It was wonderful body music, its primitive, pulsing drums sending waves of energy through us. Soon we were all up on our feet, dancing around the room—together, but also into our own head-trips. I tried whirling around once, but it was too much. I felt as if my head was going to come unscrewed. Tony snatched up his bongos and rapped on them as he danced. Claire's movements were slow and dreamy, half time to the music's beat. Mina was the most uninhibited. She gyrated sensuously around the room, weaving in and out among us, a rippling embodiment of the Latin rhythms. Watching her was arousing, but the effect of the mescaline was to distance me from my own arousal. There was no impulse to act on it.

We danced our way through the entire album. Our bodies were worn out, but our heads were clear and alert.

"I've got an idea," said Claire. "Come into the kitchen."

We followed her and she sat us all down around the kitchen table. Then she tiptoed into Jonah's room and came out with a familiar-looking box, but she hid the words on the cover, so we couldn't see what it was. She opened the box on the counter, unfolded sheets of smooth, shiny paper and set one in front of each of us. She filled a bowl with water and set it in the middle of the table. All of this without a word of explanation. Mina was the first to catch on.

"Fingerpaints!" she cried.

And sure enough, Claire next set out containers of red, yellow, green, and blue paint.

It was a magical, sensuous experience to fingerpaint while on mescaline. It engaged body and mind. The brilliant colors seemed to flow from our fingertips as we moved them sinuously across the wet paper, laying down areas of color at random, shaping images inside them, then changing the images with a few swipes of our fingers. We made blue roads, red trees, multi-colored rainbows. Each sheet was a world of its own, full of possibilities.

Claire left us after a while to feed Jonah. Then she brought him in and laid him down on a blanket on the floor to watch us. Eventually, he fell back to sleep. And still we worked, hardly speaking to one another, aside from exclamations of pleasure over our inventions.

When the special fingerpainting paper ran out, we used shelf paper. We put Jonah back in his bed, moved the kitchen table aside, and rolled out one long sheet, so we could all work together. We kept on painting and rolling out more paper, until, when we finally quit at midnight, we had a strip forty feet long, full of trees and flowers and hills and dancing figures. It was beautiful!

Then we realized that we'd unconsciously painted a celebration of the Woodstock Festival. With great ceremony, we carried it into the living room and taped it around the wall, then stood facing it, arm-in-arm, spellbound by what we'd created.

"Far fucking out," said Tony.

Eventually, with some reluctance, we detached ourselves from one another and stood around, not sure what to do next. Then Tony turned on their old black-and-white TV and found a W.C. Fields movie. Mina put on the headphones and laid back on the floor to listen to more Santana. Claire announced she was going to the kitchen to make popcorn. I said I'd join her.

While she got out the pan and started heating the oil, I cleaned up the mess we'd made with the fingerpaints. She and I didn't speak, at first, but I found myself inordinately thrilled to alone with her for the first time in several days. I kept pausing to watch her move around the room, from the cupboard to the refrigerator to the stove. She seemed to glide like a skater on a pond, her movements deft and sure. No doubt the mescaline enhanced this perception. That and the fact that I was in love with her. For it was then a realization that had been dancing around on the periphery of my consciousness leaped into full view. I was thrilled being with her because her being thrilled me.

As she stood at the stove, tending the popcorn pan, I had a sudden, intense desire to throw my arms around her. Instead, I kept wiping the same spot on the table, over and over again, as I stared at her back. She must have felt my gaze. She turned around and gave me a quizzical look.

"That's enough, John," she said.

For a second, I thought she'd read my mind. Then I realized she was talking about the table.

"You're going to rub a hole in it if you don't stop."

"Oh," I said, feeling sheepish, but unable to take my eyes off hers.

"Are you all right?" she asked.

"Me? Fine."

Her eyes searched mine for a moment, and we exchanged a confidence, but one so volatile that neither of us dared accept it. It was as if cupid had shot arrows toward our hearts but we'd turned them insubstantial before they could strike home.

The popcorn began to pop, and Claire turned back to the stove to watch over it. I went to the sink and rinsed out the paint-filled sponge, which discharged spurts of color as the water flowed through it. From the street below, I heard the sound of someone leaning on his car horn. It mixed with the sounds of running water and popcorn popping madly, until it was one big sound that grew and grew inside my head. Just as it was about to drive me over the edge, the car horn stopped abruptly. Then the popping slowed down. I shook my head, turned the water off, tossed the sponge onto the back of the sink, and turned to Claire, who was melting butter in a tiny saucepan.

"Anything I can do," I said, trying to sound casual.

She replied without lifting her head. "You can see if anybody wants a beer."

I wanted desperately to say something meaningful to her, but I had no idea what it should be.

We all ended up in front of the TV with the lights out, eating popcorn and watching W.C. Fields. Because of the mescaline, everything Fields said seemed swathed in innuendo—even the things that weren't intended to be. My mind turned a pretty straightforward comedy into a Moliere-like word play. I was almost totally engrossed by it. Occasionally, I looked over at Claire, hoping to catch her eye. In the blue glow of the television, she looked more wraithlike than ever. She never looked back—at least, not while I was looking at her.

The mescaline was beginning to wear off as the movie ended. It was time to call it a night. Tony had already promised to take Mina home, and I was relieved when he offered to drive me home, too. I wouldn't have felt comfortable staying over that night. Claire and I said a curt goodnight, and the rest of us made our way down to Tony's old yellow Bel Air, which was parked on the street.

We dropped Mina off at her parents' house, a few blocks west, then circled back to catch Lake Drive. Soft summery air flowed through the open windows as we drove past the huge houses along the lake. It carried the pleasant scent of flowers from rich people's gardens, and the sweet odor of lake water. There was enough of the mescaline high left to heighten my senses.

"Did I ever tell you I have a brother in 'Nam?" Tony asked suddenly.

Snapped abruptly from my reverie, I sat up straighter. "No, you didn't. I think you mentioned you had a brother in the service, but you didn't say anything about his being in Vietnam."

"I think about Joe a lot on nights like this. He loved to bomb around on his Harley all night when the weather was like this."

"What's he doing over there?"

"He's a Marine, a grunt—the worst job going. He joined up a year after high school. He was in Okinawa for a while. Then they sent him to 'Nam. He's been there for nine months, now. We hardly hear from him anymore."

"That's tough. My brother's there, too, but he's in the Navy, so he's not in too much danger."

"Smart guy. Kolvacik's best friend is a grunt, too."

"I assumed you were his best friend."

"I suppose I am, now. He and Mickey had a big falling out when Mickey joined up, right after high school. Tim told him he was stupid and Mickey didn't appreciate it. They didn't write each other at all, until this month, when Mickey got shipped over to 'Nam and started writing. I guess he figured he'd be needing a friend, and luckily Tim wasn't an asshole about it. I think he's really worried about Mickey."

"It sucks, all these good people getting sent over there to get their asses shot off."

We turned off Lake Drive and drove the four blocks to my street. It was overarched with majestic elms that formed a natural cathedral ceiling. The effect was emphasized by the headlights, which seemed to carve space out of the darkness.

"This is far out," said Tony.

"Isn't it fine?" I said proudly. "The sad thing is, Dutch elm disease has taken hold in the neighborhood. They say it could hit this block any day. It makes me want to cry. Here's my house."

We pulled up in front of the simple, white-sided house that had been home for most of my life. It had a small lawn in front, reasonably well cared for, but worn from use by the neighborhood kids, who always felt welcome there. The house was nestled in-between its neighbors, separated from them only by driveways. It looked cozy and secure. I thought of Marion, Ruth, Steven, and George, all fast asleep; Dad snoring away; Mom, who would wake up the second I walked in the door. I knew I would have to leave them soon, leave that house, strike out on my own, but it was not going to be easy.

Tony put a hand on my shoulder. "Take it easy, my man," he said.

We clasped hands. "I will. Thanks for the ride. I'll be in touch, soon."

I got out of the car and waved to him as he drove off. Inside the house, I reported in to Mom, then went upstairs. As I tiptoed through George's room in the dark, to get to my own, he suddenly said, "Hi, John," as if it were the middle of the day and sun was shining. I started.

"What the hell are you doing awake?" I asked.

"I can't sleep."

"Sorry to hear that."

I continued toward my room.

"John?"

I stopped, reluctantly.

"What? I'm tired."

"Are you high?"

"Jesus, George . . . A little. Why?"

"I was just wondering what it's like to be high on marijuana, that's all."

I wasn't about to mention that it wasn't marijuana I was high on. I was afraid the word mescaline would freak him out entirely.

"It's pleasant, that's all. Your senses are heightened. Like alcohol, but more interesting. I don't know. I can't describe it."

My tone was full of irritation.

"Okay, okay. I'm just curious. Hey, tomorrow morning's family brunch, you know."

Family brunch was a tradition that had started when I was ten or eleven, before Steven was even born. The last Sunday of every month, the whole family went to Mass, then came home and prepared a big brunch, everybody pitching in, one way or another. We always had a lot of fun.

"You're going to get up and go with us, aren't you?"

"That means I'd get about four hours of sleep. And then I'd have to sit through Mass. I don't know . . ."

"C'mon, John. You've missed the last two, you know. You'd make Mom and Dad really happy, and the rest of us would love to have you there, too. We hardly ever see you anymore."

"I'll try, George. That's the best I can do. Wake me when you get up. Now, good night. I'm beat."

In my room, I stripped quickly and lay down to sleep. As I lay there, my head danced with images formed with fingerpaints flowing from disembodied fingertips: Claire holding Jonah, Mina nestled in my lap, Tony beating on his bongos, my family lined up in a church pew. Finally, it all ran together and I fell asleep.

To MY SURPRISE, I felt pretty good when George woke me in the morning, so I decided to get up and join the family. I hoped to make up for the fight on the front porch the week before. As George had predicted, everyone seemed delighted to see me (though I think amazed comes closer to my parents' reaction). They all fawned over me in little ways. Marion complemented my new shirt. Mom gave me half-and-half for my coffee. George insisted I finish the last of the Welch's grape juice, which we hardly ever had in the house because it was so expensive. It was almost embarrassing.

Going to Mass at St. Veronica's was the true test of my resolve. The gigantic barn of a church evoked unpleasant memories of boring Masses, every day before school as well as on Sunday. That regime had taught me to hate going to Mass, and the whole experience still set my teeth on edge. I was anxious to leave from the moment I walked in, so it was a very long hour. I played a little "footsie" with Steven, who'd insisted on sitting next to me, and smiled bravely whenever Mom looked in my direction.

But, finally, it was over and we went back home to start brunch. I kicked Mom and Dad out of the kitchen, insisting that they read the Sunday paper while the rest of us cooked. Ruth made the coffee and orange juice. Marion tended the sausages, and Steven was put in charge of the toast. I made eggs, while George made home fries. It was a little crowded at the stove, but we managed to stay out of one another's way. Mom couldn't resist popping her head in to check on us. I think she was touched her children were working together so closely, and she didn't want to be left out of the scene. Despite our protestations, she ended up sitting at the kitchen table, watching us. But she managed to let us do all the work and she looked happy as could be.

We always ate family brunch in the dining room, because it was a special occasion. Dad led grace, and I noticed he was looking a little ashen-faced. I wondered if his heart was bothering him again. But it also struck me how attractive both he and Mom still were at what seemed to me the advanced age of fifty. Dad still had a full head of brown hair that matched his eyes, and his craggy face was handsome as ever. He was proud of his erect posture, which showed off his broad chest and shoulders. Mom's hair was graying uniformly, so it looked quite comely, especially with her blue-gray eyes. She was the one who enforced the diets that kept them both trim. She was quite a bit shorter than Dad and slightly stooped from years of childbearing and housework, but she exuded the dignity that comes from serving others with humility.

"Hey, John," said Ruth, halfway through the meal, her pudgy face beaming beneath blonde curls, "are you going to take us to a movie today? You've been promising to do that for weeks."

"Yeah," Steven chimed in, excitedly, "you have."

"I've got exams this week. I ought to study. Maybe George can take you." I looked to George to rescue me, but he didn't return my gaze.

"George always takes us," said Ruth, pouting. "We want you to take us."

"Yeah," said Steven again, imitating Ruth's pouty face.

Mom spoke up in my defense.

"Now, don't you kids bother your brother if he has to study. You can go to the Fox Bay this afternoon, on your own."

"We're tired of the Fox Bay," said Ruth. "We want to go out to the new shopping center"

"Maybe George can take you, then," said Mom.

"I've got things to do, too, you know," George protested, shoving his glasses up his nose with particular emphasis. "I'm working full time this summer."

"All right, all right," I said, raising a hand. "I don't want to start a fight. I can take a break this afternoon and drive you out there."

Steven and Ruth cheered. Marion looked pleased, too.

"Let's see *Pinocchio*," said Ruth.

Steven seconded the motion. I said it was fine with me. *Pinocchio* was one of my favorite Disney movies. It had just been re-released in the theatres.

"Do you want to go along?" I asked Marion. "Or are you too old for this kind of stuff, now?"

She blushed.

"I'll probably go. I don't get to do things with you much, anymore."

"How are your summer classes going, son?" asked Dad.

"Okay," I replied.

"Just okay?"

"I mean fine, just fine."

"What kind of grades do you expect to get?"

I knew he was pushing me. We'd gone around about grades many times before. He knew I couldn't care less about them. I didn't want to take the bait, but I was too tired to resist. "I don't know and I don't particularly care."

"You don't care what kind of grades you get?"

The tension was beginning to build in the room. Everyone could sense another argument brewing. They grew quiet and concentrated on their food, perhaps hoping that if they ignored what was going on, it'd go away.

"No, I don't care what kind of grades I get. I care about whether I like the classes and whether I'm learning anything from them."

"How do you know whether you're learning anything if you don't get good grades when you're tested on the material?"

"Frank . . ." said Mom, warning him.

He ignored her.

"I know in here," I said, tapping my head, "and in here," I continued, tapping my heart.

"And how is a prospective employer supposed to find out what's in your head? And why should he give a damn what's in your heart?"

"Employers don't give a damn about grades, either, Dad. All they want to know is that you have a degree."

He saw an opening and went for it, like a fencer touching with his rapier. "Well, Mr. Know-It-All, if you don't pay closer attention to your grades, you won't get your fancy degree, will you?"

"Damn you!" I said, standing up and accidentally knocking my chair over backwards. "I'll get my goddamn degree—don't you worry about it! Why don't you just get off my back?"

I stormed out of the dining room, through the kitchen, and started up the stairs toward my room. I heard Mom telling Dad he just didn't know when to quit, but I couldn't understand the reply he growled back at her. When I got to my room, I slammed the door and kicked a few things before dropping onto the bed, exasperated. It seemed my dad and I couldn't spend ten minutes together without getting into an argument. I hated it. But I wasn't going to let him bully me. I knew my way of looking at things worked for me, and I was ready to defend it.

Eventually, I calmed down enough to start studying. I sat on the bed with a pillow propped up behind me and reviewed my sociology book and class notes. I had been at it for several hours and was getting a little bleary-eyed when there was a knock on my door.

"Come in," I said wearily.

The door opened, and Marion stepped halfway in.

"Sorry to bother you, John, but it's three-thirty. We've got to go to the four o'clock movie if we're going to get home in time for supper."

"Okay," I said, snapping shut my notebook. "I need a break, anyway."

I dragged myself up off the bed and stretched. My legs were half-asleep, so I rubbed them. Marion stood in the doorway, watching me with a concerned look.

"What is it?" I asked.

"I don't know," she said. "I just wonder about you and Dad. Why do you always fight?"

"We just seem like oil and water, these days. We have very different ideas, and both feel strongly about them. He fought in a war and I'm refusing to; he's devout about religion and I'm an agnostic; he thinks grades are important and I think they're bullshit—excuse my language. Where's the mystery?"

She looked at me with big, sad, brown eyes but didn't speak.

"Look," I said, "I really hope to be able to move out, soon, but until then, he and I will probably—"

"I don't *want* you to move out, you know."

"I know. But I have to. Nothing's going to change between him and me, and we're making the rest of the family miserable. You know that."

She nodded gravely.

"You know he likes you more than any of us, don't you?" she said.

"What?"

"It's true. That's why he gets so angry with you. You're so much alike."

"Yeah, well . . ." I said, not wanting to believe her. "Let's get going to this movie or we won't make it."

We had a great time at the movie. George decided he'd go, too, so all five of us were alone together, for the first time in a long while. We'd all seen *Pinocchio* before—including Steven, who'd seen it as part of a birthday party, the week before—but that just made it more fun. We anticipated the exciting moments and sang along with Jiminy Cricket on "When You Wish Upon a Star" and with Pinocchio on "Got No Strings to Tie Me Down." We drove the people around us crazy, but we didn't care. We were in our own little world.

Afterward, we all piled back into the big Pontiac station wagon. Then, I had an idea. I turned around in the driver's seat and, with a sly look on my face, said "How about ice cream, gang—before supper!"

"Backwards Day!" cried Steven.

The others were all for it, too. We piled back out of the car and walked to the Baskin-Robbins, not far from the theatre in the new shopping center, where we sampled about half of the thirty-one flavors among us. By the time we got home, we were feeling a little sick, but we didn't let on. Mom couldn't figure out why we all ate so little, when she'd made us our favorite spaghetti and meatballs.

After supper, the spell seemed to break, and we all went our separate ways—Steven to bed, Ruth and Marion to the family room in the basement, George to his room to read, and I to mine for more studying. At nine o'clock, Ruth and Marion came in to say good night.

"That was fun today, John," said Ruth. "I wish you could be home with us every weekend."

George appeared in the door behind them in his summer pajamas. He had to be at work at seven o'clock the next morning.

"I wish you could, too, John," he said. "It's not the same around here without you. If you could just get along with Dad and Mom . . ." His voice trailed off. We both knew it was impossible.

"Thanks," I said. "I miss all of you. I wish I could feel comfortable being around more."

Marion picked at a sliver of wood on the doorframe, while George and Ruth gave me long looks. No one knew what else to say. Finally, George said goodnight. Marion and Ruth quickly followed suit. When they left, closing my door behind them, the little room suddenly seemed big and lonely.

-5-

N A CHARACTERISTICALLY generous move, Tony went with me to my arraignment for the shoplifting charge, during the first week of fall classes. He'd been through it before, during a wild period in high school, and he knew how scary it was, especially the first time.

At the courthouse, downtown, we were directed to a large room with wooden benches full of people waiting. In front of the room was a wide, beat-up oak table and chair. The room was windowless. Tony explained that the court clerk would call me forward, read the charges against me out loud, and ask for my plea. Then he would give me my court date. The expression "court date" sent a shiver up my spine. I couldn't believe I was going to have to face a judge—it just didn't seem real.

Ten minutes later, the clerk finally appeared. He was a short, balding man with his sleeves rolled up, his tie loose, and wet cigar stub protruding from his mouth. Clearly, he didn't feel the need to impress us with his appearance. Almost before he hit the chair, he barked out the first name on a list he'd brought in with him. When no one responded, he went on to the next. It wasn't until he read the third name, Gladys Murray, that a thin black woman in a short, tight red dress muttered, "Das me." She rose languidly and took her time getting up to the desk. Before she got there, the clerk started reading her indictment in a loud voice. She had been arrested for prostitution. His tone was essentially indifferent, with a tinge of self-righteousness, communicating that the accused was akin to the dirt under his fingernails. It was a tone that did not make me feel any more comfortable.

Gladys Murray pleaded guilty and was given a court date. As she ambled away, I heard the words "John Meyer." It took a second for me to connect the words to myself. I raised my hand and said "Here," as if it was a classroom roll call. The clerk eyed me, trying to figure out if I was being a wise guy. Apparently, the fear in my eyes convinced him I wasn't.

"Step forward, Mr. Meyer," he said in his monotone.

Tony whispered, "Good luck," as I rose to go. I smiled nervously at him, then stepped out into the aisle and made the long walk to the big table. Up close, the clerk was not nearly as intimidating. He looked small and round behind the huge slab of oak and his nose had the bulbous, rosy quality of an alcoholic's. He read the indictment swiftly, not looking up, then asked for my plea. I pleaded guilty.

"As a first offender pleading guilty, Mr. Meyer, you are eligible for Judge Duffy's community service program. This program allows you to work off your debt to the community by doing social service work somewhere in Milwaukee County. Are you interested in this program?"

This was a complete surprise. I'd never heard of Duffy's program, but it sounded a hell of a lot better than a big fine or time in jail. I told the man I was interested.

"Then you are to appear in Judge Duffy's court on Thursday, September 24th, at 9:30 a.m. Failure to appear will render you ineligible for the program. Any questions?"

I said no. Without telling me I was done, the clerk barked out the next name on his list. I walked back to Tony, who was beaming. As soon as we were out of the room, he slapped me on the back.

"Good work, man! You sure picked the right time to get into trouble. I'd heard about Duffy's program, but I forgot all about it. If all goes well, you won't even have a police record."

"Seriously?"

"Seriously. You lucked out, man!"

On the way back to Tony's house, we bought two bottles of Boone's Farm apple wine to celebrate. Claire was more than happy to celebrate with us. We sat in the living room, Jonah lying on the floor between us, pretty much entertaining himself. Occasionally, one of us shook a rattle for him or moved him back onto his blanket, but otherwise he was happy.

We were soon happy, too. The alcohol loosened our tongues, and we spent hours sharing stories about our past. I found out that Claire's father was a recovering alcoholic who had caused her a lot of grief as she was growing up—mostly mental grief, but with an occasional slap in the face when she opposed him too vociferously. She was the second oldest of five children. She had an older sister, then three younger boys who were still at home, with a much better life since their father had taken the pledge. It was a psychiatrist at the rehab center where her father went to dry out who turned Claire on to medical school.

I heard more about Tony's wild period, too. He'd "borrowed" cars for joy rides a couple of times, painted graffiti on his high school building, and participated in a few serious brawls with kids from other high schools. All of this had happened during six months when his father was out on strike with the rest of the county laborers. Tony laughed it off, but it was apparent there was a lot of pain behind the laughter he wasn't about to go into.

My big revelation was about having been a fat kid for most of my life. Claire was absolutely shocked when I showed her a picture of myself in eighth grade. (I carried it around in my wallet as a constant reminder I had to be careful about overindulging.) I was surprised by Claire's response, since, at the time, I still thought of myself as still being a bit too "stocky," as my mother always put it. But Claire, bless her heart, said she would never have guessed I'd been fat.

The more I drank, the more clearly I realized how in love with Claire I was. I was intoxicated by her. Feeling terribly disloyal, I fantasized about what might have happened between us if Tony hadn't gotten to her first. She seemed so open and gentle and caring. I wanted to tell her everything about myself, good and bad, because I felt she would take it in without judging me.

Throughout the day, I stayed as close to her as I could. I sat next to her on the floor as we all chatted, accompanied her to the grocery store when suppertime rolled around, stood at her elbow as we fried chicken, tossed salad, and mashed potatoes, sat across from her at the table, so I could stare into her deep green eyes while we ate. Tony hardly existed for me that day, but he didn't seem to notice my lack of attention to him or my excessive attention to Claire. He seemed happy to be off in his own little world. After our initial conversation in the living room, he went into a corner with a joint and a Dashiell Hammet mystery and didn't come out until supper was on the table.

What was it about Claire that drew me in so swiftly and inexorably? What made me love her, the moment I saw her? I've thought about that often, since then. Besides her beauty, which certainly provided the initial impetus, it was the sense of mystery that surrounded her. She seemed unfinished, a ghostlike figure awaiting something, or someone, to give her greater definition. I was convinced I could be the one to complete her, to make her whole, and that, in turn, she would make me whole, for I, too, felt ill-defined. She was one of those people who seem utterly receptive, simply because they listen so well and speak so little. It would never have crossed my mind not to trust Claire. She was an open vessel, into which I poured my feelings, knowing they would be safe.

With Tony, on the other hand, I knew from the start I could only go so far, only reveal so much. He didn't want to know too much. He believed in the traditional male friendship model, only slightly moderated by the more open psychology of the day. We'd hug and talk about relationships in a general way, but we never made ourselves truly vulnerable to one another. I never knew his real hopes and fears, and he never knew mine. Perhaps he sensed my feelings for Claire early on and never fully trusted me.

Despite our differing ways of relating, Tony and Claire and I got on well on the surface. We talked and laughed easily, worked together with instinctual smoothness, loved to eat and drink and be merry. We became a family almost instantaneously, incestuous longings and all. For a while, I provided a buffer between them while they sorted out their own confused feelings about being married to one another. But I was never content being in the middle.

That evening, Tony went to bed early again. Claire was sleepy, too, from the alcohol and the heavy supper. She lay on her back on the floor and, during a lull in our conversation, drifted off to sleep. I looked down on her from the sofa, her breasts rising and falling beneath her turquoise tank top. Raw Sienna was weaving its erotic spell again and a warm breeze blew in the window. She turned onto her side, her back to me, still sleeping. I almost convinced myself it would be okay to lie down behind her, put my arms around her, press my body against hers, and let nature take its course. I came very close to doing it, and scared myself so badly I left without waking her.

I stood at the bus stop down the street, shaking my head, hating myself for even considering such a thing with a friend's wife. But I also found myself looking back toward the apartment and fantasizing about what might have happened if I'd just had the courage to go through with it.

THE SESSION IN JUDGE DUFFY'S court, at the end of September, was relatively painless. He lectured me for a few minutes, then sentenced me to twenty hours of community service. If I did the service and wasn't arrested for a year afterward, my police record would be wiped clean. The only other thing I had to do was meet with the court chaplain immediately—and for as many sessions afterward as the chaplain deemed necessary.

Father Nussbaum was one of those rumpled, alcoholic-looking, middle-aged, Catholic priests who seem to have seen it all—as someone attached to the courts, he probably had. But, instead of making him hard, his experiences had made him gentle and compassionate. We sat in his tiny office, which looked out on a dimly lit airshaft, and chatted easily, while he chain-smoked Lucky Strikes. Occasionally, he would drop a gray ash on his black pants without noticing it.

He asked me about my family and about what had led me to shoplift and about what I felt, now that I'd had a chance to think it over. I told him I felt good about my family, but that things were rough between my parents and me. I explained what was happening the morning I lifted the book and told him I thought I'd learned my lesson and wouldn't do it again. He seemed to accept that, but he wasn't going to let me off the hook quite so easily.

"One thing I must insist on is that you tell your family about this."

My stomach did a flip.

"I don't suppose you've done that already?"

"Hell no!"

"I thought not. I think it's important you do. I can tell by the way you talk about your family they mean a great deal to you. If you don't confess to them and get their forgiveness, you'll always feel tainted around them. It'll hurt your intimacy."

I didn't answer him right away. Instead, I asked him for one of his Lucky Strikes. He shook one part way out of the pack and held it toward me. I took it, and he lit it for me with a dented stainless steel Zippo, exactly like the lighter my father used to have, before he quit smoking. I leaned forward, my elbows on my knees, and stared at the floor. I took several drags from the cigarette before I spoke. "How about if I just tell my brothers and sisters?"

"I think you need to tell your parents, too."

"But they'll use it against me. They already think I'm a fuck-up—excuse my language."

"Do you really think they'll do that?"

"Maybe not. I don't know. Are you really going to make me do this?"

Father Nussbaum brushed the ashes from his lap as he spoke. "I'm not going to ask you for a note from your parents to prove you've done it, but I will ask you about it the next time we meet." He stopped brushing and looked up. "I think I'll know if you're telling me the truth."

I knew damn well he would, too.

"I suggest you do it soon, sometime when the family is all together—perhaps even at supper, tonight."

"My father will kill me."

"He doesn't sound like a violent man to me. I think you mean that it will kill you to admit this to him. But that's exactly why you must. You'll feel cleansed, I guarantee."

I hated to admit it, but I knew he was right. He opened a little black appointment book on his desk. "Let's meet next week, at the same time, if that's convenient for you. I think it's important you tell your family by then."

I'd already decided I'd take his advice and tell them that night. I'd feel like a condemned man until I got it over with.

"The same time next week is fine. But what about the community service bit? I'd like to tell them how I'm going to pay for my mistake. That might ease the shock a bit."

"It's pretty wide open. You just need my approval for where you do your service. Do you have any ideas about what you'd like to do?"

"I've been thinking about doing some volunteer work for the Social Action Center, over on the East Side."

"I've heard of them. It's a Quaker organization, isn't it?"

"I guess so. I met the guy who runs it. He says they have a halfway house and a soup kitchen. He asked me if I'd like to do volunteer work for them, sometime. I guess I'll take him up on it."

"That sounds fine."

He fished out a sheet of paper from a side drawer in his desk.

"Take this form with you. Have whoever supervises your work fill in the number of hours for each day you work. When you've got twenty hours, bring it back to me."

I thanked Father Nussbaum for his help. He shook my hand warmly and wished me good luck with my family.

I worked at Siegel's for a few hours that afternoon, then went home for supper. My stomach seemed to get tighter with every block the bus traveled in the direction of my house. The walk from the bus stop home felt like a death march. I mumbled hello to my parents as I walked through the kitchen and went up to my room. I lay down on the bed and closed my eyes, but I couldn't relax. I opened my eyes and stared at the ceiling. How the hell was I going to justify what I'd done? I rehearsed a dozen ways to explain it, but they all sounded artificial. Finally, I decided I'd just have to speak from the heart and see what came out.

Mom called me down for supper. As I came down the steps into the kitchen, I saw that everyone else was already at the table, Mom and Dad on the ends, Marion, Ruth, and Steven on one side, and George on the other. My chair was between George and Dad. I sat down quickly. Dad led grace. For once, I prayed, too. I didn't have much faith, so I said to myself the only prayer I knew that made any sense to me, "Lord, I believe. Help my unbelief." It brought me the first peace I'd felt all afternoon, so I decided I'd speak up as soon as I had a chance.

The food started circulating the table. I cleared my throat. Marion looked across at me, sensing something.

"Ah, I have something to tell everybody."

The dishes stopped passing. Everybody looked at me. I'd tried to sound casual, but clearly my discomfort had communicated itself. I felt my bowels churning.

"A few weeks ago, I needed to read a book for one of my classes, really fast. There were no copies in the library, and when I got to the bookstore to buy it, I realized I only had fifty cents in my pocket. I didn't have time to scare up the money—I only had an hour to read the whole book—and it was only a ninety-five cent paperback, so, I . . . I took the book without paying for it."

"You stole it?" said George bluntly.

"I . . . took it, yes. The security guard saw me and he . . . arrested me. I had to go to Judge Duffy's court this morning. I'm sorry to ruin everybody's supper, but I thought I should tell you."

There was a seemingly endless silence. I stared down at my empty plate, dying for someone to say something—anything. Finally, Dad realigned his napkin, which he hadn't even put in his lap, yet.

"Well, we appreciate your telling us, John," he said. "This is quite a shock. None of our children has ever been arrested before. I don't know quite what to say."

"Do you have to go to jail?" asked Steven, wide-eyed, almost gleeful.

"No!" I said, more sharply than I'd intended.

Steven's smile died.

"I have to do twenty hours of community service work."

"Is this Judge Duffy's new program for first offenders?" asked Mom, a newspaper junkie always up on what was happening in Milwaukee.

I said it was.

The word "offender" sounded so harsh. It seemed to bring home to my dad the reality of what I'd done.

"So, you just went into the bookstore and stole a book, huh? You couldn't just wait and pay for it, the way decent people do?"

"I told you, Dad. I needed it right away. It was less than a dollar and I didn't think the store would miss it. I needed to read it for an English test."

"I thought you weren't worried about tests and grades and that kind of thing? Yet, you're ready to steal so you can do well on a test? I just can't figure you out, son."

"There's nothing to figure out. It was stupid and impulsive. I shouldn't have done it."

"I'll say," said my mother. "You kids think you can do whatever you want, these days. There are some rules you have to follow, you know."

"I did a report on shoplifting for my economics class," said George. "Did you know that prices go up because merchants have to make up for what they lose through shoplifting? You're not just hurting some big, rich company or institution when you shoplift, John. You're hurting all of us—including yourself."

For all his stodginess, George sometimes had real insight. In fact, I did justify my shoplifting, the few times I'd done it, as an almost Robin-Hood-like activity, stealing from the rich, who didn't need it and wouldn't miss it, and giving to the poor, in the person of myself. What he said destroyed that self-serving rationalization.

"George is right," said my dad, in a less combative tone. "You can't just think of yourself. Maybe your community service will help you consider others more. What are you planning to do?"

"There's a place called the Social Action Center, down on Brady Street. They run a soup kitchen and a halfway house for runaways. I think I'll volunteer with them. The good thing about Judge Duffy's program is that, if you stay clean for a year afterward, you don't have any police record."

"You should thank God for that," said Dad. "I just hope you've learned your lesson from this experience. And I hope you other kids have learned from it to. Your brother is lucky he didn't have to go to jail. He would have had a hard time finding a job if he had a criminal record."

Dad looked back to me and there was real tenderness in his eyes— something it seemed I hadn't seen for a long time.

"We really appreciate your telling us about this, son. We're not happy about it, but we're glad you didn't try to hide it from us. And we're glad you're making amends for it. Community service will do a whole lot more for you than jail, anyway."

The rest of the meal was unusually relaxed and enjoyable. I felt closer to my dad than I'd felt for some time. I knew it wouldn't last, but it was good to reclaim the warmth that once characterized our interactions. Sometimes I wished I was a little kid again, looking up to him as a hero, instead of seeing him as a man with questionable social, political, and religious ideas.

I slept well that night. The next day, in-between my morning and afternoon classes, I took the bus to the Social Action Center. The entrance to the building was on Brady Street. It opened onto a set of wooden steps so old they had wide grooves where people had tread on them. The steps led up to a long, narrow hallway. The Social Action Center was behind the first door on the left.

I opened the door to a large, unkempt, and sparsely furnished living room area. It had a bricked up fireplace, a threadbare, fake Oriental rug, a battered green sofa, two director's chairs, and a huge industrial cable spool, set on its side between the sofa and chairs to serve as a coffee table. Boxes of literature lined the walls and spilled out into the room. A large bulletin board across the room from the door displayed notices and hand-scrawled notes. A bay window to the left looked out over the busy intersection of Brady and Farwell.

"Hello," I called out.

Carl Lindstrom appeared in the doorway beside the bulletin board. He had on worn blue corduroy pants and a torn gray V-neck sweater over a yellow, button-down shirt. Again he was unshaven. And again I was struck by how thin he was, like someone with a debilitating disease.

"John," he said warmly. "I didn't think I'd see you here so soon."

I was amazed—and flattered—that he remembered my name.

"Well, you got a little help from Judge Duffy. I'm here to work off my debt to society."

"I see. Do you want to tell me what you did, or would you rather not say?"

"I don't mind telling you about it. Can we sit down?"

"Sure. Come on into my office."

I followed him through a small kitchen area and into a room that had once been a small bedroom. Now, it held a huge old wooden desk, piled with papers and magazines, and, along the walls, more boxes of literature. A narrow rollaway bed was tucked into a corner.

"Do you live here?" I asked.

"I do. It's not much, but I don't need much. And it's free."

"Not a bad deal."

"No. Except on nights when there are community-organizing meetings in the living room that go on until the wee hours of the morning. I can't go to bed until they're out of here."

"You rent that space for meetings?"

"Not rent, give. It's available to anyone in the community who wants to use it for a non-commercial venture. We have everything from writing groups to communist cell meetings. It's lively. Now, tell me about this debt to society you're obliged to pay."

I told him the whole story of the shoplifting arrest and its aftermath.

"I'm glad you've chosen to do your work with us," said Carl, when I was done. "We can use you. Would you rather work at the soup kitchen or the halfway house? The soup kitchen is up the street, in the basement of St. Anselm's. The half-way house is over near the tannery."

"The soup kitchen sounds right. I'm not sure I'm old enough to handle teenage runaways."

"We wouldn't ask you to take charge of anything, just to help keep the place in shape and spend some time with the kids."

"I still think the soup kitchen is better. It's such a tangible way to help people."

"Okay. When can you start? We serve meals every evening at 6:00. It's a two-hour gig, so you'll have to go ten times to cover your service hours. We can work out a schedule right now, if you want."

"How about Mondays and Thursdays for five weeks?"

He examined the schedule.

"That will work after next week. We've got enough people to cover those days through then. Shall I put you down?"

I said yes and then asked him if he could answer a draft question. I said I definitely wanted to drop my student deferment, and asked what I had to do. He dug out two pieces of paper stapled together from among the piles on his desk and handed them to me. They contained instructions on writing your draft board and included a section on dropping your 2S deferment. It still made me nervous to contemplate it.

"You're sure this will work?" I said.

"I wouldn't advise you to do it if I wasn't absolutely certain. Even if there's a crisis in Vietnam, they have enough draftees still eligible under the current number to handle it. There'll be no more numbers called this year."

I stared down at the paper.

"Far out."

~6~

TONY AND CLAIRE AND I were nearly inseparable over the next few months. Jonah began to be as comfortable with me as he was with his parents. They even joined me at St. Anselm's, dishing out food for street people. Jonah would sit in a high chair at the end of the serving table while we worked. I noticed Claire looking on anxiously whenever one of the street people approached him, but, from what I saw, no one ever even touched him. They would just look at him and smile, and Jonah, who was an outgoing kid, would smile back warmly. He became the mascot of the group on Mondays and Thursdays. We enjoyed being there so much that, after my five weeks of obligatory service, we all decided to continue.

I still had strong feelings for Claire, of course, but I sublimated them. I dated other women—even brought them to Tony and Claire's apartment—but nothing clicked with any of them. Maybe I was just going through the motions, trying to prove to myself—and perhaps to Tony—that I didn't want Claire.

Claire, Tony, and Jonah became a surrogate family for me, and that was good, because things were deteriorating rapidly at home. After a brief hiatus, when I first started working at the soup kitchen, we went back to our old ways.

As I'd predicted, Benjamin Grob's war against Port Publications for printing *Kaleidoscope* was escalating, and it became a major bone of contention between my mother and me. It wasn't long before Port Publications was hurting from the boycott, but they refused to knuckle under to the pressure. My mother called them stubborn pornographers; I called them heroic defenders of the First Amendment. We called one another any number of unflattering names. It got ugly, much to the chagrin of my siblings, who were innocent bystanders. Even George had enough sense to keep out of that one.

The war in Vietnam was escalating, too, much to my dad's pleasure. He believed that a full-scale invasion of the North was in order. I, of course, believed our troops should be going the other direction, leaving Vietnam to work out its own destiny. I had no illusions about the North Vietnamese. I could have accepted the U.S. aiding the South Vietnamese army, even advising its leaders—which was how we'd started out there, in the early sixties—but neither I nor any of my friends felt Americans should be drafted and forced to fight in a war that had no direct bearing on the fate of the United States.

It seemed that every time Nixon showed his homely face on TV to announce yet another escalation, Dad and I were watching together, just itching to mix it up. The usual result was a shouting match that sent my brothers and sisters scurrying for cover.

By Thanksgiving, things were intolerable. My parents and I were barely speaking to each other. My siblings tensed up the moment I walked in the door. I felt like a leper.

Somehow, at a Thanksgiving celebration with all my relatives, I ended up telling an older cousin about the situation. Jerry was a small-time architect in Chicago, a down-to-earth, practical kind of a guy. So, when he started telling me about the benefits of Transcendental Meditation, as taught by the Beatles' guru, Maharishi Mahesh Yogi, I listened a little more closely than I would have to a lot of other people.

He told me I couldn't change anyone but myself, so I might as well concentrate my energy there. He promised if I started meditating, I'd bring so much positive energy into the situation everyone would change as a result. He related a number of anecdotes about young people who'd seen this happen when they started meditating. He also said the learning process was simple and quick and I didn't have to become part of any organization in order to be allowed to learn. If I wanted, I could learn the technique, then go off and meditate alone for the rest of my life.

It was appealing, the simplicity and independence. I was ready to try almost anything to ease the tension at home and inside myself. But the Beatles connection made me wonder if the Maharishi was just a publicity hound. Jerry assured me that the Beatles had approached him, and there was nothing the Maharishi could do about the press's avid interest in them. "Anyway," he said, "it's the technique that's important. It helped change my life, and it could do the same thing for you. What have you got to lose?"

As I lay in bed that night, I seriously considered trying meditation to help relieve the tension as home, but, as it happened, help arrived in another form the very next day. Tony called to inform me that he and Claire had a line on a four-bedroom house for rent on Downer Avenue, just a few blocks south of the university. The rent was reasonable for a place that size, but it was still much more than they could handle alone. They had a friend of Kolvacik's committed to one of the bedrooms, but they needed somebody else to commit in order to make it go. He said they knew I wanted to get out of my parents' house and he and Claire would be pleased if I would live with them. We could all move in on New Year's Day.

I was flattered to be asked. It reinforced my feeling that Tony and Claire and Jonah were family. And the idea of moving into a house was much more appealing than moving into an apartment. It would give us all room to get away from one another, when the need arose. Figuring it quickly in my head, I calculated that, on my part-time income, I would just be able to make the rent and have enough left to pay for food and school. There wouldn't be any extras, but I found my entertainment with people, not expensive activities, so I didn't foresee a problem. And, if worse came to worse, I could work more hours. I accepted on the spot.

It wasn't until I got off the phone that it hit me. I was moving away from home for the first time in my life—probably forever. My stomach fluttered. Could I really make it on my own? Was I really that grown up? I had my doubts. But then I recalled my most recent fight with my parents.

I'd been arguing with my Mom over the *Kaleidoscope* boycott and made the mistake of swearing at her. My dad happened to be walking into the kitchen just then and he exploded. He pinned me to the wall with one of his huge hands and started screaming in my face, like a prison guard reading the riot act to a recalcitrant inmate. I think he came closer to hitting me at that moment than he ever had. I was truly frightened, as was Mom, who tried to pull him away. But he wasn't going anywhere until he was through. When he was, he stormed off to his room and slammed the door.

At supper, he looked thoroughly shaken. Right after grace, he apologized to everyone in the family and broke down in tears. I cried, too. So did Mom and Marion. After that, it was a long, quiet supper. But the handwriting was on the wall. I had to get out of there, for everybody's sake.

I announced my decision at the supper table the day of Tony's call. There was almost an audible sigh of relief from all gathered before the protestations began. They'd miss me; it wouldn't be the same family without me; would I really be able to make it on my own? It was kind of them to say those things, but I knew their heart wasn't in it. Inside, they were jumping for joy, and trying to imagine what it would be like to live in a household that wasn't in danger of blowing up at any moment. It was tough to be thought of as the troublemaker, the thorn in everyone's side. I felt more on the outs than ever.

We had an unstated holiday truce from then until the end of the year. Neither the war nor *Kaleidoscope* was mentioned. Dad offered to lend me money for school, if I came up short. Mom kept finding old things around the house—dishes, glasses, towels, silverware, and so on—and insisting I use them at my new house.

I found special Christmas presents for them—farewell gifts, I guess you'd have to say—expensive perfume for Mom and a big illustrated book on the Green Bay Packers for Dad, in which I wrote an inscription about how much I'd miss watching the games with him. They gave me a generous check—to help me get started the card said, since they wouldn't be there to look after me, day to day. The momentousness of what was about to happen hit home as we sat around the family Christmas tree. We all cried over our gifts. Their card said I was welcome to return, any time I wanted to, but we all knew I wouldn't be coming back.

On New Year's Eve, Claire and Tony and I went to a party at Kolvacik's. He and Mina had gotten married over Christmas and moved into a rundown townhouse apartment near her family's home on the lower East Side, which Kolvacik immediately dubbed "The Mansion." Usually, New Year's Eve was a meaningless holiday to me, marking the end of one arbitrary division of time and the beginning of another. But that year, when the clock struck twelve, I felt the weight of the world fall from my shoulders. I was no longer eligible for the draft and I was moving out of my parent's house.

No longer would I have to face the prospect of exile from my own country. No longer would I have to answer to someone else for the way I lived my life. I was safe. I was free. My life was my own. I kissed Claire, I kissed Mina, I kissed everyone in sight. I felt ready to take on the world.

The next day, on an overcast, frigid January 1st, 1970, the dawn of a new decade, Claire, Tony, Mina, Kolvacik, and Jonathan, the other room-mate, and I were at the new house, unloading the truck Tony had rented. We'd partied all night, but we were so excited about our new home that we were ready to work all day to set it up. Tony put Jonah in a playpen, borrowed for the occasion, situated so he could watch the action as we brought things through the front door. This kept him content most of the time, and when he wasn't, one of us would take a break to entertain him.

The house was wonderful, the kind of house I'd always dreamed of living in. It was a late Victorian covered in olive green clapboards with huge windows and a porch that ran around two sides. The front door was solid oak with a beveled glass window on top. The foyer was paneled from floor to ceiling in gumwood, a soft burnt-honey color that glowed in the light of a glass hanging lamp.

Straight ahead was a hallway that led to the kitchen. On the right was the staircase to the second floor with gumwood paneling all the way up. To the left was the living room, and beyond it, through a wide arch, was the dining room. The dining room had gumwood wainscoting, while the living room used the same wood for the moldings, top and bottom.

All the floors were oak, even in the kitchen, which was wide enough to hold a full-size kitchen table. The floors were a little worse for wear, but, after years in homes and apartments with wall-to-wall carpeting, we found them beautiful, anyway. The walls had recently been painted off-white throughout, so we wouldn't have to repaint unless we chose to.

All four bedrooms were upstairs, the two larger ones in front, both with bay windows, the two smaller ones in back, one on either side of the bathroom. Jonathan and I insisted that Claire and Tony have the largest bedroom, then we flipped a coin for the next largest one, which adjoined theirs—oddly enough, with an inner door connecting them, along with the standard doors that led from each room out into the hall. I wasn't sure if I wanted to win the toss or not. The thought of being separated from

Claire only by the thickness of a door excited me, but I wasn't sure I could bear overhearing her and Tony making love. I left my fate up to the toss of a coin. I called heads, and heads it was.

The house was so large that, if it hadn't been for a stroke of luck, we wouldn't have had enough furniture to make it looked lived-in. Claire had mentioned the house to a patient at the nursing home who was quite fond of her. The old woman lit up as Claire described it, saying it sounded just like the house she'd lived in all her life, until she'd come to the nursing home. She told Claire that she'd stored every stick of furniture from the house and insisted that Claire have it all.

Claire demurred, it being against the rules for staff to accept gifts from patients, other than simple things, such as flowers or candy. But the woman told her son, who approached Claire and insisted he would clear it with the management. He also told Claire there was considerably less furniture than his mother remembered, much of it having been sold at auction to help pay her nursing home bills. But there was a dining room set, a double bed, an easy chair, a rocking chair, assorted side chairs, a couple fake Oriental rugs, a phone table, a few lamps, and two end tables—enough to fill out our house in a way we never could have afforded to do on our own.

Working hard together, we had the furniture in place and most of the boxes unpacked by suppertime. We bought pizza and beer and collapsed in the living room. Kolvacik rolled a few j's, which mellowed us out considerably. It felt marvelous to be in our own house. I could tell that Kolvacik was jealous of the arrangement. I'd heard from Claire he'd nearly backed out of marrying Mina at the last minute, and he was already chafing under the restrictions of domestic life. He had told Tony if he'd had the chance to move in with them before the wedding arrangements had gotten so far along, he would have chosen that. Neither he nor Mina had looked too happy all day, and they seemed to be smoking a little too enthusiastically that evening.

As we sat around chatting, I got to know Jonathan a bit. He was tall and gangly—he seemed to fold himself into a chair when he sat down—with long red hair and a thin red beard. He was a serious sort of guy, though not without a sense of humor. He didn't smoke with us, and he didn't say much, but if you addressed him directly, he answered without reticence.

I knew he worked with Kolvacik out at the Harley-Davidson plant and that he'd just transferred from the University of Wisconsin-Madison to UW-Milwaukee the previous semester as a political science major. I asked him why he'd made the unusual transfer, Madison being much better known. He said he was interested in political organizing and that there was a lot more to be done on the Milwaukee campus than in Madison. He was certainly right about that. UW-Milwaukee had a well-deserved reputation for being apolitical—or apathetic, if you wanted to look at it that way.

Jonathan had grown up dreaming of going into traditional politics—he was from Boston and was weaned on the exploits of John F. Kennedy—but he'd lost interest in that. He said, somewhat vaguely, he was searching for alternative political solutions. Being from Boston, he had no family in the area, which was what had attracted him to living in the house with Tony, Claire, Jonah, and me. He'd lived in a group house in Madison and liked the family feeling of it.

It wasn't long before the work and excitement of the day—not to mention the beer and the dope—started to get to us all and conversation began to fade. Jonathan checked out early and went up to his room. I wasn't far behind. As I went up the stairs, Claire and Tony were announcing their intention to go to bed, too. Kolvacik protested, calling them wimps and party-poopers in a futile attempt to get them to stay up. Mina told him to cool it and get his coat. The last thing I heard before closing my bedroom door was Kolvacik calling her a bitch and telling her to get off his back.

It felt good to be in the quiet of my own room, though I always felt a little insecure being alone when I was stoned. I turned on the standing lamp beside my bed to warm things up. Having less furniture than anyone, I'd inherited the lamp from Claire's old lady friend, along with her bed, one of her rugs, and her rocking chair. I sat down in the chair and started to rock. If I rocked too fast, I felt dizzy, but if I rocked slowly, it felt soothing. My mind wandered off, and sometime later—five minutes or half-an-hour; I couldn't say—I heard Tony and Claire enter their room. They were discussing Tim and Mina, and I was a little shocked at how clearly their voices carried through the connecting door. None of us was going to have much privacy.

"I still say Tim never should have married Mina," said Claire.

"What the hell could he do?" asked Tony. "Her old man would've kicked the shit out of him if he'd called it off."

"Oh, you're exaggerating. Sure, he would've been pissed off, but he wouldn't have beaten Tim up. That wild man act of his is phony—it's like when a gorilla beats his chest."

"Well, I don't know about you, but I wouldn't want to cross a gorilla!"

"You know what I mean, Tony. It's all for show. He's never hit anybody in his life."

"How about shot?"

Claire ignored him. "I just hate to see them so miserable," she said. "They were both such happy people before."

"Well, nobody ever said marriage was easy."

"What's that supposed to mean?"

"I have to tell you what it means?"

"I guess not . . . Do you wish we weren't married, Tony?"

"Naaah. It's okay. No marriage is perfect."

"Geez, thanks for the vote of confidence."

"Well, are you going to contradict me?"

Claire didn't answer.

"I didn't think so," said Tony.

I cleared my throat.

"Hey," said Claire, a different tone in her voice, "you don't suppose he can . . ." I knew she must be pointing toward the door that connected our rooms.

"Maybe," said Tony. "We probably ought to put something over it. I don't want to talk anymore tonight, anyway. I'm beat."

I listened to the muted sounds of them undressing and their footsteps going to the bathroom and back, in turn. Finally, I heard the click of the bedroom light switch and the soft sound of their bodies sliding in under the sheets. Suddenly, I was hot with jealousy and desire. I wanted to be the one to share late-night chats with Claire. I wanted to be the one to slide under the sheets with her. I was tired of being on the outside. And then I was just tired. Without bothering to visit the bathroom, I stripped and crawled into bed, falling asleep almost instantly to the whoosh of cars passing by on Downer Avenue.

I ALWAYS THINK OF THOSE next few months, from January through April, as the party months (somewhat guiltily, I must admit—I'd planned to become more politically active, but once my butt wasn't on the line anymore, I let it slide). Due in part to Kolvacik's influence, our house became the center of nightly gatherings of friends and acquaintances. I got the feeling he spent more time at our house than he did at his own—without Mina, as often as not—and he often brought his buddies along. Tony and Claire never complained to him, although I heard them complaining to one another, late at night, sometimes. Jonathan never complained, either—he was usually off at one political meeting or another until all hours. And I was having too good a time to complain.

I enjoyed the constant availability of marijuana. It seemed to be part of the deal that we provided the space and Kolvacik provided the dope. It was always good stuff, too. I was drifting through life at that point, away from my family for the first time, unsure of my career plans, and without a girlfriend. It was easier to lose myself in a haze of marijuana than to deal with my feelings about any of those things.

It got so that Kolvacik depended on me to stretch out the evenings for him. Despite working early at the Harley-Davidson factory, he never seemed to want to quit. Tony and Claire generally went to bed long before he left. Even his buddies usually moved on before he was ready to call it a night. But I was never in a hurry to end the fun—especially with Tony and Claire in the bedroom next to mine. I preferred to know they were well asleep before I went to bed. So, for the first time since I'd met him, Kolvacik turned his full attention to me. I discovered that, when he needed you for something, Kolvacik had a way of making you feel special.

First, he set me apart from the others, praising my endurance and willingness to experiment. Then he told me more about himself, a kind of pseudo-self-revelation that made me feel trusted. He cooked up little escapades that bonded us to one another—like the night he took me to what he said was a special tree for him, overlooking the lake, and had us climb it together, thoroughly stoned. I'd never been a tree-climber, and I couldn't quite believe it when I found myself at the top, staring down the steep bluff and out over the dark lake. That was another talent Kolvacik had, talking you into doing things against your better judgment. He took perverse pleasure in my discomfort. But at least he didn't desert me—most of the time, anyway. It took him the better part of an hour to talk me down out of that tree, but he did it. And I've never been afraid of tree climbing since.

We also talked by the hour—sometimes in the living room and sometimes on long walks around the East Side or along the lake—about everything from education to politics to art to music to the nature of consciousness. Kolvacik was an inventive conversationalist, always presenting radical points-of-view that challenged my preconceptions. And he never failed to praise me for an original insight. It was difficult to pin down his real attitudes, his gut feelings, about things, though. Just when I thought I'd established his position on something, he'd swing around to the other side. It was dizzying, but it kept the conversation lively. Sometimes we talked right through the night.

During those party months, under Kolvacik's tutelage, I twice dropped acid. I would never have tried it with him alone—I was savvy enough not to trust him entirely—but there were always others involved. The first time I tried it, the experience was similar to the time I took mescaline, only more intense, more spiritual. It was easy to understand why Timothy Leary, the guru of LSD use (not to mention Aldous Huxley, many years before him), saw it as a door to spiritual perception that should be available to everyone.

While on acid, the boundary between myself and the rest of world blurred. At one point, we went outside and explored our little backyard. As I stood on the brown winter grass, I felt the energy that was my legs and the energy that was the earth flowing back and forth across the imaginary boundary at the bottom of my feet. Then we walked over to the river to watch water spill over a small dam. The rushing of the water was one with the rushing of my blood, both processes powerful and full of life. Even the stones along the riverbank, which I'd always thought of as cold, inert masses, sprang to life, revealing to my inner eye the ever-changing play of their energy.

The culminating experience was watching the sunrise from a landing at the top of a long set of steps leading from the end of Brady Street, at the top of the bluff, down to the footbridge over Lincoln Drive. Lake Michigan stretched out before us, vast as an ocean, matched only by the vastness of the dim sky above it. The light grew by degrees—and, truly, it did seem to grow, like something organic, one band of color sprouting from the previous one, forming a broad rainbow of pastels that stretched itself out above our heads, further and further from east to west, until we nearly fell over backwards trying to follow it.

And then, like the god humans took it to be for thousands of years, the sun began to come up, a molten red-orange disc, rising out of the vast lake like Poseidon from the ocean's depths. It grew and grew, sweeping the pastel from the sky, its red-orange light overtaking everything. Like a giant rising from sleep and unexpectedly levitating, it lifted itself out of the water and up into the sky. When we were finally able to tear our eyes away and look around, everything had been awakened by the light. The bare trees were defined by it. The glass of tall apartment buildings reflected it. Great clouds of birds flew out across the water toward its source, as if the light itself would feed them. And perhaps, I thought, it did feed them, perhaps it fed us all in ways beyond the obvious ones of giving us warmth and making things grow.

The second time I took acid—again supplied by Kolvacik—I made the mistake of watching a horror movie. It started out innocently enough. We were all gathered in the living room, enjoying the high, when Kolvacik turned on the *The Tingler*, one of Vincent Price's many B movies. At first, it was so absurd everyone enjoyed making fun of it. The premise of the movie was that, if someone experienced mortal terror and was unable to scream and release the terror, his spine would be crushed by a thing called *The Tingler*. The movie included a scene where Price, silhouetted behind a hospital screen, surgically removed a Tingler from a victim's back. It looked like a giant, wriggling centipede. The whole movie was utterly ridiculous—except for one scene.

In that scene, a man set out to frighten his wife to death. He hid in a closet and suddenly thrust his hand out toward her, through the partially opened door. The poor woman was dumb, so that, when she screamed, no sound came out. At that moment, the camera focused on her face, a mask of terror, her mouth wide open, her eyes hideous with fear.

I can't tell you a thing about the rest of the movie. That frightful image stuck with me for the rest of the night. I found myself terrified to go to the bathroom alone. When our visitors left, and everyone else in the house started upstairs to bed, I was panicking inside, but I managed to hold myself together. I went to my room and lay on the bed with all the lights on. Still, I was terrified, though I couldn't have said of what—of terror itself, I suppose.

I was all right as long as I could hear Tony and Claire rustling around in their bed, but eventually they fell asleep and the house became utterly quiet. Though the room was brightly lit, all I could think about was the darkness outside and the unnamable terrors it held. I couldn't imagine ever facing it alone again. I was certain I had crippled myself mentally for life, that I would never again be capable of being alone at night.

What have I done to myself? I kept thinking. *What am I going to do?*

Panic seized me again. Not caring what they would think if I woke them up, I turned off all but one dim light in my room, my heart pounding fiercely in the near-darkness, and opened the door to Tony and Claire's room. I couldn't see their faces. All I could make out were the two humps formed by their bodies under the quilt. But it was enough—barely enough—to stave off the panic. I dragged my rocking chair to the threshold, sat down, and stared at those reassuring humps on the bed. I knew then I would make it through the night. I wouldn't sleep, but I would make it.

Sunrise was a blessed event. I experienced first-hand the relief primitive humans must have felt when the light arrived each morning, relieving them of their real and imaginary terrors of the night. I was still worried that each night would bring the terrors back to me, but luckily I was wrong. Once I came down from the acid, the feeling passed. But it was not an experience I cared to repeat. I never took acid again.

Despite some bad experiences, I came to depend on Kolvacik's escapades to add excitement to my life. I found myself disappointed on those rare evenings when he didn't show up. The more time I spent with him, the less attention I paid to Claire. I knew she was disappointed, but we never spoke about it. I think she and I had both assumed that, living in such close proximity, we would grow closer. But at the outset it distanced us from one another. I felt I couldn't compete with Tony and Jonah. She felt she couldn't compete with the excitement Kolvacik's companionship offered me.

She also told me I was more distant when I was stoned, which was certainly true. In some part of me I knew that by smoking so much I was running away from her. I couldn't have her as a lover, and I couldn't bear just being her friend. The few times I awoke in the middle of the night to hear her and Tony making love, I was paralyzed with jealousy. I lay on my back, my body stiff, feeling like someone laid out on the rack. Every groan of pleasure I heard from their room was like a turn of the torture wheel. I wanted to scream, to leap up and pound on the connecting door—anything to shut them up. But I couldn't speak or move. All I could do was lie there and listen, tantalizing and torturing myself.

One night, in late March, I awoke to something else—the sound of a heated argument between Claire and Tony. I couldn't imagine how it had gotten started in the middle of the night, but by the time it woke me it had gone well beyond intense whispers across a pillow. Light leaked under the door, and I could hear Tony pacing in his bare feet. Though they were trying to keep their voices down, they often slid over into full vocalization.

The first thing that recorded itself in my hazy brain was Claire's voice saying, "Don't run away from me, Tony. You've got to deal with this."

"With what? All I hear is the usual bitching. What do you want from me?"

"I want you to listen to me, and I want you to talk to me. I don't know who you are anymore. And I don't think you know who I am."

"I haven't changed, Claire. There's nothing to talk about."

"You don't just talk when things change, when something dramatic happens. You talk every day. You share your feelings. I don't know what you're thinking about, anymore. I don't know what's important to you."

"I work at the fucking docks, okay? What the hell is there to talk about? 'Today I loaded a couple tons of ball-bearings, honey.' Is that what you want to hear? It's just bullshit."

"I don't mean that. I mean, what were you thinking about while you loaded them? Were you thinking about us, about Jonah and me? Were you thinking about school? Were you thinking about what you want to do with your life? That kind of stuff."

"I don't think about shit."

"I don't believe that, Tony."

He stopped pacing.

"So you don't fucking believe it. That's your choice. But it's true. I'm too goddamned bored and tired to think. What do you want me to do, make something up to entertain you?"

"I don't want to be entertained, Tony. I want to be loved. I want you to share yourself with me. It's like there's a wall of glass between us, lately. I see you, but I can't touch you."

"I don't have any energy left, Claire. I work my butt off at the docks, I go to classes, I study, I take care of Jonah, and I fall into bed. That's all I can do, right now. I don't have any energy for self-examination. If you're so sure there's something going on with me, why don't you tell me what it is."

"I'll tell you what I think it is. I think you're bored shitless—not just with work and school, but with me and maybe with Jonah, too."

"That's not true!"

"What, the Jonah part or the me part?"

"Well . . . both."

"Nice try, Tony. You just confirmed what I'm saying."

"Oh, fuck, I don't know what's going on! No, I don't feel that close to you, right now. I don't know why. I thought sharing the house would liven things up, take the pressure off of us, but I think it's just made it worse."

"I know. Now you have lots of new ways to avoid talking to me."

"Look, Claire, I'm tired, and I have to get up in a couple of hours. We can talk about this another time."

"When?"

"What do you mean, when? Some other time. Tomorrow."

"What time?"

Tony laughed. "What time?" he said.

"I'm not kidding, Tony. I won't let this slide."

"Jesus. All right, let's go out for supper. Maybe John will stay with Jonah. You can talk to your heart's content."

"*We* can talk, Tony. *We.*"

"All right, *we.* Can I go to sleep, now?"

Claire grudgingly agreed to end the discussion. The light went out, Tony got back in bed, and all was quiet. I don't know how quickly either of them got back to sleep. I wasn't able to drop off until after the sky had started to lighten.

I did babysit Jonah the following evening. He was at a delightful age. We'd celebrated his first birthday in January, and in February he'd started walking. By March, he was confident enough on his feet I could chase him around the house, which he loved. Tony and Claire left at six o'clock. I fed myself and Jonah. Then the fun began. Claire had warned me about getting him too worked up when he had a full stomach, but he wasn't about to be denied.

"Wun, wun," he kept saying, toddling down the hall and back again to tug on my hand. "Wun, wun."

The routine was for me to chase him from the kitchen into the living room, where he'd throw himself on the sofa and I'd tickle him. He'd let out a high-pitched giggle that never failed to crack me up. Then it was back to the kitchen, where we'd start all over again.

We must have done it three dozen times that night, until, finally, even he'd had enough. When I'd finished tickling him for the last time, I lay down on the floor on my back, weak from laughing. He lay on his belly on the sofa, staring at me, his soft brown hair disheveled, his big brown eyes shining with tears of laughter. I felt quite close to him in that moment, and I sensed he felt close to me. I'd looked into his eyes before, of course, but this time, with both of us relaxed and unguarded, I looked deeper than ever before.

What I saw is difficult to describe, but seeing it was one of the most profound experiences of my life. I saw not a child but a mature being, a soul, if you will, with experiences far beyond those Jonah had lived in a year. It was a being whose knowledge of life was equal to my own—perhaps even superior. It's an understatement to say it was an adult consciousness, but it was at least that, and I'd never seen anything like it in the eyes of a child.

Suddenly I knew, with the force of a revelation, that none of us enters this life a *tabula rasa*, as behaviorists would like us to believe. We bring with us a distinct, full-blown personality, perhaps in the genes, perhaps in some less definable area of consciousness, which makes us, from the beginning, more than we can communicate, more than anyone can perceive—except in an extraordinary moment such as the one I experienced with Jonah.

I'd always loved Jonah, as much for himself as for his blood connection to Claire, but this deepened my feelings for him. The prospect of caring for this little soul, nurturing him into adulthood, was suddenly very attractive. For the first time in my life, I knew for certain I wanted to raise children. I also knew that, if it came down to it, I wouldn't shrink from the task of raising Jonah.

This added a new dimension to my feelings for Claire. Combined with what I'd heard through the bedroom door the night before, this realization made room for a possibility I'd only entertained fleetingly before. Now it re-entered my mind and settled down for a long stay. What if Claire and

Tony broke up? What if Tony ran off to the west to avoid the draft? What if I married Claire and adopted Jonah? The possibility was terrifying and thrilling. It was more than I could bear to contemplate for long. But suddenly it became a possible future, something that might really happen.

When Claire and Tony came home, a few hours later, Jonah was asleep on the sofa, clutching the dirty remnant of a receiving blanket that was his frequent companion. The two of them looked happier together than they had for some time, but somehow that didn't bother me. Only time would tell if they belonged together anymore, and that long look into Jonah's eyes had given me a much-expanded sense of time. I could wait.

The three of use stood over Jonah as he lay there on his back, the blanket pressed against his cheek, his belly rising and falling with each breath. I think we felt closer, more like family, in that moment than we ever had before and ever would again.

~7~

HE PARTY ENDED IN MAY. I recall the exact moment. I was leaving for class on the morning of May fifth, a clear, beautiful spring day. As I came out the front door and down the steps, Jonathan was coming up the walk, looking tired and disheveled. Previously, when our paths had crossed at that hour, he'd only nodded and continued on into the house, where, I assumed, he went straight to bed. But this time he stopped in front of me, blocking the walk. He looked wild-eyed and determined.

"Do you know what happened, yesterday?" he said.

I said I didn't.

"Four students were killed by the National Guard at Kent State University in Ohio. They were demonstrating peacefully, unarmed, and they were shot down. Dead. This is it, John. They've gone too far. There's going to be a national student strike. We're shutting down the universities tomorrow, all over the country. School is bullshit. It's time for people to sit up and take notice. It's time to end this fucking war."

Without awaiting a reply, he pushed by me and up the steps. I was too shocked to try to stop him. Non-violent student protestors shot and killed? On a college campus in the United States of America? By National Guardsmen—citizen soldiers like . . . my father? It didn't seem possible. Did the misunderstanding between our generations run that deep? Were they ready to shoot us down for thinking differently from them?

I had to know more. I ran down to the convenience store on the corner and bought a copy of the *Milwaukee Sentinel*. There, on the front page, was the photo that was to become emblematic of the event: a woman rising from beside the body of her dead friend, turning toward the camera, screaming and crying. It had happened. It had really happened. Four students shot down in cold blood by men who could have been their fathers or brothers. No one was safe anymore.

I ran back to the house with the paper. Claire sat at the kitchen table feeding Jonah, who was in his high chair. The baby spoon in her hand was filled with strained peaches.

"Look at this," I said, my voice dulled by shock.

I dropped the paper onto the table beside her. She read the headline; she looked closely at the picture. Jonah reached for the spoon full of peaches. "How?" she said. "Why?"

"Nobody seems to know. It's not clear if an order was given. Apparently, the guardsmen aren't saying much."

"This could be one of us," she said. "This could be Jonathan or Tony or you or me. It's crazy. The world's gone crazy."

Jonah started squawking. Claire brought the spoon to his mouth. He gobbled down the peaches and immediately started agitating for more.

"Jonathan says there's going to be a student strike, starting tomorrow."

"Oh, great! So more people can get shot. You're not going to get involved, are you?"

"I don't know. Probably. I feel like things have gone too far, this time. First, the bombing of Cambodia, now this. Even that guy gunning his car into the crowd at the Street Festival on Sunday, right here in Milwaukee, and getting away with it. People are ready to kill us to stop us from thinking the way we do. I'm not going to let them scare me."

Claire was feeding Jonah furiously, now, spooning the food into his mouth so quickly he could hardly keep up.

"Goddamn men," she said. "Do you have to be such fucking idealists? You can't make them like you. Why don't you just stay away from them?"

"Why don't they just stay away from us? We don't want their fucking war!"

"Then don't go. But don't get yourself killed here, instead. What good will that do?"

"I'm not planning to get killed. But sometimes you've got to let them know that you're watching them, that they can't push you around."

"But they *can* push you around. They can push you around all they want. You can't change that."

"That's what they told black people during the civil rights movement. But when enough people got involved, they had to listen."

Claire was furiously tearing up a piece of toast over Jonah's tray. "Sure, after they killed a few dozen people. It just isn't worth it."

"How do you know if it's worth it? You've never had to worry about the draft."

"Never had to worry about the draft? I have a husband who could be taken away any minute if he fucks up in school!"

"Such as he is," I murmured, regretting the words immediately.

"What the hell is that supposed to mean?" she said, throwing the last bit of toast down in front of Jonah.

"Oh, don't play coy with me, Claire. I hear you two arguing at night."

She glared at me as she brushed the crumbs off her hands onto Jonah's tray, but didn't speak. Then she got up, went to the sink, and started washing her hands, her back to me.

"I'm sorry," I said. "That was a stupid thing to say. I try not to listen in, but, the fact is . . ."

I wanted to say it. I wanted to say, "The fact is I love you and I care about what's happening to you." But I was afraid of verbalizing something so explosive. Claire dried her hands on a towel lying on the counter, her back still to me. When she turned around, tears were running down her cheeks.

I went to her, took her in my arms, and started kissing the tears from her cheeks. Then I kissed her on the mouth and she kissed me back. Our arms encircling one another, we pressed our bodies together, kissing passionately. Now that the border had been crossed, we touched each other hungrily. If we'd been alone, I believe we would have made love right then and there. But suddenly Claire interposed her hands and pushed me back.

"No, John. We can't. Look."

I looked over my shoulder to see Jonah staring up at us, fascinated and bewildered. I winked at him and he smiled. "See," I said. "He doesn't mind."

I stepped toward her again, but she put a hand flat on my chest.

"No. This is wrong. I could do this so easily. But it's wrong."

"It's not wrong if we love each another."

"Yes, it is. You can't just marry someone and have a kid and then start falling in love with someone else."

"Sometimes you can't help it."

"I can help it. I can say no."

"Claire, I've got to tell you—"

"No! Don't tell me. I don't want to hear it. We've got to live in the same house together, you and me and Tony and Jonah. I don't want to hear something that'll make that impossible. Things have been going fine. You've been hanging out with Tim. Tony and I have been going to bed early—together. That's the way it should be. That's the way it has to be."

I had the feeling she was trying to convince herself, but I had the good sense not to say that. "Okay. If that's the way it has to be, I'll back off. But I'm always here for you, in whatever way you need me."

"John," she said, moving in closer again, "promise me you won't get involved with this strike."

"I can't promise that, Claire. I've been ignoring things for too long. I have to do something. Just because I got lucky with the draft, I can't pretend the problem has gone away. People like Tony and Tim can still get drafted, our brothers and friends are still over there. I owe it to them to protest what's going on."

"What about me? Don't you owe me anything? I thought you were about to say you loved me."

"That's a low blow, Claire. You have no right to push me away and then use my feelings against me. I'm going to school."

I picked up my knapsack, turned on my heels, and walked down the hall and out the front door. When I got to the sidewalk, I heard the door open behind me, but I kept walking.

"John," said Claire from the porch, "I'm sorry. That was stupid."

I stopped and looked toward her. A gentle spring breeze blew her long, fine hair across her face. She pushed it back.

"I'm sorry, too, Claire. Really sorry."

I walked on. I should have been thinking about Kent State, but all I could think about was Claire standing on our porch, her lovely hair blowing in the breeze, and the feel of her body pressed against mine. I considered turning back and trying to convince her to make love with me, but I was afraid of being rejected again.

The campus was buzzing. There were clusters of people all over engaged in heated discussions. When I got to my English class, late, they were not discussing the history of American literature but current American reality. A small woman with red "Afro" hair—not a regular member of the class—was standing in the aisle, arguing vehemently with the professor, a middle-aged man always neatly dressed in a white shirt and tie. That day, his tie was loose and his sleeves rolled up, revealing thick salt-and-pepper hair on his forearms. He was so agitated he didn't even notice me come in.

"I still don't see what good it'll do anybody to shut down this campus," he was saying to his adversary. "Education's what people need in order to fight ignorance in this country. It's ignorance that leads to wars like this—ignorance of other cultures, ignorance of human motivation, ignorance of our own historical shortcomings. What good will it do to stop people from learning?"

"Schools aren't the only place to learn, professor. There's a big world out there. We can't just pretend it doesn't exist. We've got to learn to deal with it. Any guy in this class could be sent over to Vietnam. What good would American literature do him if he got himself killed in a jungle on the other side of the world? Let's make sure that can't happen, first, then we'll get back to American Lit."

Most of the class, including me, cheered this speech. It even made our professor pause and think. But he couldn't quite believe the rationale.

"Are you proposing that universities just stop dead until the war ends?"

"No. But they can teach about something relevant to what's happening in the world. We want classes on Southeast Asian culture, on the history of U.S. involvement in Vietnam, on the military-industrial complex, on U.S. imperialism. We want to learn about the politics determining our fate. We're tired of learning for the sake of learning."

Again, we cheered her on.

"What do the rest of you have to say about this?"

"I'm for it," I said. "I'm not sure schools should teach only that stuff, but they ought to teach more of it. Maybe it'll take a strike to convince them of that."

"No more 'business as usual,'" said a guy on the other side of the room.

"This is bullshit," said a guy in the front row disdainfully. "I'm not paying to learn about contemporary politics here. I can read about that in newspapers and magazines. I want to be an English teacher. Learning about the military-industrial complex won't help me do that."

"But maybe it'll help keep you from getting your ass shot off," said the redhead. "Isn't that worth the price of admission?"

"You say it'll help me do that. I'm not convinced. I think we ought to—"

His words were drowned out as half-a-dozen people started talking at once. In the confusion, I could only make out bits and pieces of what people were saying.

". . . don't give a shit about the war, I want . . ."

". . . this is more important than that . . ."

". . . Only people with a good education can change what's happening . . ."

". . . and my folks would kill me if they thought I was . . ."

". . . cut off from the rest of the world. We've got to stay in touch with . . ."

"Okay, okay," the professor finally called out.

The room gradually quieted down.

"Whatever we think about all this, ultimately, we're clearly not going to get anything done today. If you want to stay and keep talking, fine, but anybody who wants to can go. For those not inclined toward political discussion, head on over to the library and read some of the articles I put on reserve—they'll be on the final exam. Barring a strike, I'll see you all at our next class."

About half the people in the class left, including our redheaded agitator, who undoubtedly moved on to another class to stir things up. The rest of us had a serious and volatile discussion about whether a student strike would serve any purpose. Some felt a strike would be a waste of time. Others, like me, felt that it would be a significant gesture in the wake of the Kent State shootings. It would say to the establishment we weren't going to ignore the issues, weren't going to be frightened away from our concerns by the death of our fellow students.

Some people were just worried about grades—they didn't want to waste the work they'd done all semester. I found this pathetic. It wasn't as if UWM was an expensive school. I asked them how losing one semester of credit compared to the fate of the Kent State students. It was an unfair question, but it shut them up and allowed us to concentrate on deciding if a student strike would serve a real purpose. After an hour and a half of discussion, most of us had decided it would.

By the time I got out, bright red flyers had been tacked up all over the place calling for a student strike at UWM in conjunction with a national student strike. It called on everyone to gather the following morning at 9:00 a.m. on the lawn in front of Mitchell Hall. As I was reading one of the flyers, Carl Lindstrom appeared at my elbow.

"Kent State's really got people riled up," he said. "I think there'll be a big turnout for the rally. Are you going?"

"I'm planning on it. How about you?"

He smiled faintly—the only way he ever smiled, it seemed. "I'm one of the organizers," he said. "It may cost me my draft counseling office here, but what the hell. I can always set up in the Episcopal center, across the street. The pastor there's on the organizing committee, too. We're meeting down at the Social Action Center tonight at seven. Want to join us?"

"Me? Help organize? I don't think I'm ready for that."

"I think you underestimate yourself, John, but you shouldn't take it on if you're not ready. Why don't you drop in tonight and see what it's all about?"

I told him I might. We promised to see one another in front of Mitchell Hall, the next day, if not before.

WALKING HOME FOR LUNCH, I entertained fantasies about leading a demonstration as part of the strike. I kept thinking of that Romantic painting of Victory leading the forces of France into battle. But demonstrations were supposed to be non-violent—at least, that was my image of them. I had been weaned on the non-violent philosophy of Martin Luther King, who had been killed in May two years before, the month I graduated from high school. To me, the participants in the civil rights movement were more heroic than soldiers. Unlike soldiers, they'd had nothing with which to defend themselves in the face of attack. And, yet, they'd marched on—from

Selma, Alabama, to the South Side of Milwaukee—insulted, threatened, spat upon, attacked with nightsticks, rocks, water hoses, police dogs, sometimes beaten, mutilated, and killed. But they were not moved from their goal. I wasn't sure I had that kind of resolve.

When I got back to the house, I found that Claire had gone off somewhere with Jonah. Jonathan had just gotten up, after only a few hours of sleep. I found him in the kitchen, his stocking feet up on the table, eating a carton of plain yogurt. He had no idea where Claire and Jonah had gone.

"Has the strike been announced?" he asked.

"The flyers were up after my class. Are you involved in organizing it?"

"Yeah, sort of. Part of it, anyway. Are you going to participate, or are you going to be a scab?"

"I'll be there."

"Where? In your classes or out on the lawn?"

"On the lawn, of course."

"Good man."

He swung his feet down, stood up, tossed the yogurt carton into the trash and his spoon into the sink. Then he tore a banana off the bunch on the counter and headed for the door.

"See you tomorrow," he said.

"Wait," I said, stopping him in the doorway to the hall. "Do you know something about the plans for tomorrow? What's going to happen?"

"Oh," he said, purposely being vague, "I don't know. A big demonstration, that's all. We're going to try to shut the place down."

"And what if people don't participate?"

He smiled knowingly. "We'll try to convince them that it's not a good idea to go to classes anymore."

"You going to the meeting at the Social Action Center tonight?"

"How do you know about that?"

"Carl Lindstrom told me about it."

"You know Carl?"

"He was my draft counselor last fall. He thinks I might be good at organizing."

"You offering to help?"

It was my turn to be vague. "Possibly. I don't know."

"Forget it, then. You've got to be sure. If you're not part of the solution, you're part of the problem. It's too risky otherwise—for everybody."

He started walking away.

"I think I'll come, tonight," I said, straining to please. "I know I support the strike."

He stopped with his hand on the front doorknob and turned to me. "It takes more than that to help lead it, but suit yourself. Just don't tie up the meeting with a lot of stupid questions, okay? We've been working toward something like this for a long time and we don't want amateurs fucking it up."

Without waiting for my reply, he was out the door. It wasn't until I looked into the refrigerator to find something for lunch that I realized it was my yogurt and banana he'd eaten. No doubt he felt he'd "liberated" them for the sake of the revolution.

I LEFT FOR WORK BEFORE CLAIRE RETURNED. As I made my deliveries for Siegel's, I listened to news about the Kent State incident and about the student strike being planned across the country. The shootings had politicized many students who'd previously been indifferent to Vietnam War protests, and widespread cooperation with the strike was expected. As always, there were those on the far right who felt the students had gotten what they deserved, but virtually everyone else, from moderate to liberal, felt the Guardsmen had seriously overreacted.

The radical left used the incident as evidence that it was time to take up arms against the establishment, but there weren't many buying that argument either. The vast majority of people wanted less violence, not more.

Listening to the news accounts inspired me and, by the time I was through with work, I'd decided I had to go to the meeting at the Social Action Center. I wasn't ready to commit to leading anything, but I wanted to see what was going down.

When I arrived, the main room was so full I could barely squeeze in the door. People filled the sofa and perched across its back; they sat on the floor, on tippy piles of boxes, on windowsills. Every inch of space was occupied. Those who arrived after me were forced to stand in the hall, although the Gray Panther representative, John Ascher, a man with shoulder length gray hair who was a head taller than anyone else in the room, kept warning us to close the door. He was worried, naively it seemed to me, about possible political enemies overhearing our plans. Any serious political enemies could have walked into the middle of that room while it filled up—and probably had.

I caught glimpses of Carl conferring with Ascher and with my roommate Jonathan and a few others in the vicinity of the industrial spool coffee table. I assumed these were the strike organizers. I recognized a black man, Jimmy Sommers, the head of SDS at UWM. He was the brother of a woman I'd dated briefly. He had a permanently angry look on his face that had always intimidated me when I visited their house.

Finally, Jimmy helped Carl up onto the spool. They were a study in contrast, Jimmy a broad-shouldered, stocky-legged man in a red flannel shirt and jeans, who could have passed for a lumberjack, Carl looking like the proverbial reed in the wind standing up there, as if the energy of the assembled multitude could knock him right off his perch. But I suspected that, despite his frail body and gentle demeanor, he was sure enough of himself to handle the crowd.

"All right," he said quietly. "Let's get started here."

Conversation ended abruptly and all eyes focused on him.

"We've got a lot of work to do tonight, if we want to bring off this strike tomorrow. It's a big undertaking at a school the size of UWM. We have an ad hoc committee here that's done some planning, but we want to know what all of you think about our ideas, so don't be afraid to speak up. And don't be afraid to ask questions, either. There's no such thing as a dumb question here."

I happened to look at Jonathan when Carl said this and saw him roll his eyes. As he'd made clear to me earlier, he was not so sanguine about the usefulness of less-than-perceptive questions.

"We have representatives of several different political groups on the committee, all of whom have a stake in the strike and the political upheaval we hope it will cause. We don't all agree about what we want to happen, once the strike is successful, but we've agreed on what we'd like to do to make it happen. That's what we're going to tell you about tonight, in the hopes we can hammer out a practical, intelligent plan and give people concrete tasks that'll make the strike happen.

"I've committed the Social Action Center as a meeting place for those involved in organizing the strike. Once the strike is successful, we want the Student Union to be strike headquarters, but until then—and in case we get pushed out—"

Here several boos were heard. Carl paused and put up his hand.

"I know, I know, none of us wants to think about it not working out, but we don't know what'll go down. Just in case, it's good to have a gathering place off campus, and this will be it. We'll try to have someone manning the phone at all times, to give out information and control rumors. The phone number is on a mimeographed information sheet we'll give to anyone who wants one.

"The way we're going to work things tonight is that each of us on the committee is going to present part of the plan. Actually, I'll present an overview of the plan and then each of the others will go into more detail about how we're going to organize specific segments. Let me remind you again to ask questions or make suggestions at any time. We don't want to run this meeting like fascists, so feel free to jump in."

No one was moved to jump in at that moment, so Carl went on.

"The major goal of the strike is to shut down the university in order to call attention to the idea that it shouldn't be business-as-usual in this country when a lot of people are dying unnecessarily over in Vietnam. We plan to open the strike with a rally and march, tomorrow morning at nine. At the end of the march, we'll go to the Union, take it over, and turn it into strike headquarters. Then we'll break up into smaller groups and make our way around the campus, confronting students and professors who aren't honoring the strike. We'll also issue press releases on the state of the strike from the Union. If all goes well, we'll reconvene in front of the chancellor's office at an appointed time—probably late in the afternoon, and take that over, too.

"The plan is to stay put in the Union and the chancellor's office until the university takes seriously our demands for more education on topics related to the war. In the Union, we'll demonstrate what we have in mind by holding seminars and staging performances on war-related issues. We have no idea how long this could take, so we need a sizeable core of committed people. I'm glad there are so many of you here tonight, but each of us will have to recruit more people tomorrow to make this feasible. We'll talk about how to do that later.

"Right now, I'd like to introduce Jimmy Sommers, the head of SDS at UWM, who'll talk about the rally that'll kick off the strike. But before Jimmy gets up here, are there any questions?"

"How do you think the pigs will respond to all of this?" asked someone across the room.

"The city police may not be involved at all. We have information that they'll have a sizeable contingent in some far corner of the campus, just in case they're needed. We'll see what the chancellor thinks constitutes needing them. He may see the size of the rally and panic immediately, or he may let us take over the Union. We just don't know."

"But what's our strategy if we do encounter them?" said a tough-looking guy in an army jacket with a unit patch and a Vietnam Veterans Against the War emblem on his sleeve. "Are we going to take them on or back off?"

This was the first time Carl looked unsure of himself. He looked down at Jonathan and Jimmy, standing below him, as if asking their permission. They both looked grim.

"This was a point of disagreement among the committee members," he finally said. "I, personally, want only non-violent action. So do a majority of the committee. But a couple others have different ideas. We agreed that they should be allowed to air those ideas here, even if we don't agree with them. You'll hear what they think about this issue when they get up to speak about the strike."

When no more questions were forthcoming, Carl introduced Jimmy, who leaped up onto the spool.

"First, let's get this rally shit out of the way, then I'll tell you what I think needs to go down tomorrow. The rally will start at nine sharp in front of Mitchell Hall. That big cement porch in front will be our stage. We'll have speakers from all different kinds of groups—SDS, Black Panthers, Gray Panthers, Gay Coalition, Vietnam Vets Against the War, etcetera, etcetera. They'll each talk about their perspective on the war. While that's happening, we'll be handing out literature telling people what we plan to do and why—with a big emphasis on the why. We need to convert people at this rally. We need to convince them there are more important things than going to class, that they can't keep their head buried in the sand any more. This country's coming apart at the seams. The quicker we can make the old order collapse, the sooner the new order can take its place. We might be able to do that peaceably for a while, but the Man isn't going to let us for long. He's gonna come down on our heads hard, and we've got to be ready for him. I say we don't lie down and let him pound us. I say we fight back—maybe just with rocks and the sticks from our protest signs, but, one way or another, fight back. We'll still get our heads busted, but we'll let 'em know that we mean business. And people will see—"

At this point the room erupted with voices, some saying "Right on" but most protesting, telling Sommers he was crazy, that we'd get ourselves killed, that this approach was stupid. He kept on talking, but I couldn't hear what he was saying anymore. People were arguing all around me. I saw Jonathan tug on Sommers's arm until he bent over to listen. Sommers nodded his head and got down from the spool. Jonathan climbed up. He didn't attempt to speak. He just stood there, surveying the room with a commanding expression. Gradually, the arguments began to die down, and it wasn't long before everyone was looking up at him. Soon, the room was silent, and still Jonathan had not spoken. It was fascinating to see my quiet, reserved roommate take control of a roomful of people. When he finally opened his mouth, he spoke very quietly, but he had total attention.

"You're supposed to hear about forming groups to disrupt classes, now, but that can wait. There are a lot of petty things—petty bourgeois things— that can wait. It's time to stop pussyfooting around with this government. It's time to bring it down. That's what we in the Communist Party intend to do, and we'd like any of you who are serious about changing things to join us."

Despite my abhorrence of the anti-Communist crusades my parents participated in and of the "Red-baiting" that characterized political discourse in the country at the time, I was shocked to hear Jonathan reveal himself as a Communist Party member. It was partially that I lived with the man and knew nothing about this, but it was also that, because of my upbringing in the fifties and early sixties, and despite the fact I didn't believe it intellectually any more, the idea of being a Communist still carried overtones of almost mythological evil in my mind. Jonathan Bradford, the guy across the hall from me, was actively engaged in activities designed to overthrow the U.S. government. I couldn't quite believe it. I was so distracted by this realization I missed several minutes of what Jonathan said.

I shook my head to clear it and tuned in again, just in time to hear him wind up.

"I'm not going to waste any more of your time talking about this bull-shit strike. This is meaningless. What a bunch of bourgeois students do and don't do will have no impact on the revolution that's about to happen. It's the workers who need to organize, not the intelligentsia. Our job is to serve the working people, to help them do what is so hard for them to do while they're under the thumb of capitalist bosses—organize to end their oppression. That's where it's happening, my friends. Not at UWM, not at Madison, not at Columbia or Berkeley or even at Kent State. Workers have been dying for the cause for a century. Now that we've lost a few of our own, we're finally concerned. Well, if you're really concerned, follow me out that door and down to Communist Party Headquarters. We are the people who are going to make a real revolution. Join us."

He jumped off the spool, parting the crowd as he walked toward the door. He seemed to be looking right at me as he approached, but his gaze went through me. A few people followed him, but only a few. When they'd left, the room erupted in conversation again. Carl got back up onto the spool and waited for things to quiet down again.

"Well," he said, "we're off to a flying start. If this keeps up, we won't have a strike committee left by tomorrow. Moving right along, I'd like to ask Bill Fleischer of the Vietnam Veterans Against the War to tell us about how we plan to occupy the Union."

Fleischer was pretty straight looking with his short blond hair and olive-green fatigues with the patches removed. He stood very straight, look-ing—and talking—more like a drill instructor than a war protestor.

"We expect the Union will be pretty well cleared-out when we get there—if the administration plans to let us have it, that is; but we'll get to that in a minute. If it's open, we'll proceed to the ballroom, then divide into smaller units and liberate the various areas—these will be the same units that'll eventually move on to the classrooms, by the way, but I'll let John Ascher tell you about that. We'll set up a communications center in the ballroom and assign areas around the building for teach-ins, street the-atre performances, draft counseling, food, and so on. We'll also have sen-tries posted at key doors and windows, so the police can't take us by surprise. The plan is to keep the place neat and clean—for a change, huh?—so nobody can complain we did any damage. We'll have people patrolling the place constantly to prevent trashing."

"Booooo!" said somebody near the window.

"Hey, we're not animals," said Fleischer hotly, his fair face reddening with dramatic swiftness. "If you wanna trash something, trash your own house. We want people to focus on the issues here, not our lack of hygiene."

"So, what *does* happen if the pigs won't let us into the Union?" asked the same guy who'd asked earlier about the police.

"We block it off," said Fleischer. "We lay down in front of the doors and prevent anyone from entering. We only let people out."

The questioner persisted.

"What if they start clubbing us and hauling us away? Do we help each other out or lie there like pussies and take it."

"Hey, asshole," said a voice from the back, which, it turned out, belonged to the Afro-haired redhead from my English class. "Keep your sexist comments to yourself. Having a vagina—and that's *vagina*, pal, not *pussy*—doesn't make me any less courageous than you. And while we're talking about courage, it takes a lot more of it to sit still and take a beating and make a point than it does to fight back."

"Bullshit," said her antagonist.

"Okay, troops," said Fleischer, cutting things off before they could get out of hand, "have your philosophical arguments somewhere else. We're trying to get things organized here. The fact is, the committee has decided on a non-violent approach. We want to make friends, not create more enemies than we already have. If you're not comfortable with that approach, you might as well leave, because we'll be wasting your time."

"Count me out," said the heckler, shouldering his way through the crowd. "You're all a bunch of pussies." He paused and looked back toward the redhead. "And I do mean *pussies*, sweetheart," he said.

He continued out the door, pursued by catcalls.

The rest of the evening was spent on the nitty-gritty of strike organization and techniques of non-violent protest, though occasionally someone burst into a political diatribe of one kind or another. It was as if each of these people had a personal agenda they couldn't bear to put aside, even for one evening. To be more fair, perhaps it was the first time most of them had found an opportunity to speak their mind in public.

Whatever the reason, it made me less than sanguine about the rally. There were already half-a-dozen speakers on the docket. Add to those the spontaneous speakers sure to emerge, and we could lose our audience long before we were ready to move them toward the Union. I could only hope someone sensible like Carl or Bill would monitor the microphone and keep things under control.

I volunteered to lead a group to liberate the snack bar, though I was not entirely sure I could handle the job. The eating area there was an important space in the Union, with a sunken central section perfect for political performances by groups such as Theatre X. I believed that art and drama were important tools for winning people over to the cause, so I was motivated to secure a space for those activities. I was also committed to preventing the kind of abuses—theft and vandalism—bound to tempt some demonstrators in a place as familiar and fully of "booty" as the snack bar. I agreed completely with Fleischer it was important not to distract people from our purpose by acting like juvenile delinquents.

By the time the meeting broke up, it was two o'clock in the morning. I managed to get a lift back to the house on Downer. As we pulled up, I noticed a light burning in the living room window. I guessed Kolvacik was there, and I was not thrilled at the prospect of having to get by him to go to bed. He'd want me to play with him all night long, no doubt, and I was beat. I sighed, said goodnight to the others in the car, got out, and walked slowly toward the door. As I mounted the steps to the porch, I looked through the bay window into the living room and saw, not Kolvacik, but Claire sitting on the couch in a brief pink nightie, her long, slender legs crossed, her brows knitted in thought. My mouth went dry and my heart started to pound.

With shaky hands, I managed to unlock the front door and go in. I entered the living room. Bathed in the light of a pole lamp beside her, her blonde hair shimmering, Claire looked particularly angelic, but the pink nightie set off her flesh, too, its low-cut neckline emphasizing the swell of her breasts, its arrested hemline revealing the entire length of her thighs. Neither of us spoke. I stood in the archway, staring into her eyes, looking for a clue about what I was supposed to do. In reply, she uncrossed her legs and opened her arms. I went to her quickly and knelt down between her thighs. She took my face in her hands, studied it for a moment, then leaned forward and kissed me, a long, deep kiss whose message was perfectly clear.

The rational part of my brain was sending out panicky messages: *You can't do this with Claire—certainly not here, not now! What if Tony comes down? What if Jonathan walks in? What will happen afterward?* But the rest of my body wasn't listening. Claire and I made love—right then, right there on the sofa, not even bothering to turn out the light. My body felt as if it had come home.

After making love, we lay in each other's arms on the couch. We had yet to utter a sound, outside the mumbles and moans of lovers. Initially overwhelmed with passion, then confused and exhausted, neither of us had even said, "I love you." I spoke first, moving strands of pale hair off her face as I did. "I want to be able to do this with you forever—you know that, don't you?"

She nodded.

"What are we doing to do, babe?" I asked.

"We can do whatever we want to," she said. "Tony's moving upstairs."

"What do you mean, upstairs?"

"The attic. He's going to build himself a room up there."

"Alone?"

"Let me get a cigarette, and I'll tell you about it."

I let her up. She picked up her panties and nightie from the floor and put them on. With her slow, languid, cat-like movements, it was as exciting to watch her put them back on as it had been to help her take them off. My penis began to swell again. She noticed and smiled.

"Put that thing away, will you. It's too distracting."

I pulled on my jeans but left my shirt off. Claire lit a cigarette. When I asked for one, she lit it off of her own and handed it to me. We sat on either end of the couch, our feet touching in the middle. She held the big green ashtray on her lap. I collected my ashes in the palm of my hand. A warm, gentle night breeze blew the sheer curtains in the bay window.

"Tony and I had it out this afternoon," she said. "He came home from work in a foul mood, the way he always does lately. I just wouldn't take it. We started arguing about something stupid, and it went downhill from there. Luckily, Jonah was over still over at Susie's. When we were through, he drove off to the lumberyard. He came back with a load of two-by-fours sticking out the car window. He hauled them up to the attic and started pounding away. He wouldn't even come down for supper. His sleeping bag's up there. I assume he's sleeping in that."

"What does this mean?"

"It means we're separated."

"Living in the same house?"

"We can't afford to do it any other way."

The simple practicality of this answer left nothing more to say on that subject.

"How do you feel about it?" I asked.

She took a long drag on her cigarette, tilted her head back, and blew the smoke into the air. Then she shaped the ash on the edge of the ashtray. I leaned forward and dumped the ashes from my palm into the ashtray.

"Relieved, I guess," she finally said. "I'm tired of trying to make it work with him. I don't really believe it's over, but it might be. This could be the beginning of the end."

She took another drag of her cigarette, blew the smoke out and sniffed a few times. I wondered if she was going to cry, but I didn't see any sign of tears in her eyes. Suddenly, a wave of concern and tenderness washed over me. I leaned forward and wrapped my free hand around her foot, which was calloused on the bottom from walking barefoot, but incredibly soft on top.

"Claire," I said, to get her to focus on me.

Her eyes met mine, and once again I noticed how they seemed to glow like a cat's. "I love you," I said.

Her cat's eyes became kittenish for a moment, but the wary glow quickly returned.

"I want to love you, John," she said. "But I don't know if I can love anyone. Relationships are so fucked up . . ."

My stomach dropped. I could have dealt with tears and anguish, but I was afraid of her confusion. I wanted it to be simple. I wanted her to want me, instead of Tony. I let the disappointment pass before I spoke, allowing a saner voice to prevail in my head. Still, I found myself having to subdue fearful feelings in order to speak what that voice said to me.

"Of you course you don't know what you want," I said, squeezing her foot. "It's all brand new. It'll take time. But I'm here for you. I really do love you."

Claire searched my eyes. My throat was constricted with emotion as I tried to hide my fear she would reject me. She looked away without revealing anything, stubbed out her cigarette in the ashtray, and held it out to me, so I could put out mine. I was afraid to look in her eyes. I put out the cigarette. She set the ashtray down on the floor beside her. Then, to my surprise, she slid down onto the sofa, opened her thighs, and reached toward me.

"Make love to me again, John," she said quietly.

Tears welled up in my eyes. I went to her.

After making love again, we fell asleep, but luckily I awoke in time to get upstairs before Tony came down to go to work. I wasn't ready for that confrontation, yet. I left Claire sleeping on the couch, but not before putting a blanket over her and pausing a long moment to look at her. She was so beautiful! I felt privileged to be her lover. It was like a dream come true. But then I thought of Tony and realized that it could rapidly turn into a nightmare.

Up in my room, I fell onto the bed, exhausted, but my mind was full of thoughts about Claire and about the student strike, and I couldn't get back to sleep. I heard Tony clump downstairs to the kitchen in his work boots. Soon, I heard him go out the back door, start up his car, and drive away. I was thinking of going down to Claire again when sleep finally overwhelmed me.

~ 8 ~

WAS AWAKENED BY THE SOUND of Jonah crying in the kitchen. It took a few minutes for reality to set in, to comprehend that I had really made love to Claire and committed myself to helping lead a student strike. How could so much have happened in one night? It had seemed like a romantic drama by moonlight, but in the harsh clarity of sunlight, it was frightening. A knot of tension formed in my stomach.

I pulled on a red t-shirt over my jockey shorts and wandered downstairs, looking for reassurance from Claire. But I found her flying around the kitchen in her white uniform, which was rumpled from having sat in the dryer all night. She was trying to make herself a lunch while feeding Jonah breakfast.

"Oh, John, I'm so glad you're up," she said, sliding a banana into her lunch bag and folding over the top. "I was just going to come and get you. Susie will be here in five minutes to give me a ride to work and take Jonah to her house. I haven't even brushed my hair. Would you feed him his pears?"

Before I could answer, she was on her way out the door and up the stairs to the bathroom. Jonah, who had been momentarily distracted by my entrance, realized I was the only source of food in the room and started squawking at me. I stared after Claire.

"Of course I'll feed Jonah his pears," I muttered under my breath as I sat down in front of him. "What else could I possibly have on my mind after last night? Huh, Jonah? All I did was make love to your mother. But that's okay. No need for her to worry about my feelings. I'll be just fine."

109

Jonah's only thought was for his food. He watched intently as I opened the little jar of strained pears. His eyes followed the spoon back and forth, each time I filled it and brought it to his mouth. Only when we reached the bottom and his appetite was sated did he pause to look into my eyes. He seemed to be looking for something in them. Perhaps he sensed that something had changed, that somehow I was connected to him in a way I hadn't been before. I had no doubt children were capable of picking up such things, but, on that occasion, I could have been imagining it. I wanted some kind of affirmation of what had happened.

A car honked at the front of the house. I handed Jonah a piece of melba toast that was sitting on the edge of the table and went to the bay window in the living room. Susie saw me and waved. I waved back. Claire came flying down the stairs, trailing her purse and a diaper bag.

"Did you wipe Jonah's mouth?" she said, dropping the bags at the bottom of the stairs.

"He's still eating melba toast," I replied coolly.

Claire had taken a step toward the kitchen, but my tone stopped her. She turned to me.

"Look, John, I'm sorry I can't be more responsive, but this is my life. If you're going to do a hurt dance every time things get hectic for me, we might as well forget it right now. I don't need it."

She continued on into the kitchen and returned, a moment later, with Jonah in her arms, still chewing on his now-slimy melba toast. I picked up her bags and started toward the door.

"Thanks," she said, "but just put them over my shoulder. In case you haven't noticed, you don't have pants on. I don't want to scandalize my sister."

I looked down and laughed. She laughed too. Then Jonah joined us.

I hung the bags carefully over her shoulder, then leaned past Jonah and kissed her full on the mouth. She resisted for a second, then her lips melted into mine. When I pulled back, Jonah looked back and forth from me to Claire with a curious expression.

"Will you be home for supper?" Claire asked.

"Well . . . probably not, actually. I never got a chance to tell you, but I'm helping lead the student strike today. By suppertime, we'll either be occupying the student union or a holding cell downtown."

I smiled. Claire was not amused. Her sister honked again, this time more insistently.

"I can't believe it," she said. "After everything I said to you yesterday morning? After what happened between us last night? I don't have time to deal with this, now. Call me at work before you leave."

She marched by me and yanked open the front door.

"And don't forget!" she called over her shoulder.

After returning to my room to put on a pair of jeans, I went to the kitchen, poured myself a bowl of cornflakes, and cut up a banana on top of it. I went out onto the front porch steps to eat. It was unusually warm for early May. The sun on my face was summer-like. The sense-memory of making love to Claire lingered in my body, making it feel relaxed and languid. In the sun, even my mind began to relax. I had no idea what the day would bring, but instead of worrying about it, I let it go. By the same time the next day, I could be in jail, with Claire kissing me through the bars, or the strike could have failed entirely and Claire could be back with Tony. Who the hell know what was going to happen. As the song said, "*Que sera, sera.*"

The cereal barely made a dent in my appetite, and I didn't know when I'd get a chance to eat again, so I made two pieces of toast, slathered them with peanut butter and jelly, poured a glass of milk, and returned to the porch. I was halfway through the second piece when the phone rang. I returned to the kitchen to use the wall phone.

"Okay," said Claire, starting right in, "I only have a couple minutes. What's this about you leading the strike?"

"I'm just going to help out. I think it's important that colleges start paying attention to the war. The strike will let them know that they can't go on as if nothing is happening."

"Four people got killed at Kent State. Isn't that important?"

"Think of all the guys our age getting killed in Vietnam! Not to mention all the Vietnamese they're killing. It's worth it if it helps stop that."

"But it won't!"

"How do you know? And even if it doesn't, we still have to protest it. Do you believe the Germans should have protested their government's oppression of Jews, even though they might not have been able to stop it?"

"Of course. But that's different."

"The point is, when you believe your government's behavior is morally wrong, you have a responsibility to protest it. I think the war and the draft are morally wrong, so I have to protest them."

"Oh, quit being so fucking logical, John. You don't have to convince me. I'm just trying to tell you I'm worried about you."

My heart skipped a beat. "No need. I'm not a hero. If anybody pulls a gun, I'll head in the other direction."

"It's not funny, John. Not any more."

"I know. Look, I'll be careful. I promise. Will you and Jonah come and visit me at the Union, this afternoon, if it all works out?"

"We'll see. Only if I'm sure it's safe."

She paused.

"About last night, John . . . I don't want you to get your hopes up. I don't know what's going to happen."

"I understand. But I do love you, Claire. You know that, don't you?"

"I know you think you do."

"Do you think you love me?"

Another pause.

"Don't ask me that, right now, okay? It's too soon. I know I care for you a lot. I have since the night we met. But I don't know what that means for the future. I've got to go, now. I can hear Mrs. Millowski screaming down the hall, and I'm the only one who can calm her down."

"I'll call you from the Union—or from the police station."

"Don't say that!"

"Okay. Goodbye. I love you, Claire."

"You probably shouldn't say that, either."

"But I do love you. Even if we're 'just friends,' I still love you."

"If you mean it that way, I guess I can say it, too. I love you, John. Goodbye."

The line went dead, but I didn't hang up. The sound of Claire saying "I love you" lingered in my ear until the dial tone broke the silence. I hung up. She loved me! Whatever it meant ultimately, it was enough for the time being. I floated out to the porch to finish my toast, then floated back into the kitchen to wash up the dishes. I floated all the way up Downer Avenue to school.

It was exactly nine o'clock when I joined the crowd massing in front of Mitchell Hall. A microphone and large speakers were set up on the wide porch in front of the building. I saw Carl Lindstrom, Jimmy Sommers, Bill Fleischer, and John Ascher huddling a few feet behind the microphone. There were about a dozen homemade signs poking up out of the crowd, and people around the fringes were working on new ones with magic markers and poster board. In the unseasonably warm air, the gathering had a festive feeling about it.

Surprisingly, the police were not in evidence, yet. I didn't think the chancellor would hesitate to ask them in. More than one campus had been trashed by demonstrations that had gotten out of hand. But I had a good feeling about this one. UWM was not Berkley or Columbia or Madison, where large demonstrations had been happening for years. It was a commuter school, where most of the students went home to their old neighborhood and their high school friends at the end of the day. It had taken the Kent State killings to mobilize them. The crowd was growing by the minute. Students seemed to be streaming in from all directions, on and off campus.

Someone tapped me on the shoulder. I turned to see Tony standing there, grinning, in his characteristic black t-shirt and black jeans.

"Hey, bro," he said. "Just like old times, huh?"

I felt as if I'd been punched in the chest. I was totally unprepared to see him. Perversely, the image of Claire pulling her nightie up over her head came into my mind's eye and I couldn't shake it. I was speechless.

"What's wrong with you?" he said.

I was saved by Carl's voice, which boomed out over speakers turned up much too high.

"Would those of you leading contingents—"

I whirled around to face the front. Carl paused while Bill Fleischer ran to turn down the volume. Then he started up again.

"Sorry. Would those of you who'll be leading contingents to the Union please come up here for a moment."

I turned back to Tony. "I've got to go up there."

"You're helping lead this thing? Far out!"

"Just the group that'll liberate the Snack Bar—assuming we get into the Union in the first place."

Tony got a determined look on his face.

"We'll get in," he said. "Can I be part of your group?"

"If I have anything to say about it, you can."

"Kolvacik is coming, too."

"The more the merrier," I said, trying to sound lighthearted. But my voice cracked as I said "merrier." I saw it written in my mind as "marry her."

"You okay, man?" asked Tony. "You look tired."

You don't know the half of it, I thought. "I'm fine. How did you get out of work for this?"

"I just got lucky. There wasn't much work today, so my number never got called."

I went up front, where eight or ten people were gathered around Carl and the other rally organizers. Carl quickly reviewed the plan for securing the Union, asking each of us to gather twenty people to assist us in our area. As soon as each area was secure, the leader was to send a representative to the ballroom to report in.

"There is to be no trashing—anywhere," he said emphatically, "and it's your job to prevent it. This is not a fraternity prank. It's a political action. Anything we do that reflects badly on us weakens its political impact. Understand?"

We all nodded.

"Let's get started, then. You go out and gather your people, while we get things going up here. The plan is to be on our way to the Union in forty-five minutes."

I returned to where I'd left Tony standing. Fortunately, he was engaged in a lively discussion with a tall, pretty black woman in a dashiki with a plunging V neckline.

"John," said Tony, "this is Alicia Bolton. She's in my Ed Psych class. John lives in the same house I do."

Alicia and I grasped palms and checked each other out. She looked familiar.

"Hey," she said, "I know you! You used to go out with Miriam Sommers!"

"That's where I know you from," I said. "We met at a party, once. How is Miriam?"

"She's good. She should be here, soon. Jimmy told her she'd better get her sorry black ass out here today or he'd personally come and get her."

"I bet she didn't like that!" I said.

"Damn straight! She hates it when Jimmy bosses her around. And she could care less about politics. She's an aaahhhhtist. But he was dead serious about today."

"As I recall, he was dead serious about which way the toilet paper should be put on the roller."

Alicia laughed loudly.

"You do know the man, don't you? Anyway, I think Miriam will show for this one. She knows it's important to Jimmy. And she does love her brother, different as he is from her."

Carl's voice came over the loudspeakers again. "Welcome everyone! We're ready to get started here, so listen up."

He paused for a moment. The crowd slowly quieted down and all eyes looked to the stage.

"Hey," I whispered, "I've got to recruit people for my contingent. Can I count on you two and Kolvacik—and maybe Miriam?"

"I'll talk Miriam into it when she shows," said Alicia.

"Thanks. I'll be back in a few minutes."

As Carl recapped the situation in Vietnam—taking the opportunity to educate those who hadn't thought much about the war until Kent State woke them up—I went around asking quietly for volunteers to join us. I asked a few people I knew, but most of them were strangers. I approached a variety of types, from obvious hippies to neatly dressed suburbanites. A few of them looked at me like I was crazy, but most were eager to participate. I told them where I'd be standing and asked them to gather around me when the rally ended and the march began.

When I got back to Tony and Alicia, Miriam and Kolvacik had arrived. They both gave friendly nods, but we didn't say anything, because Carl was finishing up his speech with an impassioned plea for discipline and restraint during the demonstration.

"They're just looking for excuses to write us off," he said, "to call us hoodlums and ignore what we're trying to tell them. Let's not give them an opportunity to do that. We all grew up watching the civil rights movement on TV.

We know non-violence works. Let's shout out our message loud and clear, but let's not hurt anybody or destroy anything. Let *them* be the bad guys.

"We can do it. We can protest until we force them to end this damn war. Because we're the ones being forced to fight it. And we're not going to fight it anymore, are we?"

"No!" shouted the crowd in unison.

"You don't mean 'No,'" said Carl, "you mean 'Hell no!'"

He started chanting, "Hell no, we won't go! Hell no, we won't go!"

The crowd picked it up immediately, and soon there were hundreds of voices chanting it as signs waved above our heads. With movie script timing, the police appeared, a great blue-black mass moving up Kenwood Boulevard, which ran along the side of Mitchell Hall. They did not march, as National Guardsmen would have, but swarmed, looking, in their riot helmets, like some kind of strange, hardheaded insects. Their commanders were careful to keep them at a distance, so there was no implication that they intended to break up the rally. But their presence inflamed the crowd. The chanting, which had been directed toward the stage, was now directed at them, the whole crowd turning to face them and increasing the volume.

"Hell no, we won't go! Hell no, we won't go!"

The police stared us down. A young man in faded jeans with no shirt and long, greasy hair, broke out of the crowd and raced toward the police line. He stopped ten feet in front of them, turned around, dropped his pants and bent over, showing them his naked ass. It was a stupid and crass thing to do. I hoped it wasn't an indicator of the general level of intelligence among the demonstrators. The police ignored him. A moment later, a few of his friends came out of the crowd to retrieve him.

Eventually, Jimmy Sommers took the microphone and quieted the crowd with his low, authoritative voice. I watched Miriam as Jimmy did his stuff, and I could see the admiration in her eyes. I sometimes wondered if it wasn't my being intimidated by him that had put her off. She wanted a man with his kind of authority, which wasn't my style. She looked particularly beautiful that day, with a green, blue, and yellow paisley bandana tied around her short hair. It accentuated the almost Native American quality of her features, especially her strong, prominent nose and broad forehead. She looked like an African queen. I sighed. One that got away . . .

Jimmy's speech was shorter than Carl's and more hard-hitting. He as much as said that if the war didn't end soon, he saw no way for the UWM SDS to remain non-violent. But he reiterated the strike committee's commitment to non-violence, telling people that this was where things stood for the time being and that they had to act in unison.

Next, Bill Ascher spoke for the Gray Panthers, as an elder supporting the protests of the young, relating the oppression of the young to the oppression of the old. He was followed in rapid succession by representatives of the Black Panthers, the Gay Liberation Front, the Vietnam Veterans Against the War, and on and on, until people started to drift away. The rally had been going on for an hour and fifteen minutes. It was exactly what Carl had feared.

Just when it felt as if a mass exodus was about to begin, Bill Fleischer took the microphone and galvanized the crowd by asking if anyone was ready to march. A great roar of approval went up. He quickly described the route the march would take: down Kenwood to Maryland; up Maryland and through the west end of the campus; across on Hartford Street, in front of the library; back down Downer to the Fine Arts building, then into the great plaza at the center of the campus and across it to the Student Union.

"Then," he said, in a quiet but firm voice, "we will occupy the Union, and the student strike of 1970 will officially begin. No more 'business as usual'!"

Another roar went up from the crowd. I know Bill intended to say more about the logistics of the Union take-over, but the crowd had had enough. We started moving, en masse, toward Kenwood Boulevard, which also happened to be in the direction of the police. Someone started chanting, "Hell no, we won't go!" again and the crowd took up the chant. Bill and Carl and the other strike leaders had to hustle to get in front of everyone.

Most of the people I'd recruited for my contingent found me as the crowd surged forward. I was near the front, myself, and I could feel the tension in the police line as we approached. I saw one officer squeezing hard on the handle of the billy club in his belt. They were being ordered back by their commanders, but they were hesitating. I had the sense they would have welcomed the opportunity to give us a good whipping. But they backed off, blocking Kenwood where it met Downer to keep cars from coming through. We turned away from them and marched down the street toward Maryland Avenue, which had already been blocked off by police cars.

As we marched, more students joined us, while others watched from the lawn and from the wide concrete balconies of the Student Union, a building that filled almost half of the block between Downer and Maryland. A cluster of male students in tank tops waved an American flag from the second floor porch of their fraternity house, across the street from the Union. When some of the demonstrators called for them to join us, the flag-wavers gave them the finger in unison and called out something about "commie fags"—not the most original epithet. But we didn't care. The day was ours.

I was thrilled to look back and see demonstrators filling both sides of the boulevard and spilling over onto the sidewalks, dozens of protest signs waving above their heads: "End the Draft!" "U.S. out of Vietnam!" "What if they gave a war and nobody came?" *Maybe this is it, I thought. Maybe demonstrations like this all over the country will make people sit up and pay attention to us. Maybe we'll all refuse to go and they won't have anybody to fight their stupid little war. It was exhilarating to think that we might be able to alter the course of the nation's history by saying no to an immoral war.*

The "we won't go" chant, which seemed to capture the feeling of the day, continued as we turned the corner onto Maryland Avenue, in the shadow of the Union. I couldn't help wondering what would happen when we had circled the campus and returned to occupy the building. I was all for non-violent protest, theoretically speaking, but the prospect of being clubbed over the head and dragged to a paddy wagon terrified me.

For years, I'd had recurring dreams about being in the power of people who didn't care for me as an individual, who only wanted to punish me as a representative of something they hated. It was quite possible I was on the verge of confronting that nightmare in real life. And beyond the terror of being beaten was the fear of becoming an outcast. I was on probation for my shoplifting offense. If I was arrested and convicted of even a minor infraction of the law, I'd have a permanent record as a criminal with not one but two offenses. Would I ever be able to get a decent job?

I mulled all this over as the march swept me along. I could just step out of the crowd and walk away, if I wanted to. The march would go on without me. But would I be able to live with myself if I did, if I ignored my conviction that, as Hamlet put it, something was "rotten in the state of Denmark"? I didn't think so. As Carl had pointed out at the rally, we were a generation weaned on images of civil rights demonstrators standing up to snarling police dogs, blasting fire hoses, rock-throwing crowds, firebombs, and Klan threats. Month after month, year after year, we'd watched incredibly courageous black people—and whites, too—put their lives on the line for what they believed. With that example in the forefront of my mind, how could I run away from the responsibility of standing up for what I believed, no matter what the consequences might be? The answer was clear. I couldn't.

Part way up Maryland, we veered left, funneling between a couple of buildings into the west end of the campus. Our numbers continued to swell. I'm sure some people just came along for the ride, as if joining a Mardi Gras parade, but I sensed others were joining because, as the organizers had intended, the march acted like a clarion call to their conscience, making them realize, finally, that they did oppose the Vietnam War and the draft, and it was time to do something about it. How many of them would be willing to face down the police and help to take over the Union remained to be seen.

When we reached Hartford Street, we turned right and headed up the gentle slope that led past Columbia Hospital. Doctors, nurses, visitors, even a few patients in hospital gowns, stared down at us from the windows. A few flashed peace signs, but most looked as if they were watching a freak show. I suppose we looked a motley crew—bearded, long haired, shirtless hippies beside plaid-skirted co-eds; professors in ties beside professors in tie-dye; blond boys in button-down, pale-blue shirts beside black students in wildly colored dashikis. But it was the variety of participants that gave me hope. If the protest cut across social lines, they could no longer pass us off as a radical fringe.

Suddenly, Miriam appeared at my side and slipped her arm through mine.

"It's amazing, isn't it?" she said. "All it took to get you white folks out was having a few of your own shot down. You notice that nobody took to the streets when those eight black students were shot down at South Carolina State."

Miriam had always loved to catch me off guard with provocative statements about whites.

"They weren't protesting the war, were they? I think this is the first time that anti-war demonstrators have been shot down. And the fact it was done by our own soldiers shocked people, too."

"I still think it's because they were white. A lot more people started paying attention to the Civil Rights Movement when whites started getting killed, too."

"I suppose. How the hell are you, anyway? I haven't seen you around much, lately."

"I've been doing a couple independent studies, so I'm not on campus as much. Do you miss me?"

"Of course I miss you. It wasn't me that broke us up, if you recall."

"If you're going to start in about that again, I think I'll go back and talk with Alicia." She slipped her arm out of mine.

"Just don't go too far," I said. "You're part of my contingent you know."

"Aye, aye, captain," she said, mock-saluting me. Then she winked and dropped back to join her friend, who was walking arm-in-arm with Tony.

We were in front of the library, by then. A large group of students had left their books behind to come out and see what was up. As we passed by, a good number of them fell in with us. The crowd had gotten more rowdy as the march progressed. The chant had gone from the relatively mild "Hell no, we won't go" to the more aggressive "One, two, three, four, we don't want your fucking war!" We were definitely feeling our oats. It was a good feeling, a feeling of empowerment, whether it was indicative of any real power or not.

At the corner where we turned back onto Downer, a block from where we'd started, the front of the crowd slowed up, bringing the rear of the crowd in tighter, until people were swarming across every inch of the intersection. The chant grew louder and louder. Slower and more tightly packed, the crowd approached the opening on the right that led between the library and the Fine Arts Building and onto the cement plain in front of the Student Union. We funneled through the opening, our voices reverberating off the buildings and saw the Student Union dead ahead. There were no police in sight. Spontaneously, we started jogging across the plaza toward the building. We continued to chant, faster and faster, as we trotted toward the main doors. Carl managed to stay in the lead and, as soon as he got to the entrance, tried one of the doors. It was open. Others pulled open the rest of the doors. As we swept by him, Carl cried out, "Find your leader! Follow your contingent! Otherwise, go to the ballroom!"

Tony, Alicia, Miriam, Kolvacik, and the rest of my contingent found their way to me. I led them through the hall and then two floors down the free-standing cement staircase to the main lobby. It was deserted. We crossed the lobby and entered the snack bar, whose doors were, somewhat to my surprise, wide open. I had half-expected everything but the main lobby to be locked up. Perhaps the administration's theory was that the more access we had to various rooms, the less likely we were to do damage trying to get into them.

It was strange to enter the snack bar, usually the liveliest place on campus, and find it empty. I finally realized the police must have cleared the building just before we arrived and then cleared out themselves. It seemed the administration was doing its best to avoid a confrontation. We passed the row of vending machines that lined the wall on the right, after which was the entrance to the food-serving area. That area had been closed off with a metal grating, as it always was when hot food wasn't being served.

"Damn," said Kolvacik, "and here I wanted to get a cheeseburger."

The others laughed, somewhat nervously, it seemed to me.

I peered in through the metal grating, then turned to survey "the pit," the depressed area full of tables in the middle of the snack bar.

"Well," I said, "I guess we've liberated the snack bar."

A pair of stragglers who'd apparently followed us in stood before one of the soda machines.

"In that case," said the larger of them, "let's liberate a few snacks."

He lifted a boot—a combat boot, I noticed—and kicked the face of the machine. Cans rattled inside, but nothing came out.

"That's enough, guys," I said, trying to sound authoritative.

"Fuck you," said the smaller one, not even bothering to look at me. He kicked the machine, too.

Tony walked up to them.

"Look, guys," he said, "if you want a can of soda, I'll buy it for you. But if you just want to bust something up, go someplace else and do it. We're not trashing this place."

The bigger guy—and he was several inches taller than Tony and much broader—turned to face him.

"Fuck off, shrimp," he said.

Tony laughed. "No," he said, "I think it's you who's going to leave. Unless, that is, you'd like me to demonstrate how I earned my black belt in karate."

"Bullshit," said the big guy.

"Whatever you say," said Tony, cool as could be.

The two looked at one another and then at Tony, who looked perfectly relaxed, yet utterly immovable.

"Ah, let's not fuck with this asshole," said the little guy. "He's not worth the trouble."

Without another word, the pair left. Tony watched them go, then turned and flashed a big smile.

"Jesus H. Christ, Tony," said Kolvacik. "And I thought I was a bull-shitter."

"You mean, you don't know karate?" I asked incredulously.

"The only black belt he owns is the one holding up his pants," said Kolvacik.

Tony's smile widened. He winked at me.

"I got pretty good at my verbal game back in high school. I'd fight if I had to, but I tried to avoid it. It hurts to get punched!"

"Far out, man," said one member of our contingent.

"My hero," said Alicia, only half kidding.

She took Tony's arm again. He didn't seem to mind her attention.

"Thanks, Tony," I said. "Would you mind holding the fort here, while I go up and report in to Carl?"

"Not at all. I don't know about the rest of you, but I'm feeling dry after all that walking and chanting. Sodas on me!"

I made my way up to the ballroom on the second floor, a long, wide, high-ceilinged room with a south-facing wall made entirely of glass, which let in wonderful light all day long. Glass doors in the wall led out onto a cement porch that ran the length of the ballroom. It was wall-to-wall people inside, all milling about as if unable to stop moving after the exhilarating march. On a low-rise bandstand at the opposite end of the floor, Carl and the other strike leaders were huddling while someone set up the sound system they'd used at the rally. I worked my way through the crowd toward them. Just as I stepped up on the bandstand, the huddle broke. I stopped Carl as he was about to step off the bandstand.

"Everything's fine in the snack bar," I said. "We even foiled a couple of vandals."

"I'd hoped we wouldn't have to deal with that kind of thing so soon. I'll tell Bill. He's going to set up patrols to wander the building."

If Carl was aware of the irony of our having to "police" a building that we had illegally taken over, he didn't show it.

"What happens next?" I said.

"Just hold your area, for now. I'm going to talk to the crowd, soon, and introduce Theatre X. While everyone's being entertained—and educated, too, I hope—I'll take a contingent over to the chancellor's office."

"I'd like to be part of that," I said.

"I didn't think you would, being on parole. There's a much bigger chance we'll get arrested for this one."

"There are more important things than that."

Carl smiled. "Then put someone you trust in charge of watching over the snack bar and meet us outside the draft counseling office in fifteen minutes. We suspect the chancellor doesn't think we'll try to take his office, since he gave us the Union. We want to surprise him."

I returned to the snack bar, drank a soda, asked Tony to take charge, and went up to the office where I'd first met Carl. He was standing outside it with Jimmy Sommers, John Ascher, and about a dozen other people. He'd left Bill Fleischer behind to handle the rally in the ballroom and to organize contingents to demonstrate in classes. If Jimmy remembered me, he didn't let on. He looked right through me. But, then, he'd done that most of the time when I was dating his sister, too.

"This is everybody," said Carl. "We don't want to arouse any suspicion, so we'll leave discreetly, some individually and some in pairs, and rendezvous in front of the chancellor's office in ten minutes. Got it?"

We all nodded.

"Okay, pair up with somebody, or just take off on your own. Some of you should go down through the lobby and out that way." Carl looked at me. "John, why don't you and I go that way."

Everybody scattered. Carl watched them go, then looked at me.

"Our turn," he said.

We walked in silence until we were out of the Union and on our way up Maryland Avenue. The silence gave me time to consider what I was about to do. My stomach started doing flip-flops.

"I admire you for taking this risk, John," said Carl, as if reading my mind. "Not everybody would do it."

"Maybe I'm just stupid," I said.

"If you are, this country needs a lot more stupid people."

"Since I am taking the risk, mind if I ask exactly why we need to take over the chancellor's office. I trust your judgment, but I'd like to know what the goal is."

"The chancellor won't talk to us. We tried to get in touch with him yesterday and early this morning to talk about closing down the university officially, but he refuses even to discuss it with us. I think his plan is to let us have the Union but come down hard on us if we try to disrupt classes. We want to confront him directly and force him to show his hand."

The chancellor's office was in an ivy-covered building more like a small European villa than an administration building. Again, we were surprised to see no police. Perhaps the chancellor had been overconfident about the effect of giving us the Union. When we were all assembled, Carl led us in through the heavy front door and into a round marble lobby with iron-railinged staircases curving up both sides. A lone security guard—an unarmed middle-aged man, I was relieved to see—sat at a table set between the two staircases.

"What the hell?" he said, standing up as we entered. "What do you kids want?"

"We just want to speak to the chancellor," said Carl, ignoring him and starting up the stairs. We followed him.

"You can't go up there!"

"Why not?" asked Carl, not pausing to wait for an answer.

The guard came around the table after us.

"Because he's not in, for one thing."

Carl paused for a second, then said, "We'll wait for him," and continued on up. "He's expecting us."

We trouped after him, amused at the guard's bewilderment. As we went through the door off the landing, which led to the chancellor's anteroom, we heard the guard call someone on his walky-talky. The chancellor's secretary was not in, either. Carl strode by her desk, grasped the knobs on the double doors that led to the chancellor's office, and pulled the doors open wide. We entered a large, tastefully decorated room with leaded glass windows behind a substantial desk, ivy peaking in around the window edges, and bookshelves lining the walls. The cream-colored carpet felt springy under my feet. Carl went to the desk, but instead of sitting in the chancellor's big, green, leather chair and putting his feet up, as a more egotistical leader might have done, he sat down on the carpet in front of the desk, facing us. Taking our cue from him, we all sat down, forming a circle in the middle of the room.

"So far, so good," said Carl. "Anybody want to back out? I fully expect the police to show up momentarily. This is your last chance."

Everybody stayed put.

"We have one demand, that the chancellor talk to us. That's it. We'll sit here until he's willing to hear us. If police come, they'll have to drag us out."

The prospect of being dragged down one of those marble staircases was not a pleasant one.

"Just go limp," Carl continued. "Make them do all the work."

We sat looking at one another, not quite sure what to say. I felt strange being in the chancellor's private office without his permission. It felt like when I was a kid and I'd sneak into my parent's room. I had a powerful urge to start looking into drawers.

Within ten minutes, we heard someone talking with the security guard in the lobby, then footsteps on the marble stairs. My stomach started to churn. Someone appeared at the door—not a policeman, but a thirtyish man with red hair and tortoise-shell glasses, wearing a charcoal gray suit.

"Gentlemen," he said, "I'm Marvin Klein, the chancellor's administrative assistant. The chancellor is tied up in a meeting right now, so I'm acting in his place. What can we do for you?"

"We'd just like to talk to him," said Carl. "He hasn't bothered to respond to any of our calls, so we came to see him in person. We'll be here when he's ready to talk to us."

"But you must understand that you can't be allowed to invade the chancellor's private office. I'm sure he would be happy to meet with you, but not under these circumstances."

"All right, then, you arrange the circumstances. It doesn't have to be here, but it has to be today, by 1:00 this afternoon."

"And you would be . . . ?" said the administrative assistant with a hint of scorn in his voice, although he tried to conceal it.

"Carl Lindstrom, representing the UWM student strike committee."

"Can you speak for the whole committee?"

"Two of the other three members are right here. I trust they'll speak up if I say anything out of order."

"So, let me get this straight. You'll sit here until the chancellor returns or until he agrees to a meeting somewhere else before 1:00 this afternoon. Correct?"

"Correct."

"Then I'll contact the chancellor as soon as I can and relay that message. I'll bring you his reply."

Mr. Klein left. I had to admit I was impressed with the administration's way of handling the situation, up to that point. At other universities, demonstrations had been handled with much less tact. I began to think Carl might even convince the chancellor to allow some sort of moratorium on classes.

Half-an-hour later, just after the grandfather clock opposite the chancellor's desk had struck half past noon, Mr. Klein returned.

"The chancellor has agreed to meet with the four members of the strike committee here in his office at 1:00. His only conditions are that the committee wait in the anteroom, as he would ask any visitors to his office to do, and that the rest of this group disperse. Is that agreeable?"

Carl looked at John and Jimmy, who both nodded.

"One o'clock it is," said Carl. "John," he said to me, "will you tell Bill to join us here then?"

I said I would.

"Then, gentlemen," said Mr. Klein, "can we please vacate the chancellor's office."

We all rose and walked out past Mr. Klein. He had a satisfied look on his face, as if he'd rid his boss's office of vermin. I wondered what it had cost him to remain civil to us. The security guard was waiting in the anteroom and Klein directed him to escort those of us who weren't staying out of the building.

"Are you sure this is all right, Carl?" I asked.

"We'll be fine."

The guard led us down the marble steps and across the lobby and pushed open the big entrance door. As we stepped out, we found policemen in riot gear lining both sides of the walkway that ran across the front of the building. They had the facemasks of their helmets flipped up and their faces were none too friendly. We had to walk between them. Though they said nothing, many of them gave us looks that embodied the expression "if looks could kill." Another large contingent of police was gathered at the side of the building. For a moment, I wondered if the chancellor was setting a trap for the strike committee, planning to have them arrested in the hope that the strike would die without their leadership. But my gut said that the way he'd handled the situation so far made it unlikely.

Back in the Union, we found the ballroom nearly deserted. Bill Fleischer sat at a long table along the wall, marking up a map of the campus. I told him the situation, gave him Carl's message and mentioned my speculation about the possibility of it being a trap. Fleischer agreed it was unlikely.

"By the way," I said, "where is everybody?"

"They're out demonstrating in classes, trying to wake people up to the need for this strike."

"You put them to work fast!"

"No other way to do it. If you let people sit around on their butts, they start forgetting the point of the exercise. They say people learn better by teaching, so I think we'll have a more committed core of people after this.

"I'd better get over to the chancellor's office, if the old man is going to meet with us. Can you hold down the fort here? A few reporters have come by to find out what the story is. All I'm saying is that the strike has been successfully launched and that we're hoping to convince the administration to declare an official moratorium on classes for some period of time."

"Seems to be about all there is to say."

"I'll be going, then," said Fleischer, getting up. "Wish us luck."

I sat down in the hard metal folding chair he'd vacated. Only then did I realize how tired and hungry I was. I'd been flying high all morning and I was ready to crash. But it was not to be. Minutes after Fleischer left, a local television reporter appeared, accompanied by a cameraman with one of the small, shoulder-mounted cameras that had become so popular for capturing the action at demonstrations. Someone pointed her to me and, despite my protests to the contrary, she was convinced I was "somebody" in the strike—or maybe she just wanted a story fast. Finally, I gave up arguing with her and agreed to answer a few questions about it, though I was certain the footage would end up on the cutting room floor. The camera started rolling.

"Are the strikers satisfied with having taken over the Student Union, or do they have bigger plans?"

"The Union is strike headquarters. The purpose of the strike is to stop 'business as usual' across the campus and convince students and teachers to spend time studying the war and its impact on Vietnam and our society."

"How long do you expect the administration to suspend classes?"

"That hasn't been determined, as far as I know."

"What if the administration won't cooperate with your plan?"

"We'll go ahead, anyway. We think we'll win the support of the majority of students and professors."

"How will you go about winning that support?"

"We'll go into the classrooms and talk to people."

"What if a professor doesn't want you there?"

"We still think students should hear what we have to say, so we'll say it anyway."

"What good will this strike do?"

"As I'm sure you know, it's part of a national student strike that we hope will change attitudes across the country. It's our generation that's paying in blood for this war and we think our peers should know what the war's really about. That's enough questions, now. As I said, I'm not on the strike committee, I'm just filling in while they meet with the chancellor."

"They're meeting right now?"

"Yes."

"What are they discussing?"

"Whether the university will declare an official moratorium on classes for some period of time to allow students to learn about the war."

"Where are they meeting?"

"It's not my place to give out that information."

"Are they in the chancellor's office?"

"It's not my place to give out that information."

"Okay, Frank," said the newswoman. "We're not going to get anything more out of him."

Frank turned the camera off.

"The man who sent me over here said your name was John Meyer. Is that M-e-y-e-r or M-a-y-e-r?"

"With an e."

"Now, off the record, John, where's this meeting taking place. I've got a big chance to scoop the competition here. I'd like to take advantage of it."

"Sorry. I can't help you."

"Were you told not to tell anyone?"

"No."

"Then why won't you tell me?"

"Because I wasn't told I *could* tell anyone, either."

"I think I'll try the chancellor's office."

"Suit yourself."

She and Frank scurried off to find the big secret meeting. I wished I hadn't opened my mouth about it, but there didn't seem to be any harm in people knowing it was going on. Other reporters had probably followed the chancellor back to his office anyway. It wouldn't take a rocket scientist to figure out that there would be action there, at some point.

As I watched the TV people leave the ballroom, I saw Claire enter, pushing a stroller and trying to hold onto a struggling Jonah in one arm. She had a big straw bag hanging from her shoulder. Just seeing her sent a thrill through my body. When I waved to her, she put Jonah down and pointed him toward me. He came running in my direction, a big smile on his face, and let me pick him up.

"Decided to brave the big strike, huh?" I said when Claire drew near.

"I listened to WUWM. They said it was all pretty orderly, so I thought I'd come down."

"I'm glad you did. How was work?"

"Exhausting. All the old folks were cranky. I'm glad I only had a half day."

"Tony's here, too," I said. "Apparently there wasn't much work at the docks."

"Where is he?"

"Down in the snack bar. At least, he was. We liberated that, first. Tim's there, too—and Miriam, my old girlfriend."

Jonah, tired of being ignored, was squirming to be let down.

"You can just let him run around," said Claire.

I put him down and he took off, making a big arc around the huge expanse of floor—a toddler's paradise. Occasionally, he glanced back to make sure we were still there.

As Claire watched him, I watched her. She caught me staring.

"What?" she said.

"I love you," I said.

She blushed. "You shouldn't say that to me."

"It's true."

"I know, but . . . I don't know."

She started fishing around in her shoulder bag and came up with a pack of Kools.

"What's going to happen, Claire?"

She took out a cigarette, but before she could slip the matches out of the plastic sleeve around the pack, I snatched the pack from her hand. I pulled out the matches, lit one, and held it up to her. She brought the flame to her cigarette by gently guiding my hand with her fingertips. Her touch sent a shiver through me. She inhaled deeply and blew the smoke up into the air.

"Let's just play it by ear, okay?" she said. "I have to see how things develop between Tony and me."

We shot the breeze for a while, watching Jonah explore the ballroom. Then, I looked over Claire's shoulder to see Tony entering the ballroom with Alicia on his arm. Claire saw me looking and turned to see what I was looking at. At the same moment, Tony noticed her. He paused for a half step—I could almost see the wheels turning in his head—but then he continued on. It was so quick that Alicia didn't even notice. He walked right up to us, his arm still entwined with hers.

"Hey, Claire," he said, looking nervous in his attempt to act casual. "This is Alicia. She's in my sociology class. Alicia, this is my wife, Claire."

Alicia did not appear to be surprised.

"Hi, Claire," she said. "Tony's told me a lot about you. Where's Jonah?"

"Here he comes," said Tony.

Jonah, having just noticed his father's arrival, was barreling toward him. When he arrived at Tony's leg, he threw his arms around it. Tony let go of Alicia's arm and lifted him up.

"Hey, little guy, what are you up to? Have you come to join the strike?"

"He's so cute!" squealed Alicia in that patronizing way that people without children have when they're trying to ingratiate themselves with someone who has children. "Look at those little overalls!"

She poked at his belly with her index finger. Jonah slapped her hand away.

"Be nice, now, Jonah," said Tony.

Jonah wriggled in his arms. Tony put him down and off he went again.

"So, what's happening with this strike?" said Tony. "We've been sitting on our asses in the snack bar for a couple of hours, now. What's the point?"

"Who's still down there?"

"Just Kolvacik. The rest of them split. I told him I'd go find out where the action is."

"Didn't anybody ask you guys if you wanted to demonstrate in classes?"

"Nobody said anything to us. We've just been shooting the breeze and drinking sodas and keeping the vultures away from the vending machines. What happened in the chancellor's office?"

"He wasn't in. His administrative assistant came by and told us the chancellor would meet with the strike committee at 1:00."

"You don't really think he'll shut the place down, do you?"

"What do you think?"

"Do you know what 'fat chance' means?"

"Don't be so cynical, Tony," said Claire. "Maybe they'll work something out."

"Yeah, I'm sure the trustees would go for him ending the school year a few weeks early. He'd be out on his ass if he made a deal with us."

As if on cue, the members of the strike committee appeared, fresh from their meeting with the chancellor. None of them said a word. Jimmy Sommers threw himself into a folding chair and crossed his arms tight over his chest.

Carl plopped down in the chair beside him and stared across the ballroom. John Ascher leaned against the wall and looked down at his feet while Bill Fleischer paced. Suddenly, Jimmy slammed his fist down on the table.

"Damn it!" he said. "I told you. you can't trust the Man!"

"What happened?" I asked.

"As I suspected," said Carl, "he let us have the Union but has no intention of cooperating with us in any other way. While we were talking with him, his administrative assistant called him out of the room and told him strikers were disrupting classes. He came back in like the wrath of God, demanding to know who we thought we were pulling something like that without consulting him."

"At which point," Bill Fleischer interjected, "I told him we were a strike committee, not the fucking Boy Scouts of America."

"Which did not endear us to him," said John Ascher dryly.

"Fuck endearing ourselves to him!" said Jimmy.

"It's not like we should have expected him to cooperate." said Carl, "The fact that he gave us the Union raised false hopes."

"It's war, now, man," said Bill.

"It's war we're fighting *against*, Bill," said Carl. "Let's not start talking about a non-violent protest in those terms."

"I still think we ought to disable the power plant or trash the water lines" said Jimmy. "Really shut the place down."

"Then we wouldn't be able to stay here, either," said John.

"We can manage," Jimmy replied. "This is a revolution, not a dinner party."

"It's not a revolution, either, Jimmy," said Carl. "It's a strike. It has a limited purpose. We can achieve that purpose without destroying anything."

Jimmy didn't reply. He just recrossed his arms and sat, stone-faced.

"Let's prepare a press release," said Carl. "We'll announce that the administration is refusing to cooperate with a moratorium on classes, making this officially a strike. We can take the high moral ground here, driving home the point that confronting the war is more important than finishing a few college classes."

"Preaching to the converted," muttered Jimmy.

"And if we destroy things," said Carl hotly, "we've alienated the converted, too! Give it a rest, Jimmy. You agreed to a non-violent, non-destructive approach. After the strike is over, you can organize whatever kind of political action you want."

"Don't think I won't!" Jimmy replied.

Suddenly it seemed to sink in to Carl that the committee was airing its dirty laundry in public.

"John," he said to me, "would you and your friends mind giving us a little privacy? We've got some planning to do."

"Sure," I said. "Why don't we all go down and check in on Kolvacik?" I said to the others.

"I've got to go," said Claire. "I just wanted to see how you were doing."

Tony raised an eyebrow when Claire addressed this statement to me. I wondered later if it was the first time he'd suspected there was something besides friendship between us.

"I've got to go, too," said Alicia. "I have to get to work. How about walking me to the bus, Tony?"

Tony looked at Claire, who remained impassive. I wondered how, even in their circumstances, she could watch this come-on without showing a hint of jealousy.

"Sure," he said. "I'll walk you to the bus." He looked at me. "How about I meet you and Kolvacik in the snack bar in a little while?"

I said that was fine.

"See you later, Claire," he said.

"Yeah, later," she replied. "I'll see you later, too, John," she said and kissed me quickly on the mouth, making sure Tony saw it.

"Jonah," she called.

Jonah was on the other side of the ballroom, his face pressed against the glass that separated the ballroom from the balcony. He turned and came racing toward us as we moved away from the table. Alicia and Tony were ahead of us. This time, when Alicia tried to take his arm, Tony wouldn't cooperate.

"What do you think about that?" I asked Claire.

"What?" she said.

"How do you feel watching her come on to Tony like that?"

"Confused. Sometimes I think he and I both need a break from one another; other times, I think having another relationship would kill ours."

She stopped and turned to me.

"That's why I need to go slowly with you, John. I don't know what I want. I don't know what I can give you. I have to think about Jonah, too."

As always, her pale green eyes mesmerized me.

"Take your time, Claire. I'll be patient."

It was what I wanted to believe about myself, but even as I said it I wondered if I really could wait. My desire for her was painful.

Out of the corner of my eye, I saw Tony look back over his shoulder at us. Then Jonah slammed into my leg and started giggling. I picked him up and looked into his brown eyes. "Life's not simple, is it, pal?" I asked him.

He got a serious look on his face, as if he understood perfectly what I was asking him, and shook his head.

Claire chuckled.

"This kid's no dummy is he?" I said.

We continued out the ballroom entrance.

"Why don't you put him in the stroller," said Claire. "I'm sure he's worn out from running around in there."

I lifted Jonah in while she lit another cigarette.

"Will you be here all night?" she asked.

"Depends on what comes down. I'll come home if I can."

Suddenly, I had a powerful sensation that I was talking to my wife.

I said, "Do you think we could . . ."

She drew deeply on her cigarette, her brow furrowed, and blew out the smoke. Then she smiled.

"Maybe. I need to think about it. She glanced in the direction Tony and Alicia had disappeared. He might not even come home tonight."

"I'll be there," I said, "unless something really serious comes down here."

I walked her out of the Union entrance, said goodbye again, and stood watching her push Jonah down the street, her fine blonde hair swaying back and forth as she walked. I hoped she would look back at me and wave when she turned the corner, but she kept right on walking, her eyes straight ahead.

~9~

Y TEN O'CLOCK THAT EVENING, Claire and I had made love in my bed and come back downstairs to watch the news about the strike. Jonah was asleep and no one else was home. We sat hip-to-hip on the sofa, sharing a beer and a cigarette.

The student strike was the top story and, after a few shots of the action at the better-known national schools, the focus moved to UWM. The same reporter I'd talked to was shown standing at the edge of the crowd in front of Mitchell Hall, describing the action, while Carl spoke on the platform, far behind her. Then there were shots of the march, of students milling around in the ballroom, and of the Theatre X performance. Then, suddenly, my face appeared on the screen. I nearly dropped the beer bottle.

"Far out," said Claire.

I was saying my bit about how it was our generation paying in blood for the war and about how we were hoping to change attitudes across the country. It wasn't more than thirty seconds long, and then they moved on to shots of demonstrators in the classrooms. Claire started to speak.

"Wow, that was really—"

"Wait a second," I interjected. "I want to hear this."

They described the classroom demonstrations as confrontational, disruptive, and disrespectful, and showed only the most damaging footage of demonstrators shouting down professors, standing on desks, and harassing students.

"Damn it," I said, "that wasn't all that happened! Tony and Kolvacik and I were in a class this afternoon that spent two hours talking seriously

135

about the war after the group we were demonstrating with came in. Of course, they couldn't show anything like that. That's not dramatic enough!"

A commercial appeared. I threw a pillow at the television, accidentally turning it off.

"Whores!" I said.

"You didn't really expect them to make you guys look like heroes, did you?" asked Claire.

"Yes! No. I don't know. I just wish they could be fair."

"They played what you said. That was pretty eloquent, if you ask me."

I smiled slyly. "You're not just saying that because you had multiple orgasms, are you?"

She hit me in the face with a pillow.

"Are you calling *me* a whore, now?" she said.

I threw my arms around her, pulled her to me, and kissed her deeply. Then I pulled my head back. "If the shoe fits . . ." I said, deadpan.

She punched me in the chest half-heartedly.

"See if you get anywhere with me again," she said.

The phone rang. I went to kitchen and answered it.

"John," a voice said, "this is your father."

"I'm here, too," said Mom, who was on their other phone.

"We just saw you on the news, son," said Dad. "You were very articulate. We were proud of you."

"We couldn't believe it," said Mom. "Why didn't you tell us you were going to be on?"

"I never thought I would be."

"Well," she said, "you should have told us you might be. We could have missed it."

"We don't want you to think we agree with this strike thing, son," said Dad. "You kids ought to finish your studies before you go off demonstrating. But we did want you to know we thought you presented yourself well. Maybe you ought to go into public speaking. You've always been good at that sort of thing."

"Maybe I will," I said. "Thanks for calling."

We small-talked for a few minutes, then said our goodbyes. I returned to the living room, shaking my head.

"Your folks?" said Claire.

I nodded. "Praising me to the skies because I was so articulate on TV."

"You're getting on better, now, aren't you? I told you you would."

"It isn't that that amazes me. It's that they could listen to what I said, think it was eloquent, but not respond at all to the content. If they'd really heard what I said, they'd understand what all this is about."

"I don't think that's true. People hear what they want to hear. Your folks just heard their son speaking well on TV. They can't relate to what you said, but they can relate to you. Take it for what it's worth."

"I suppose. I just can't understand how anybody can think that dirty, stupid little war is worth dying in."

The phone rang again. This time it was my siblings, miffed that Mom and Dad had called without letting them speak to me.

"You were great, John," said Marion. "My brother the TV star!"

Even George was impressed.

"Did you ever think of going out for the debate team?" he asked.

A school friend called next. "Guess you've had your fifteen minutes of fame, now, huh, pal?"

A couple other friends called, too. It was quite a lesson in the pervasiveness of television. Thirty seconds on the air and I was locally famous. Suddenly I understood why people worked so hard to get their face on the tube. It was heady stuff.

But I came down fast. When the phone calls stopped, I went to find Claire, who'd gone upstairs. Her door was closed and I could hear her sobbing on the other side. I tried to door, but it was locked.

"Claire," I said, "what is it?"

"Go away," she said.

"Why?"

"I just need to be alone."

"Tell me what's happening."

"Go away!"

I went into my room and tried the door to hers. She'd forgotten to lock it. I pulled it open. "Claire," I said gently, so as not to shock her.

She was lying facedown on the bed. She twisted around to look at me. Her face was red and wet with tears.

"Go away!" she cried. "I can't take any more of this shit!"

I went to the bed and sat down beside her. She continued to cry. I tried to caress her hair, but she batted my hand away.

"Claire," I said, "this isn't fair. What did I do?"

"Oh, go to hell!" she said. "Everything isn't about you, you know. I'm just so fucking confused. I want you. I want Tony. I want Jonah. I want to be alone. I don't know what the fuck I want. You go off to your little demonstration and Tony has his job and Jonah just does whatever he fucking pleases. But what the hell do I have? Nothing! Not a goddam thing! Now, get out of here—I mean it! I need to be alone."

I tucked my tail between my legs and went into my room. I sat in the rocking chair, hoping Claire would change her mind and call me back in, but finally it was too disturbing to listen to her cry. I went downstairs, but in the quiet house I could still hear her crying above me. I went back to my room, put on jeans and a sweatshirt, and went out onto the front porch. The spring night air was cool and refreshing. I sat down on the top step and rested my back against the wooden post that anchored the railing. I sat facing north, toward the campus, wondering if I should have just stayed overnight at the Union, as many of the strikers were doing. I could have gone, even then, but I wanted to be home if Claire needed me.

After I'd sat there for some time, my mind a muddle, a powder blue Chevelle pulled up directly across the street. I tried to see who was in it, but it was right under a streetlamp. Light reflected off the windows and threw the interior into deep shadow. After five or ten minutes, the door opened on the passenger side and Tony emerged. My stomach clutched. He stood on the curb and waved to the driver as the car drove away. I still couldn't see who it was, but I had a pretty good hunch.

Tony didn't notice me until he'd crossed the street and stepped up on the curb. "Meyer, is that you?"

"It's me. Who was your date? Alicia?"

He looked down at the sidewalk and shuffled toward me. "You weren't supposed to notice that."

"Just a lucky guess. You two getting it on?"

Tony stood at the bottom of the steps, unsure, I think, if he wanted to sit down and give me an opportunity to pry information out of him. I was enjoying being on the offensive when I'd half-expected him to start grilling me about Claire.

"Promise you won't tell Claire?" he said.

I knew I couldn't make that promise, so I tried to slide by. "She'll get it out of you, herself, Tony."

He looked up toward their bedroom window. "I suppose you're right." He looked back at me. "Yeah, Alicia and I made it over at her place. I feel kind of guilty, but, hey, Claire and I agreed this would be a real separation, even though we're living in the same house. The only promise we made was that we wouldn't bring anybody back here."

I blanched, then I realized that, in fact, if not in spirit, Claire hadn't broken their agreement. She hadn't brought me back to the house; I already lived there. Still, I wished she'd told me about their arrangement.

"Seems kind of quick to be sleeping with somebody else," I said.

I was appalled at my ability to play the innocent, under the circumstances, but there was a certain perverse pleasure in getting the scoop on Tony's situation without revealing my own.

"I suppose it looks that way," Tony said, "but Claire and I have been heading for a crash for a long time. I'm sure you saw that. Now that it's happened . . . well . . . I wouldn't be surprised if she found somebody to fool around with pretty soon, herself. You wouldn't know anything about that, would you?"

I couldn't tell if he was toying with me or if it was a sincere question. He stood with his back to the streetlamp and the light from it threw his face into shadow, so I couldn't read his expression. I fell back on a safe generalization. "She seems pretty confused, right now."

Tony didn't respond immediately. Was he searching my face, which was well lit by the streetlamp, for signs of prevarication? I tried to make my expression as bland as possible. Two could play at that game—if, indeed, he was playing a game.

"Yeah," he finally said, "I'm confused, too. But it'll work itself out, one way or another. How was Jonah, tonight? Did he go to sleep okay?"

"He went down without a peep."

"I think I'll go check on him before I go up to bed."

He put his foot on the first step.

"Tony," I said, unsure what I was about to say.

He stopped, one foot still on the walk, and looked at me. I wanted to be honest with him. I wanted to bring things out in the open. But I couldn't. It was too early. My relationship with Claire might not go anywhere, however much I wanted it to. If things developed between us, there would be time enough for truth telling, later.

"What did you think of the strike?" I asked.

He pulled his foot off the step.

"That reminds me," he said. "Did you see yourself on the news?"

"Yeah."

"Alicia and I watched it. You did okay, Meyer. I was proud of you."

"Thanks. My family called about it, too. But what about the whole thing, today? Was it worth anything?"

"Who the hell knows. Maybe it woke a few people up. I hope so. I'm damn sick of worrying about my brother over there. Every time I get a letter from him, I wonder if it'll be the last one. He's been in dozens of firefights. It's such a fucking waste of people and money. Like we don't have anything better for those guys to do, or anything better to do with the millions of dollars in bombs we're dropping on North Vietnam. The whole thing sucks. You going back, tomorrow?"

"Until I have to go to work in the afternoon. I don't think old man Siegel would approve of his driver skipping out for a demonstration. Anyway, I've still gotta eat."

"Don't I know it. I've got a feeling there'll be more than enough work at the docks, tomorrow. I'm going to bed. Take care, man."

He went in. My butt was going to sleep on the hard wood, so I followed Tony in, but just long enough to get one of Claire's cigarettes from the pack on the coffee table, where she'd left them when we sat together. I lit one and went back out onto the porch. I paced back and forth, trying not to make too much noise. I didn't want to disturb the sleeping household. I knew I should go to bed, but I was too restless. I decided to walk up to the Union and see how things were going there. I went upstairs to check on Claire, first. She was fast asleep. I turned off the lamp beside her bed and tiptoed out.

Once I started walking along Downer Avenue, I found myself breathing easier. Only then did I realize how tense I'd been at the house. I considered sacking out in the Union overnight; I'd probably sleep better. But then I thought of Claire getting up in the morning and wondering where I was and thought better of it.

When I turned the corner onto Kenwood Avenue, I saw lights from inside the Union glowing out into the night. It looked as if no one was asleep there, yet. As I approached the building from the opposite side of the street, I saw that someone had painted S-T-R-I-K-E and a clenched fist in red in the seven huge glass panes that walled the ballroom on the second floor. The sight stirred my blood, the way a flag stirs the ardor of a soldier. I went in through the main entrance and heard music coming from the snack bar. I found a party going on in there: a three piece rock band played in the pit, with dancers all around them. Small groups were sitting at tables or on the floor around the pit smoking joints and passing bottles of wine. A woman was painting faces and other body parts at a table near the entrance. Not being in a party mood, I turned to go up to the ballroom. Then I noticed the glass front of a vending machine had been smashed in and all the candy stolen. I wondered if our friends from the morning had returned.

Things were quieter in the ballroom. Dozens of strikers lay sacked out in sleeping bags on the floor along the glass wall, despite the lights still being up high. Just as I walked in, somebody dimmed them. The strike committee table was in the same spot and had several desk lamps lighting it up. I saw Carl behind one of them, writing something, and went to him.

"Writing the UWM manifesto?" I asked.

He looked up. "John, what are you doing here? I thought you were gone for the night?"

"I'm staying at home, but I thought I'd check in. How's it going?"

"So far, so good. We visited a lot of classes, today, and I think we really got to some people. Made a lot of them angry, too, of course. By the way, that was some performance on the news. You did a great job, but you probably should have warned us. You sounded like a spokesperson for the strike. Jimmy was pretty angry about it."

"I told them I was nobody, but they stuck the camera in my face and wouldn't take it out until I said something. I made it clear I was just a participant in the strike, not a member of the committee, but, of course, they cut that part. I did mean to tell you. Sorry."

"If that's the worst glitch we have during this strike, I'll be delighted. Everybody they interview about the strike should be so articulate."

"What's the plan for tomorrow."

"More of the same: confronting people in classes, trying to get people in here to educate them about the war. Speaking of which, we need people to lead informal discussion groups here in the Union, tomorrow morning. Can you take one? We're trying to get as many leaders as possible, so we can keep the groups small. You wouldn't have to make any kind of presentation, just get the ball rolling and try to keep the discussion under control."

"I could do that. What time?"

"Ten o'clock. Stop by here in the morning, and we'll assign you a room. Now I need to get back to this. I'm trying to write an opinion piece for the *Journal* that explains the purpose of the strike. One of the journalism profs knows the editor and can get it into tomorrow's edition if it's downtown by midnight."

I left Carl to his task, wishing I had one myself, and walked around the ballroom, looking for someone I knew. I didn't see anyone, so I wandered out into the hall and down the steps to the lobby. Still no one familiar. The party in the snack bar was in full swing, but somehow the sound of loud music and laughter made me feel lonely. I headed for home.

Back at the house, I went up to my bedroom and pulled off my clothes. By then, the feeling of loneliness was like an ache in my heart. I had to be with Claire. I locked the door to my bedroom, then slipped quietly through the door to hers. She was still asleep, turned on her side, facing the windows. Feeling both brash and shy, I lay down on the bed behind her, spooned my body against hers, and put an arm around her. She wrapped her arms around my arm and pulled it to her breasts. Finally, I felt I was where I should be.

"G'night, Tony," she mumbled.

I was momentarily hurt, but I brushed it off. If Claire was ever going to be mine, I was going to have to be patient with her. It was her life being turned upside down. She had a lot to lose. I only stood to gain. I took a deep breath, exhaled, and pulled myself tighter against her. *Que sera, sera.*

In the morning, Claire was surprised and pleased to find me in her bed. She seemed to have forgotten her outburst—or, at least, didn't choose to revisit it. We made love quickly and intensely, finishing just as Jonah made it known he was awake. Tony was long-gone to the docks, so Claire went to Jonah while I bathed. We had a seven-foot long, two-foot deep, claw-footed Victorian bathtub in the upstairs bathroom. I filled it with hot water—a time-consuming task with a tub that size—pouring in a large dollop of Claire's bath salts to make it even more relaxing. When it was finally ready, I sank down into it and closed my eyes. Immediately, I heard the door. I opened my eyes to see Claire entering in her bathrobe.

"Mind if I join you?" she said.

"Mind, hell! I'd be delighted!"

"Jonah's playing in his bed. He won't last more than ten minutes, but at least I can get cleaned up."

She slipped off her robe, revealing her lovely, naked white body, and hung the robe on the door, then turned to me.

"Wait," I said. "Just stay there for a moment. I want to look at you."

She paused, but then said, "It's too cold. Let me in there."

She came to the tub and stepped into the hot water, her skin going all goose bumps as she did. She turned her back to me, presenting me with her beautiful behind. I reached out, took her by the hips, and slowly pulled her down into the water, between my legs. She leaned back against me, her hair falling across my naked chest and into the water at my belly. I put my arms under hers and folded them across her breasts, which were half submerged in the water, its heat turning her nipples hard. She tipped her head back and we kissed deeply. Then she took the soap from the metal rack that hung over the side of the tub, opened my hand, put the soap in my palm, and tipped her head back to whisper in my ear.

"Wash my breasts," she said.

I soaped up my hands and happily did as I was told. The feel of her soft flesh slick with soap was incredibly arousing. Heat permeated my body. I kept running my hands over and over her breasts. She kissed me again. Then we heard the door opening.

We both sat bolt upright, like some sort of weird, pornographic toy. Jonah stood there, wide-eyed, in diaper and t-shirt.

"Tub?" he said.

"It's okay, sweetheart," said Claire. "Mommy's taking a bath. How did you get out of your bed? You've never done that before, have you?"

Jonah shook his head, looking rather proud of himself. Claire looked back at me. "Great timing, huh?"

"John tub?" said Jonah.

"I guess I'll have to look after him."

"I'll do it," I said.

"I think it's better if he doesn't see you get out of the tub naked. You finish your bath, then I'll come in and finish mine. I just wish we could finish together."

"You and me both," I said. "Another time."

"Promise?"

"Promise."

She rinsed off her breasts—a task I'd been looking forward to, myself—then stood up, took her towel off the rack beside the tub, and wrapped it around her. Jonah still stood at the door, watching us. Claire stepped out, dried herself off, and led him back to his room. I started to wash myself. The magic of lolling in the bath had departed with Claire.

Jonah's appearance put my feelings in a funny place. On the one hand, I loved the kid, and his seeing me with Claire that way somehow made us feel more like a family. On the other hand, his face at the door, the spitting image of Tony's, also felt like a reproach. He was Tony's son and would always be Tony's son. I had a feeling that, if it came down to it, Tony would put a lot more passion into keeping Jonah than he would into keeping Claire. I wondered if he'd feel keeping Jonah also meant trying to keep Claire. It was that bond between him and her I feared most.

By the time I finished washing, I was depressed. The whole situation suddenly seemed a hopeless muddle. Nobody knew what Tony wanted. Only Jonah's needs were clear, and I had the feeling they would be the deciding factor, which was likely to leave me out in the cold. But then I felt a spark of determination ignite in my heart. Maybe I would lose in the end, but I wasn't going to give up before I started. It could be that Claire and Tony couldn't live together anymore, even if they wanted to for Jonah's sake. It was a whole new ballgame, and I wasn't going to quit in the early innings.

I told Claire I was done and took Jonah into my room while she finished bathing. He sat on my bed, leaning on a pillow against the wall, watching my every move. Like the time we'd stared into each other's eyes on the sofa, months before, he seemed to be looking into my soul. I had a spooky sensation that some higher part of him was analyzing me, assessing my potential as an adoptive father, or perhaps just looking to see if I was sincere in my love for his mother. I'd never felt so spiritually exposed before.

When I'd finished dressing, I started wrestling with him on the bed, to distract him. We pushed and pulled and hugged each other. I let him play his favorite wrestling game, which was to push me off whatever piece of furniture I happened to be on. I always made a great show of falling and looking up at him with a surprised face, which always sent him into a paroxysm of laughter. Finally, Claire appeared at the door, looking fresh and radiant.

"All right, you two. Enough of this. Jonah's going to get an upset stomach. It's time to go to Aunt Katie's, Jonah, to see Christy and Ryan."

"Christy, Ryan," said Jonah, sliding off the bed.

"Are you going back to the Union?" Claire asked.

I nodded.

"They want me to lead a discussion group, this morning. Then I have to work, this afternoon. You working later, too?"

"From three to eleven. Tony's picking Jonah up at Katie's."

"I've got an idea," I said. "Why don't we eat supper together?"

"I don't get much time."

"Neither do I, but you're right up the street. Why don't I pick up a couple subs while I'm out making deliveries and bring them by at, say, 6:00? We can eat them on the lawn up there."

"Okay. I never know for sure when I'll get my dinner break, but I'll try."

We said goodbye, refraining from kissing each other in front of Jonah, who was clinging to Claire's leg. They went downstairs and out on the porch to wait for Katie. She arrived momentarily. After eating a bowl of cereal, I went to UWM. I found myself getting nervous as I approached the Union. After blithely agreeing to lead a discussion group, I found myself wondering what I'd do if it got out of hand. Emotions were running high around the campus. There were a lot of Vietnam veterans taking classes there, and those who weren't opposed to the war were angrier than anybody else about the strike. They felt as if they were being deprived of the education they'd more than earned by putting their life on the line in Southeast Asia. I felt intimidated by them.

I reported in at the strike committee table. Carl wasn't there, but Bill Fleischer was. He sent me to a small meeting room on the third floor, in an area where a lot of student organizations had small offices. The room held a large meeting table made of some indeterminate dull yellow man-made material. Fluorescent lights glared down on it, reflecting off its shiny surface. The room's only saving feature was a single, narrow window that overlooked the cement plain. I pulled open the bottom of the window to let in a little air, and a little air was exactly what it let in. An oversized, white-faced clock on the wall said it was 10:00. I sat at the head of the table and waited.

Ten minutes passed and no one showed up. Then twenty. At twenty-five minutes past, a young man poked his head in and asked if I was there for the science fiction club meeting. I said no. At 10:40, I gave up and returned to the ballroom. Carl was there, this time.

"Nobody showed up," I said.

He looked rather disgusted.

"Fifteen rooms with fifteen discussion leaders and exactly seventeen people have showed up. Total. We put them all in one room, down the hall, if you want to join them. Otherwise, we're organizing groups to demonstrate in classes again. They don't seem to want to come to us, so we'll just have to keep going to them. Sometimes the apathy around here makes me want to give up."

"You seem tired," I said.

Carl peeled off his wire-rim glasses and lay them in front of him, then rubbed his gaunt face with his hands.

"I'm exhausted. I haven't done a thing at the Social Action Center for days. Luckily, the Quakers are behind the strike, or I'd probably be out of a job."

"Is anybody down there?"

"I've got someone tending the place, but he can't make any important decisions, and he's not exactly a whiz with administrative details. I've got to let it go, though. This comes first."

He put his glasses back on.

"Thanks for listening to me complain," he said. "I've got a lot on my mind. Now, about the classroom demonstrations. We've sent several contingents out already, but there's another one forming over there. They've just had their crash course in non-violent resistance from Bill."

He pointed to the dais/bandstand, where about twenty students sat waiting for marching orders.

"Will you lead that group? I don't know any of them and you participated yesterday, so you know the routine. Enter the room chanting and take over the front. Don't try to push the professor aside and take over the podium, but if he offers it to you, jump on it. If he won't yield the floor, chant until he gives up, or just start talking over him. Don't lecture; try to get people talking to one another. That gets the best results."

"Where do you want us to go?"

"To Lapham Hall. There's a big astronomy lecture in the auditorium."

I went over to the other students, identified myself, and told them what we'd be doing. I said if we succeeded in getting people talking, they were welcome to join in the discussion, but they ought to hold back until the class was engaged. I said their first task was to disrupt the class, to stop "business as usual," so we could turn the students' attention to the war. A couple of them looked unsure about this. Another looked a bit too eager, but overall they seemed like a serious, committed group. I asked for questions.

"How do we know when we're done?" one of them asked.

"We'll be done when the class is done—or before, if everybody walks out on us, which happened in one class I went to, yesterday."

"What did it feel like doing this? It seems strange, somehow."

"It *is* strange. It goes against our everyday ideas about leaving people alone, about not interfering with their life. We wouldn't be doing something this dramatic if we didn't feel it was important."

I felt as if I was reassuring myself when I said this. If I was queasy about leading a discussion group, I was downright frightened of leading a group to break up a class. It was one thing to go along for the ride; it was quite another to be in charge of the demonstration.

There were no other questions, so we started over toward Lapham Hall. No one spoke along the way. It was as if all of us were gathering our energy to do something we were not naturally inclined to do. When we entered the lobby, we saw a few students standing around smoking, as if it were any other day on campus. I stopped my contingent outside the lecture hall and gathered them into huddle.

"Okay," I said, "let's just take a few deep breaths and start chanting. Let's do 'Hell, no, we won't go!' That tends to get people's attention. We'll walk right up the aisle and stand in a line across the front. Keep chanting, no matter what anybody says to you. I'll raise my hand when it's time to stop. Are we ready?"

They all nodded.

"Okay, let's start quietly, here in the huddle, then build up the volume. Hell no, we won't go. Hell no, we won't go."

They picked up the rhythm immediately. As the volume grew, we stood up straight, looking into one another's faces for reassurance. The smokers in the lobby turned to watch us. The chant grew louder and more energetic. When it reached a good pitch, I threw open one of the auditorium doors and led them in.

Every head in the room—and there were a couple hundred of them—turned to us. Some faces were amused, some bemused, some supportive, and others disgusted. A small, balding professor, neatly dressed in a gray suit buttoned all the way up the front, stood beside the podium. It was Dr. Keuchler, the professor I'd had for astronomy the previous fall. Immediately, I was embarrassed. Dr. Keuchler was an old-fashioned professor on the verge of retirement. He was formal and strict, but he loved his subject and his students. Even students who came out of his introductory class thinking he was going to be dull as dishwater were hooked by the end of the first formal lecture. I had developed tremendous respect for him during the semester and felt foolish breaking in on him. But it was too late to turn back.

"Hell no, we won't go! Hell no, we won't go!"

As we lined up across the front, Dr. Keuchler stood beside the podium, eyeing us, not with disdain, as I would have expected, but with real curiosity and interest. He did not attempt to continue lecturing. Some of the students in the class picked up our chant, while others started up a counter-chant.

"Go away! Go away!"

"Hell no, we won't go!"

"Go away! Go away!

"Hell no, we won't go!"

Many of them stood up, either to support us or to try to shout us down.

"Go away!"

". . . we won't go!"

As the counter-chants continued, Dr. Keuchler stood calmly at the podium, taking it all in, a half-smile on his face. He seemed to represent the experience of the ages, which had seen all this—and worse—before and was intrigued to see it again. On and on went the chants, one side against the other, neither wanting to give in. It seemed as if they would go on forever. Then Dr. Keuchler seemed to come to a decision. He picked up his briefcase from the floor beside the podium, gathered up his lecture notes, and put them inside, closed the briefcase, and started walking toward the coat rack that held his overcoat and hat. I was certain he was going to take his things and walk out, but, instead, he set the briefcase down at the base of the coat rack, and proceeded to take a seat in the front row of the auditorium.

The moment Dr. Keuchler sat down, the chanting stopped abruptly. There was an eerie silence for a moment. He sat looking at me, his face displaying the same half-smile, which now seemed to be saying, "Your move, Mr. Meyer."

"Thank you for allowing us to speak, Dr. Keuchler," I said. "And thanks to the rest of you for listening."

"Go away," someone shouted from the back of the hall.

"We'll be going soon enough," I said in the direction of the voice, though I hadn't seen who it was. "But, first, we have something important to talk about. There's a war going on in Vietnam."

"No shit!" called the heckler.

This time I spotted him. He wore a white polo shirt and was being egged on by several guys around him.

"The simple fact is, any one of the men in this room could be drafted to fight in that war."

"Not me," the heckler called out, "I'm 4F."

Dr. Keuchler rose and turned around to face the heckler. He did not speak. He just looked at the heckler until the heckler sank down in his seat, not looking remorseful, but, I suspected, not about to open his mouth again while I tried to talk. Dr. Keuchler sat down again.

"We're not here to give you answers. We're here to get you thinking about what's going on in Southeast Asia and talking to one another about it. The whole point of this strike is to get you to step outside your routine and confront an issue that affects every one of you, directly or indirectly. I've got a brother over there. He happens to be pretty safe because he's in the Navy and North Vietnam doesn't have a navy or an air force to threaten his ship. But other people aren't so lucky."

"My brother's in the jungle," said a woman in the front row.

She was dressed conservatively, in a plaid skirt and a spring sweater.

"Would you mind getting up and turning around to speak," I said. "It's hard for people in the back to hear you."

She did as I asked. "My brother's in the jungle," she repeated. "He wakes up terrified and he goes to sleep terrified and he doesn't have the faintest idea why he's there."

"He's there because he loves his country," said a middle-aged man in the back row.

"He does love his country," said the woman. "But he doesn't see what good he's doing his country over there. He says he'd be happy to defend the United States if anybody attacked it, but he knows he's not defending it over there. He says he might even be willing to fight for South Vietnam, if it had been his own choice. But he doesn't understand how a bunch of politicians can make him fight in a country halfway around the world that is no threat to our own country. He just wants to come home."

The woman sat down. No one spoke for a moment. I was just about to invite other people to speak when the middle-aged man stood up. He had gray hair and black-rimmed glasses and wore a white shirt, open at the neck. "My son is over there, too, and I'm proud of him. Hell, he doesn't understand exactly what it's all about, but he doesn't think he has to. He trusts his government and he believes it's his duty to serve when ordered to—just as I did in World War II. He'd be a whole lot safer over there—and so would your brother, young lady—if you demonstrators didn't give aid and comfort to the enemy by publicly opposing the war, making the communists think this war doesn't have the full support of the American people. I wish every one of you—"

"It doesn't have the full support of the American people," said a young man on the aisle near the wall, "and it's a lie to pretend it does."

"Don't you call me a liar, young man!"

"I'm not calling you a liar," he replied. "I'm calling Tricky Dick a liar."

"That's no better," said the older man. "You're talking about the president of the United States!"

"Yes, a president. Not a king, a politician, an elected official. I have a right to call him anything I like."

Suddenly, the room erupted with voices taking sides with both speakers. It was impossible to make out what anyone was saying. I knew it was my job to restore order, but I wasn't sure how. I went to the podium, not sure what I was looking for, and found a large textbook on a shelf inside it. I picked it up with both hands and used it as makeshift gavel, pounding the top of the podium. It took awhile for the pounding to be heard above all the voices, but finally the fracas died down and everyone looked up at me. I admit to feeling a sudden sense of power, winning the attention of such a large group. But immediately I felt inadequate to the task of directing them.

"Maybe we'd better speak one at a time," I said lamely. "It's only polite."

Only polite? That was the kind of thing my mother said. I felt like an idiot. But it seemed to work, momentarily. A female student in the middle of the auditorium raised her hand. I nodded to her. She stood up.

"I wonder if we could have a show of hands. How many people in this room think the war in Vietnam is justified and should go on and how many think we should get out as soon as possible? I'm for pulling out. How many are with me?"

Every one in my contingent raised their hand, of course, but so did at least seventy-five percent of the people in the auditorium.

"It looks to me," said the woman, pinning me with her eyes, "that you and your friends are preaching to the converted. Besides, you've made your point. Now, why don't you get out of here so we can have an astronomy class."

"Yeah!" some others shouted. "Get out of here! Let us have our class!"

This was an unexpected turn. I was at a loss for words, momentarily. Dr. Keuchler saved me again. He stood and faced the young woman. The room quieted down quickly.

"Miss Johnson," he said, "a discussion involves much more than one group of people convincing another group of people of their point of view. Even if everyone in this room agreed that the war should end, we could still learn a great deal by discussing it with one another. Why don't you share your thoughts on the subject with us."

Now it was Miss Johnson's turn to be surprised. As she stood thinking what to say, Dr. Keuchler sat down. "Well . . . I think we shouldn't be there. It's a war that has nothing to do with us."

The middle-aged man in the back spoke up again. "The Germans taking over Europe had nothing to do with us, either. Should we have just let the Nazis do what they liked? The North Vietnamese murder South Vietnamese villagers who won't follow them. Should we just ignore that?"

"Germany declared war on us," she replied, more self-assured, now. "North Vietnam didn't do that—or, if they did, it wasn't until we got heavily involved in the war. I don't think the North Vietnamese are saints or anything, but the South Vietnamese are the ones who ought to be fighting them. We can send them help—even volunteer soldiers, if anybody's interested—but I don't think we ought to be drafting our young men and sending them over there to die for something they don't believe in."

A chorus of voices rose in support of Miss Johnson. She looked pleased with herself for holding her own and sat down.

The discussion went on for the rest of the period. At the end, Dr. Keuchler stood to thank us, which led to a spontaneous outburst of applause from the class. Looking out at all those clapping hands was the high point of the student strike for me. I was happy I'd succeeded as a group leader, but, more importantly, I was happy we'd accomplished exactly what the strike was intended to accomplish, to get people to give the war the attention it deserved. At that moment, it all seemed worth it.

~10~

ATER THAT DAY, I SAT on the lawn at the nursing home where Claire worked, regaling her with my exploits as a strike leader. Cars whooshed by on Oakland Avenue. I was so caught up in my impassioned description I didn't notice when her attention began to wander. Finally, she stared for an inordinately long time at the passing cars.

"What is it?" I said, irritation creeping into my voice.

She looked at me. "It's hard for me to hear about all this when I feel like there's nothing going on in my own life."

"Nothing going on? What about Jonah? What about pre-med?"

"Jonah is . . . Jonah. He's not me. I'm just his caretaker. And I haven't been studying chemistry enough lately, so I don't know if pre-med is going to happen."

"Whose fault is that?" I said.

"What do you mean?"

"If you want to do it, you'll do it. If you don't, you won't. It's just like this strike. I could've begged off. Nobody would've cared. But I wanted to do it and did it. Nobody can stop you if you really want something."

"Is that so, Mr. Know-It-All? You try raising a kid and cleaning up bedpans for crazy old people and see how much energy you have left for making something of yourself. I'm so sick of hearing about what a hero you are in the strike."

"I didn't say I was a hero. I just said I was glad I was able to help."

"It's not what you say, it's how you say it. You puff up your chest like a rooster. You really think you're the cock of the walk since you fucked me,

153

don't you? Well, I feel like shit, and you've hardly even noticed. You're so full of yourself since this strike started you don't even see me anymore."

She stood up. "I'm going back to work, now. I'll see you at the house later. Or maybe I won't. I suppose that depends on whether they can live without you at the Union, tonight. Come back down to earth, John. I don't want a hero. I want somebody who loves me and listens to me."

She stalked off across the lawn.

"Claire!" I should have gone after her, but my own hurt and anger prevented me. "Claire!"

She kept right on going. I went back to eating. *Why should I let her upset me,* I thought. I knew what I was doing for the strike was worthwhile. I wasn't going to let her cynicism taint it. I ate the last few bites of my sub and the unfinished half of hers.

Then I started to feel remorseful. Perhaps I had been paying too much attention to the strike and too little to her. Ultimately, she was much more important to me. Perhaps that was exactly why I'd been paying more attention to the strike than to her. I was afraid of how important she was becoming to me because I was unsure if she would ever be mine.

I crumpled the greasy, white butcher paper that had held our sandwiches, carried it inside with me, and tossed it in the janitor's wheeled trash cart parked beside the reception desk. I asked the receptionist to get Claire on the phone for me. She called the floor and asked for her, then handed me the phone. It took a few minutes for Claire to pick up.

"This is John. I'm down at the reception desk, so . . ."

"I understand. You have to be careful what you say. What do you want? I'm really busy."

"I just want to apologize for not being a good friend, that's all. I know you have a lot on your mind and I haven't been very sensitive to that."

The receptionist, a small, middle-aged black woman, smiled as she listened to what I was saying.

"It's okay," said Claire. "I'm just feeling sorry for myself. But thanks for caring. Will you come back to the house tonight?"

There was a plaintive quality to her voice that precluded me from saying no, though, in fact, I'd considered staying overnight at the Union. "Of course," I said. "I'm going to the Union at nine, as soon as I get off work, but I can pick you up when your shift is over. We can take the bus home or walk."

"That'd be nice. I'll see you out in front at five after eleven. Thanks, John."

During the last few hours of my shift at the liquor store, I spent more time stocking shelves than delivering. It felt good to hoist the big cases around and let my mind wander. Making up with Claire had freed me to ponder my success as a strike leader without feeling guilty. Perhaps she was right that I overestimated my accomplishments, but it made me feel good about myself.

Just after dark, I walked over to the university from work, still feeling high. But as I entered the campus next to the library, I saw something that caused my stomach to sink. One of the huge plate-glass windows on the first floor at the back of the building had been shattered. Pebbles of glass were scattered across the pavement, sparkling in the artificial light. A janitor stood inside the window, surveying the damage. When he saw me staring, he glared at me as if I'd personally done the damage. I tried to look sympathetic and innocent, but I felt guilty.

"Why you kids do this?" he said in heavily accented English. "You have good school. You destroy it. You have free country. You won't fight for it. You all crazy."

I hurried on. I passed another hall and saw "Hell no we won't go!" painted on the brick in red paint. Then I saw more broken windows. I felt pursued by the destruction. I hurried into the Union, which showed no damage, and went right up to the ballroom. Carl was on the phone and he looked upset. As I came near, I could hear what he was saying.

"I told you, we had nothing to do with trashing those buildings."

He listened for a moment.

"No, not even SDS. You don't even know if they were strikers. As soon as we heard what was going on, we told the police. It looked to me like they were in no big hurry to do anything about it."

Again, he paused.

"What I'm saying is that they could have been vandals taking advantage of the strike to go on a spree, or they could have been police plants meant to make us look bad."

He listened again.

"I'm not paranoid. It's been done elsewhere."

As he listened the next time, he looked up and waved me to a chair beside him. I sat down.

"Yes, we want classes cancelled. We've been trying to convince you to do that since we started. But we think it'd be a mistake to do it right now, in response to vandalism. That would legitimize destructiveness."

He rolled his eyes at me as he listened again.

"Of course I'm worried it would make us look bad. In fact, I suspect that's what you're trying to do. And you know you'll look good with the parents if you discipline their bad children who broke things and wrote on the walls."

He held the phone away from his ear. I heard the garbled sound of an angry voice on the other end, then a click. Carl brought the receiver back to his ear.

"Mr. Klein?" said Carl. "Mr. Klein?"

He put the receiver in its cradle.

"That was the chancellor's man. He hung up on me. Guess he didn't like me calling his bluff."

"You really think the trashing was staged by the police?" I asked.

"Who knows. It might have been rogue strikers. I just wanted him to know the strike committee hadn't authorized it."

"When did it happen?"

"Just as it was getting dark."

"How much damage was done? I saw three or four broken windows and some graffiti."

"They've counted ten broken windows and three walls with graffiti."

"Was anybody arrested?"

"No, and that's what makes me suspicious. The vandals did pick a good time to go on their little spree, though. Evening classes were over, so there weren't many people around to witness it. The police had their guard down, because they've been expecting this sort of thing to happen in the middle of the night."

"What's the chancellor going to do?"

"I think he's going to use it as an excuse to close down the university for the rest of the semester. He's been wanting to do it from the start—not because we wanted him to, but because he didn't like the idea of anybody else in control of his campus. I think he'll boot us out of the Union as soon as he does that."

My throat went dry. I swallowed.

"Are we going to try to hold onto it?"

"Probably not. We don't want to fight over a building. We can educate people about the war someplace else. We might do better to claim victory and announce that war education will continue at other locations—the Social Action Center, church basements—wherever we can do it. In fact, I'd better make some calls right now, so I can tell the committee what our alternatives are. We're meeting at 11:00."

"Anything I can do?"

"Not right now. Check in tomorrow morning."

I wished Carl good luck and headed home, thinking I might ask Tony if I could use the car to pick up Claire. He was in the living room watching TV when I arrived.

"The chancellor was just on live," he said. "He looked like quite the stern father. He's ending classes for the semester, after tomorrow, since there are just a few weeks left. He said there's no point in keeping the school open when strikers are disrupting classes and vandalizing buildings."

"That bastard. He has no idea if strikers were responsible for the vandalism."

"He also said we'd get incompletes for our classes and would have to make up the work by the end of the summer session—take home exams and that kind of shit."

"I suppose that's fair. This won't get you in any trouble with draft board, will it?"

"One of the reporters asked if students with deferments would have trouble. He said no."

"I hope he's right."

"You and me both."

"By the way, Tony," I said, trying to sound casual, "I'm going to meet Claire after work. Mind if I take the car and pick her up?"

He was engrossed in the TV again. I wondered if he was a little drunk.

"Fine. Why don't you take her out for a drink. She's been a little touchy lately. I think she needs to get out."

Was he pushing me into her arms? I tried to sound casual when I answered him. "Sure. If she wants to."

I got the extra set of keys from the hook in the kitchen. If I left right away, I would arrive early at the nursing home, but I was worried that, with a few beers in him, Tony might start asking embarrassing questions about Claire and me.

"See you later, Tony," I said as I walked past the living room on my way out.

"No you won't. I'm going to bed in a minute."

"Tomorrow, then."

I felt light-footed as I went down the front steps and into the night, like a teenager who'd just been given the car for a date. I fired up the old Chevy and clicked on the radio to find Jimi Hendrix wailing away on his guitar—music I'd first listened to in high school. I pictured Claire waiting for me in front of the nursing home—waiting for me—and a thrill ran through my body. I couldn't believe we were lovers. It was almost too much. I backed out of the driveway and unintentionally "patched out" when I accelerated.

I turned east at the next corner, deciding I'd kill time cruising along Lake Michigan. It was a beautiful spring night, almost summer-like. I smelled the odor of flowers in the air as I passed Lake Park on the wide road that curved around it and down to the lakefront. Hendrix gave way to Santana. I turned up it. The Latin beat pulsed through my blood as I drove. I found myself wishing for a joint, but it didn't matter. I was high without it.

I drove past the parking lot at McKinley Beach, which was a popular "make out" spot. Cars lined the broad curve of the retaining wall along the back of it, windshields facing the water. I continued on past the illuminated tennis courts across from the marina, past the white clapboard Coast Guard station recently taken over by Native Americans intent on reclaiming tribal land, past the duck pond backed with weeping willows. I drove all the way downtown and started back up Lincoln Memorial Drive in the direction I'd come from. I took my time. Cars whizzed by me as I gazed off across the lake. Small, white-capped waves punctuated its broad surface.

When I arrived at the nursing home, I felt relaxed and happy. Claire sat on the wide front steps, smoking a cigarette. She had loosened her blonde hair, which fell down over the back of her white uniform, making her look angelic. Seeing her made me giddy. When she saw me pull up, she rose and came toward me. I leapt out, came around the car, and, with a great flourish, opened the passenger door for her.

"Your chariot, Madame," I said.

She chuckled.

"What's gotten into you?" she asked.

When she was in, I closed the door gently, kneeled down on the curb, and leaned against the window frame.

"What's gotten into me, madame? The sky, the lake, the moon, the stars, and, most of all, your timeless beauty."

"What have you been smoking?"

I put on a mock look of shock.

"Think you, madame, that only the evil weed can produce such effects? Fie on you! Insult not the beauty of my lady, which hath more power to affect the senses than the finest hashish in all the kingdoms of the East!"

She laughed. "You're crazy—you know that, don't you?"

"Crazy, indeed. Crazy with love for thy very own self. Kiss me, you fool!"

I closed my eyes and tilted my head.

"Not here, Romeo. Wait until we get back to the house. Is Tony there?"

"Yes, but he's had a few beers and he said he was going to crash. I think he'll sleep soundly."

"Then maybe you'll get a kiss, after all. Home, James!"

"What'er my lady wants."

I rose, went around to the driver's side, and I slid in beside her, realizing how few times I'd actually sat beside her in a car. I liked the way it felt.

We were home within a few minutes. Neither of us had spoken along the way, but that felt good, too. I liked the fact that I could just be with Claire. I pulled the car all the way up the driveway to the back of the house and turned off the engine. In the silence, a gentle breeze blew through the car, bearing the smell of damp earth and new leaves. Claire made no move to get out, nor did I. There was no place else on earth I wanted to be. Claire's hand slid across the bench seat between us and engaged mine. Her palm was warm and dry. We sat holding hands for some time, still not speaking. Finally, without turning her head to me, she spoke.

"You may have that kiss, now, sir, if you so desire."

I looked at her. She continued to stare straight ahead. With my free hand, I reached over to her chin and gently turned her face toward me. Her large, pale eyes looked vulnerable. Her breath was shallow. I slid my body over to hers, took her in my arms, and kissed her deeply. She kissed me back, tentatively at first, but then with growing desire. My hand went to her breasts. Her breath caught for a moment, but then she relaxed. I undid the big white buttons on the front of her uniform, unhooked her bra, which clasped in front, and put my hand inside it.

Our passion built by degrees as we undressed each other in that cramped space. There was barely room for Claire to lay back and open herself to me, but she did, and I entered her, driven equally by love and lust. Once I was inside her, being inside her was not enough. I wanted to become part of her. I wanted us to become one person. What would have seemed like furtive, guilty coupling to an outside observer was, in fact, the true consummation of our love. Perhaps arguing and making up had deepened our sense of commitment to one another. Perhaps the stars and planets were correctly aligned. Whatever the reason, our lovemaking in the front seat of that car took us to a place we hadn't been before. She was mine, that night—for the first time—and I was hers. When we were finished, we lay there, naked and cramped, and cried together. We said nothing, but we both knew why we were crying. The future was suddenly wonderful and terrifying.

We slept together in my bed that night, and woke early to make love again, not parting until we heard Jonah knock on the locked door to Claire's room and call out, "Mama?" She went into her room to let him in. She put on a nightgown and returned to my room, cigarettes in hand, Jonah trailing behind her.

"John?" he said when saw me in the bed. "Sweep?"

"Hey, little guy," I said. "Yes, I'm still sleeping. Your Mama has made me very tired."

I winked at Claire, who sat on the edge of the bed, lighting up a cigarette. She took a drag and held it out to me, but I declined.

"Smoke," said Jonah.

He climbed up onto the bed and sat down on the pillow beside mine, the one Claire had been sleeping on. He looked at the two of us as if expecting us to do something. I grabbed him and lifted him over my head. He looked surprised but not displeased.

"Be careful, now, John," said Claire.

"Boom," said Jonah.

"Do you want to go boom?" I asked.

"Boom!" he said again.

I lowered him down toward my chest, then up again, three times, saying, "And a one, and a two, and a three." With my arms extended, I dropped him onto the bed beside me, saying, "And a boom-de-eh!" He landed on his face and started giggling uncontrollably. It was a game my parents had played with me and all my siblings when we were little. It never failed to delight a child.

"Boom!" said Jonah with even greater enthusiasm as he crawled back into my arms. "Boom!"

So we "boomed" again—and again and again. It always amazed me how often small children could repeat a simple activity and not get bored with it. Claire watched us contentedly as she smoked her cigarette. Finally, *I* got bored with it and sent Jonah back into Claire's room to jump on the bed, despite her half-hearted protests that he wasn't supposed to do that.

With Jonah occupied, I was able to turn my attention back to her.

"Happy?" I said.

"Happy," she said. "For the moment."

"What's going to happen to us?" I said.

"I don't know. But let's not worry about it. Let's just enjoy being together."

"I wish I could."

"What, enjoy our being together?"

"No, of course not. I wish I could not worry about it. I wish I could forget that Tony is Jonah's father and your husband—not to mention my friend—my former friend, once he finds out what's going on here."

Claire tapped the long ash of her cigarette into the palm of her hand. "We have to tell him, you know," she said.

"I know. Should we do it together?"

She thought about this for a moment. "I don't think so," she said. "I think he'd feel like we were ganging up on him. I'll tell him. It's not like you and I are getting married or anything."

I smiled. "Not yet."

Claire smiled back at me. "Do you mean that?"

"I'm afraid to think about it."

"Why?"

"It feels like there's so little chance it could happen."

"You never know."

"You never do. Kiss me."

She looked through the door to her room. Jonah was happily jumping on the bed. She leaned toward me, the arm with the cigarette extended out behind her for balance, and lay her lips on mine. She kissed me softly, at first, then pressed her lips into mine and darted her tongue into my mouth. I put my arms around her shoulders and pulled her down.

"Don't," she protested, but then she kissed me again, hard and long. "Let me up, now."

I did. Jonah was standing in the doorway. He certainly had a knack for finding us in compromising positions.

"Come on, Jonah," said Claire, standing up and trying to act casual, "let's change your diaper and get you dressed."

"Poopy?" he said.

"We'll see," said Claire.

The three of us ate breakfast together and I allowed myself to imagine we were a real family in our own home with no other emotional encumbrances. I felt calmer and more purposeful than I'd ever felt in my life. I had no idea what I wanted to do with my life after college, but there, with Claire and Jonah, life took on shape and purpose. Whatever else might happen, loving them was surely something worth doing.

"We're going over to Katie's house this morning," said Claire. "Want to come along?"

"I wish I could, but I promised Carl I'd check in at the Union this morning."

"What's left to do over there? You said the school was closing."

"I don't know. Maybe nothing. He was planning to set up classes on the war in various places around the East Side. I might be able to help him do that."

"Will you teach one of them?"

"Me? I don't know enough about the war. But I can help with coordination and publicity."

"You're pretty dedicated to this, aren't you?"

There was a new respect in her voice, which touched me.

"I think it's important—more important than most things." I looked her in the eye. "Most things, but not all."

"Well," she said teasingly, "if I'm more important, why don't you come with me to Katie's?"

"If there's nothing brewing at the Union, I'll meet you there. Okay?"

"Okay. Will you wipe Jonah's face and get him out of his high chair while I get my stuff upstairs. Katie should be here, soon."

I did as I was asked. Then Jonah conned me into chasing him around the first floor. While we were at it, Katie arrived with her two children, Christy and Ryan, who stood shyly by for about a minute, then joined in the action. By the time Claire came down the steps with her purse and the diaper bag over her shoulder and her uniform on a hanger, the first floor was like a daycare center for hyperactive children.

"Oh, great," she said, "get them all riled up and then send them off with us."

"That's the idea," I said as I whizzed by, chasing Christy into the kitchen.

It took some time to tear the children away from the game, but finally everyone was ready to go. Claire hung back while the others went outside. We kissed deeply, then held one another.

"Can I pick you up after work again?" I asked.

"Oh, shoot," she said. "That's what I forgot to ask you about. Susie wants me to go out for a drink after I get off. Katie and Tony are both going out, too, so they can't watch Jonah. Would you mind?"

"Not at all. I don't have to go to Siegel's today. We'll work something out. What time will Katie bring Jonah back?"

"About seven o'clock. He should go right to bed. He's always beat after spending the day with Christy and Ryan."

We kissed once more, and she went out. I stood looking out through the thick glass window in the front door as she walked to the car, her hair gleaming like corn silk in the sunshine. She got in and they drove off. I sighed deeply and went back into the kitchen to clean up breakfast.

When I went to the university, half-an-hour later, I walked west for a change and turned up Maryland Avenue, which brought me to a side door of the Union. When I entered, I noticed immediately it was very quiet. I went up to the ballroom and found it nearly deserted. Carl and Bill Ascher sat at the usual table, but they looked uncharacteristically casual, with their feet up on the table and their chairs leaned back. Bill saw me approaching.

"Well, well, well," he said, "another loyal striker. Or are you coming from the big rally?"

"What big rally?"

"You could hardly have missed it if you came by Mitchell Hall."

"I haven't been over that way. What's up?"

I looked at Carl, but he was staring at his boots up on the table.

"The chancellor has finessed us. His little announcement about students having to make up class work and exams for this semester has everyone in an uproar. They've forgotten all about the war in Vietnam."

"I'm not following this," I said.

"It's simple," Bill said. "Nobody wants to make any sacrifices. They expected the chancellor to let them strike and still give them full credit for their courses. There are guys over in 'Nam getting their heads shot off, but these assholes can't even put in a little extra studying over the summer for the sake of waking up the country. It's pathetic."

"What do they want?" I asked.

"Are you going to make me spell out their pathetic little demand? They want to be given their mid-term grade if they were passing and they want the option to take an incomplete if they weren't. No muss, no fuss, no risk. They get to play at being political activists and pay nothing for the privilege. I'd like to strangle every one of them."

"It's human nature, Bill," said Carl, finally. "I keep telling you . . ."

"Well, fuck human nature, then!"

"Seems to me human nature is already fucked," said Carl, deadpan.

Bill was about to launch into a fierce rebuttal when Carl's words sunk in.

"Well," he said, "it's about time you admitted that."

"Let me get this straight," I said. "These people want to strike and still get full credit for their courses, the courses they haven't finished?"

"That's about the size of it," said Carl.

"Seems pretty hypocritical" I said.

"Bingo," said Bill.

"You know," said Carl, "I wouldn't mind it if this was led by people who opposed the strike. You'd expect them to be bummed about it. But it was strikers who organized this protest—overnight, it seems—and, as you can see by how deserted this place is, a lot of strikers are taking part in it."

"I wish they'd put that much energy into the strike," said Bill.

"Some of them did," said Carl. "What amazes me is they can protest this with equal energy. It's like protesting on behalf of starving people one day and the next day protesting because you didn't get cake for dessert."

"Speaking of cake," I said, "to put it another way, they want to have their cake and eat it, too."

"Here, here!" said Bill.

"What do we do, now?" I asked.

Carl dragged his feet off the table and plunked them down on the floor. He looked like a soldier about to go on a forced march.

"We hold our anti-war classes and hope somebody shows up."

At that moment, I sensed movement behind me.

"Uh-oh," said Bill.

I turned to see a half-dozen police officers in riot gear standing at the door as an officer with gold trim on his cap approached us. He stopped ten feet before us, as if we had some easily communicable disease, and looked over our head as he spoke.

"At the direction of the chancellor of university and the mayor of Milwaukee, I hereby order you to vacate these premises within the next half-hour. If you have not exited the building within that half-hour, you will be subject to arrest."

With that, he turned on his heels and strode back to his men, who parted to let him through, then followed him out.

"The chancellor isn't wasting any time," said Carl.

"He created a diversion and now he's taking advantage of it," said Bill. "He's a good tactician. The bastard."

"Is this the end of the strike?" I asked.

"We were planning to end it today, anyway," said Carl. "They can't kick us out of a place we were going to leave voluntarily. We'll just thank the chancellor nicely for cooperating with our request that the school be shut down and announce our continuing war education program. Two can play at tactics."

"We could have used a few more officers like you over in 'Nam," said Bill, smiling impishly.

Carl gave him a long, serious look.

"Okay, okay," said Bill, "so it was a lousy joke."

Carl gathered up the strike committee's papers, stuffed them into an accordion-pleated file folder, and tied it closed. The three of us walked down the steps, through the lobby, and out the main entrance of the Union, where a gaggle of local reporters converged on us and thrust microphones into our faces. Bill and I let Carl step forward to field the questions, which he did with great aplomb. By the time the reporters were ready to let us go, Carl had convinced them the strike had achieved everything the committee had intended it to.

I was almost convinced—but not quite. The news about strikers being more interested in their grades than in the strike had thrown me for a loop. It was hard to believe that so many of my fellow students were that mercenary. It had never occurred to me that I should get credit for work I'd voluntarily chosen not to complete. The chancellor's decision to allow us to make up class work over the summer seemed generous, in that respect, though his intention had been to derail the strike. Did he really suspect his offer would be protested? He'd probably realized non-strikers would be upset by it and would resent the strikers, but I couldn't believe he would have expected the strikers to be upset by something he saw as a concession. That part had been serendipitous for him. It made me angry at the strikers. Was this the meager level of self-sacrifice they were able to maintain? How could they hope to win a non-violent war against the war in Vietnam if they weren't willing to make such a small sacrifice for the sake of the cause? As Bill has said, it was pathetic.

I went with Bill and Carl to the Lutheran student center, across from the campus, to help write publicity material for the war education classes, but my heart wasn't in it. I had a feeling very few people would turn out for them. Suddenly, it seemed as if nobody cared.

In the middle of the afternoon, I dragged myself home. The day had turned unseasonably hot and humid. I installed myself on the couch in the living room, in front of a box fan, with a glass of ice water. Tony arrived soon afterward and went off to shower. When he came back, he joined me in front of the fan with a beer. I told him what had come down on campus and, to his credit, he was just as disappointed as I was. Sitting there with him, without Claire at the forefront of my thoughts for a change, I remembered how much I'd liked him when we first met—how much I still liked him.

The fact that I was making love with his wife suddenly seemed selfish and ridiculous. What right did I have to insert myself in their relationship, even if—some would say especially if—they were having problems? What kind of friend did something like that? On the other hand, Claire was my friend, too. She and I had become much closer than Tony and I had ever been, well before she and I had started making love. Perhaps my relationship with her was a natural progression from an intimate friendship.

The world was changing. Maybe more of this sort of thing was going to be happening. Maybe Tony and I would remain friends, even after he found out about Claire and me. Maybe we could even share Jonah. Maybe we would all live together—his new girlfriend might even join us—and operate as a community, instead of as isolated nuclear couples. As I sat next to Tony on the couch, enjoying his humor and his straightforward attitudes, I couldn't help hoping it could happen. I was tempted to tell him, right then and there, what I was thinking. But I couldn't summon the courage. It was easier to just hang out with him and let it slide.

The phone rang. It was Claire. I could tell immediately that she was not at work. She sounded too relaxed. It turned out she'd called the nursing home to get her hours for the next week and gotten an aide who wanted to work a double shift and take off another night, so she'd traded.

"I just wasn't up for bedpans, tonight," she said "but it's too damn hot to hang out in the house. Want to go to a movie?"

"Tony's here, too," I said, suddenly feeling guilty.

"He's supposed to have his own plans. That's why you were going to babysit Jonah."

"What about Jonah?"

"Katie's going to keep him overnight. We could see *Paint Your Wagon*. I hear it's great. Tony can come, too, if he's not doing anything else. I'm not in the mood for romance, anyway. I just want to have a good time and cool off."

"I'll see what he says."

Two weeks before this, the three of us going to a movie together would have been an event of no consequence. We did a lot of things together, with and without Jonah. But as I set down the phone and went into the living room to talk to Tony, I felt as guilty and sneaky as an adolescent lying to his parents. Tony didn't seem to notice anything, but, then, it was often hard to tell with him. It turned out that his plans had fallen through and he was hot and tired, too. Like Claire, he was ready to do anything to get out of the heat.

We picked up pizzas for supper and took them over to Katie's, so Tony could see Jonah before going to the movie. But, as it turned out, Jonah was more interested in his cousins than in his father, so we went to an early showing of the movie. We stuck to small talk in the car. The atmosphere wasn't exactly tense, but it wasn't as relaxed as it had always been when the three of us went out. I wondered if Tony noticed that. At the theater, Claire sat between Tony and me.

Knowing nothing about the plot of *Paint Your Wagon*, which had been a Broadway musical, I expected it to be pure entertainment, something to relax me and allow me to forget everything that was going on among the three of us. At first, it looked as if that was exactly what it would be. Lee Marvin and Clint Eastwood were gold miners in the Old West, living in an all-male camp with their fellow miners. They were also best friends, Eastwood playing the straight man to Marvin's crazy drunk. Then Jean Seberg appeared, looking, it struck me, not unlike the beautiful woman sitting next to me. Marvin and Eastwood both fell in love with her. They were ready to tear one another apart over her, until they realized that, if she would have them, they could both be her husband, the way Mormon men of that era often had two or more wives.

By this time, I was on the edge of my seat. *Why not?* I thought. *Why couldn't something like that work?*

It jibed perfectly with what I'd been thinking that afternoon. Why should I have to give up Tony to have Claire? Why should Claire have to give up Tony to have me? The world was changing. All kinds of new arrangements might be possible. For the first time, I felt hopeful we could all stay together and be happy.

Unfortunately, the movie plot did not follow this line. Jealousy between the men reared its ugly head, first, but that was brought under control. Then Jean Seberg's desire for respectability started to grow, a desire that did not leave room for the trio's unconventional arrangement. In the end, Lee Marvin ended up going off on his own. It was, to my mind, a sad ending, but not, I decided, an inevitable one. We were not living in an age of conventional morality. There was room for new experiments. Perhaps the three of us would be marital pioneers. I was sensible enough to know that if something like that was going to happen, it was going to happen slowly and organically, not on the strength of momentary inspiration from a movie plot. But it gave me hope.

-11-

HE NEXT DAY, I WORKED at the liquor store until nine o'clock and came home to babysit for Jonah. Tony was going out—presumably with Alicia, although he didn't say—and Claire had rescheduled her drink after work with Susie. I was happy to go home and do nothing. Between the strike and my new relationship with Claire, I was emotionally exhausted. Jonah was already in bed when I got there, and Tony was out the door in minutes. I sat in the living room reading a novel until I heard Jonah crying. I went to him right away, hoping to settle him down before he woke up completely. But he was wide-awake and upset. I had to pick him up and walk him around the dark room for half-an-hour before he finally quieted down and, slowly but surely, went back to sleep.

Even more tired by then, I went back downstairs, intending to veg out in front of the TV. I walked around the corner into the living room and nearly jumped through the ceiling in surprise. Kolvacik was sitting on the sofa, lighting up a joint.

"How the hell did you get in here?" I said.

He took a long hit, held it in, and cocked an eye at me. Then he blew out the smoke in a long, slow stream.

"I broke a window," he said.

"I didn't hear any—"

"Through the door, for Christ's sake. It was open. Sit down, Meyer, we need to talk. Want a hit?"

"No thanks."

"Suit yourself. Me, I think more clearly when I'm high."

"That remains to be seen. What's on your mind?"

"Claire."

Suddenly, my stomach hurt.

"And Tony."

"What about them."

He looked me square in the eye. "You're fucking her, aren't you?"

I looked away, then back at him.

"I'm not 'fucking' anybody."

"Fucking, rolling in the hay, boinking, making love—whatever you want to call it. It's all the same to me."

"Well, it's not all the same to me."

"Call it any pretty name you want, asshole. You're still fucking your friend's—my friend's—wife. How can you live with yourself?"

"He's not exactly being attentive to her these days, you know. He's living in another room and probably sleeping with his pal Alicia—even as we speak."

"That's about him and Claire. This is about you."

"You can't separate the two!"

"I'm doing it."

"Then I don't want to talk about it."

I stood up and headed toward the stairs.

He followed me.

"I told you a long time ago not fuck with them, Meyer, and I meant it."

I stopped at the foot of the stairs and faced him.

"It's none of your damn business, Kolvacik. You're just jealous because you want to fuck her yourself. Well, I want a lot more than that. I love her. And if Tony doesn't appreciate her enough to stay with her, I'm going to be there for her. And you can tell him that."

Suddenly, the anger seemed to drain out of him. He took a deep breath and exhaled, looking at the floor. "I'm not sure he even knows about it, yet."

He raised his head and pinned me with his eyes again. "You've got to tell him. You can't pretend he doesn't live here and you can't pretend he's not your friend. What you're doing is bad enough. Not owning up to it is even worse. That's all I came to say."

He went to the door, then turned to me again. "Even if you love her, man, it's wrong. It's just wrong."

He yanked open the door and went out. I stood where I was and listened to him start up his car and drive off. Jonah started crying again. I wanted to go upstairs, but I felt paralyzed. I stood there, rooted to the spot. Finally, I shook my head hard to bring myself back to reality and went to him. He was all twisted up in his bed sheet, sweaty and frightened. I unwound the sheet and picked him up. He put his head on my shoulder and started sucking his thumb. I sat down in the rocking chair and rocked him back and forth, singing an Italian lullaby Mina had taught me one night.

"*Nina, nana, coco la dela mama*
Nina, nana, coco la del papa"

I sang it over and over again, comforting myself as well as him. For a long time, his eyes were open. Then his eyelids began to flutter and droop, and he fell back to sleep. I was just about to get up and put him back into his bed, when I heard the front door open, then footsteps on the stairs. I was afraid Kolvacik had come back. But it was even worse. A moment later, Tony stood silhouetted in the doorway.

"How's the little guy doing?" he asked.

"Fine," I said. "I was just about to put him down."

"Let me hold him, first."

I got up and Tony came forward. I handed Jonah to him. My arms felt empty. I moved away from the rocker so Tony could sit down. I wanted desperately to leave, but Kolvacik's admonition kept replaying in my head: "You've got to tell him . . . You can't pretend he's not your friend." I sat down on the rug and leaned back against Jonah's dresser. It was dark and peaceful in the room. I wanted desperately to leave it that way. But, finally, I cleared my throat and spoke.

"Tony?"

"Yeah."

"How are things with you and Claire?"

"You know how things are. They suck."

"I mean, how do you feel about her, deep down."

"I don't know. That's why I moved upstairs. I need some distance to figure it out."

Tony rocked away in the dark, Jonah in his arms. I wanted to say it. I needed to say it. But I didn't know how to say it. I took a deep breath and released it slowly before I spoke. "You know I care a lot about her, don't you?"

"She says you're her best friend."

"Does that bother you?"

"Should it?"

"Maybe."

He stopped rocking. Jonah shifted in his arms.

"Why?"

The tension in the room was as thick as the darkness.

"Because . . ." I started, unable to complete the sentence.

"You're in love with her, aren't you?" he said.

"Yes."

"Fuck . . ." he said softly.

Neither of us moved or spoke for a moment. Then Tony started rocking again.

"I didn't want it happen," I said lamely. "I just wanted to be—"

He held up a hand to stop me. "Don't explain," he said. "Don't fucking explain."

He kept rocking.

"I'll never forget the first time I saw her," he said. "At a party in high school in somebody's basement. She was on the steps, listening patiently to her girlfriend going on and on about something. She had a beer in her hand and she was wearing white shorts and a white tube top. I watched her sip her beer, wrapping those beautiful pink lips around the mouth of the bottle. Then she looked over and smiled. That was it for me."

He paused. "Seems like a long time ago."

"If you want me to back off, I will," I said.

Tony stopped rocking again.

"That's bullshit."

"I guess it is," I said. "I wish it wasn't."

"Yeah, well, if wishes were horses and all that crap. Nobody seems to be getting what he wants around here. Except maybe you. Are you sleeping with her already?"

"Yes."

"You two didn't waste any time, did you?"

"It wasn't like we planned it. It just happened."

"You had nothing to do with it, huh?"

"I didn't say that."

"Sounds to me like you're saying you weren't responsible for it. That shit won't fly in a marriage, man, I'll tell you that. You want Claire? Fine. You've got her. But it doesn't just mean fucking her. It means living with her shit day in and day out. You haven't even begun to see her shit, yet. Or she yours, for that matter. You guys are living in a fantasy world. Playing house. It's a whole lot different when you're married and you've got a kid and you're stuck with each other all the time."

He rose abruptly and, despite his own agitation, put Jonah down in his crib gently. Then her turned to me, looming over me as I sat on the floor, his fists clenched at his sides.

"And even if you get Claire, don't get any ideas about Jonah. He's my son and he's going to stay my son."

"Are you telling me to stay away from him?"

"I know that won't happen. If you're hanging out with Claire, you'll be hanging out with him, too. There's nothing I can do about that. But if I ever get a whiff of you trying to take my place with him, I'll beat your fucking face in."

He strode from the room, opened the door to the attic, and took the stairs two at a time. I heard his boots on the floor above me.

I stayed sitting, my back against the dresser. Again I felt paralyzed. I wondered what I'd gotten myself into. I knew I loved Claire. Was that all that mattered to me? I knew that, given the choice between keeping a friend and finding a woman to love, it was no contest. I was like a knight looking for someone to champion, and Claire was the fair maiden of my dreams.

I went back down to the living room and eventually fell asleep reading on the couch. Claire woke me when she arrived.

"What time is it?" I asked.

"Two o'clock. Is Tony home, yet?"

"Oh, yeah. He's home."

"Why do you say it like that?"

I sat up, yawned, and stretched my arms.

"We had a . . . conversation."

"What kind of—You didn't tell him about us, did you?"

"I did."

"Shit."

"It just came up."

"Did he ask?"

"Not exactly."

"But you decided it was your job to tell him."

"It seemed like the right time."

"I see. I'm his wife. I'm the mother of his child. But you should be the judge of when it's the right time to tell him we're lovers. Who do you think you are?"

"I'm his friend. Kolvacik came by and he made me feel like shit for keeping it from him."

"Tim? How does he know about it. I suppose you told him, too. Is there anybody you haven't told?"

"I didn't tell Kolvacik. If you didn't, I guess he just figured it out on his own."

"Well, thanks for making my day. Now I'll lay awake all night trying to figure out what to say to Tony in the morning. I wasn't ready for this yet, John."

She pulled her Kool 100s out of her fringed leather purse and threw the purse on the couch. She extracted a cigarette and a book of matches and lit the cigarette.

"What will you say to him?" I asked meekly.

She sat down on the overstuffed chair across from the couch, pulled off her shoes, and brought her legs up under her.

"I wish I knew," she said.

She smoked silently for some time. I wanted to push her for an answer. I wanted to hear her say she was going to tell him she loved me. But I wasn't entirely certain that was the answer I'd get, so I waited. Finally, she seemed to sense my anticipation.

"Go to bed, John. I told you, I don't know what I'm going to say. It'll take me all night to figure it out."

I didn't move. I had to have some kind of reassurance.

"Will you tell him you love me?" I asked.

She took a long drag on her cigarette and blew it out slowly. "I'll tell him I care a lot about you. I don't know what love means right now."

"May I kiss you good night?"

At first, she didn't seem to hear what I said. Then it registered. "Yes," she said. "I think I need a kiss."

I went to her, knelt down in front of her, and took her free hand. "I love you, Claire. Whatever happens with Tony, I love you. I don't think I can help it."

"Then kiss me."

I kissed her, then laid my head on her breast. She wrapped her arms around my head, being careful to keep her cigarette away from my face.

"This is crazy, John. You know that, don't you?"

"I know."

"Go to bed, now. I need to think. I also need an ashtray for this cigarette."

We broke our clinch. It was difficult to let go.

"Can we sleep together tonight?" I asked.

"I need to be alone. If I'm feeling better in the morning, I'll come and visit you."

"No," I said. "You sleep in. Tony's not working, so I'm sure he will. I'll take care of Jonah when he wakes up. You can have your reckoning with Tony later on. In fact, if you want to go somewhere to talk, I'll watch Jonah for you."

"How was Jonah, tonight?"

"He woke up twice. It took some work to get him back to sleep both times. Do you think the tension around here is getting to him?"

"I'm sure it is. I wish we could spare him all this."

I said good night and dragged myself up the stairs to bed. I couldn't sleep. Much later, I heard Claire come up to bed, then the muffled sound of crying. I was just about to go to her when it stopped. Still, I couldn't sleep. Finally, I got up and went into her room.

She lay on her stomach, asleep. I wanted to lay down beside her and take her in my arms, but I was afraid to. Instead, I sat down beside her and caressed her hair. I wanted reassurance I wasn't a fool to sacrifice my friendship with

Tony—and, no doubt, with Kolvacik—for her. I knew that, if I really did wake her, she'd tell me she didn't know what she felt and couldn't make any promises. That made me afraid, and being afraid made me angry. For a moment, I hated her. I wanted to shake her and make her say she loved me. I continued to caress her fine, soft hair, trying to push away my fears. All-at-once, I realized how exhausted I was. I leaned over and kissed the back of her head, then got up and went back into my own room.

Everyone slept late in the morning, including Jonah. I woke up first, after less sleep than anyone, brought to consciousness by the sound of someone slamming the front door. I had a splitting headache, and I felt half-conscious. I dragged myself downstairs to investigate, half-hoping it was a burglar who would shoot me and put me out of my misery. I found Jonathan, our long-lost roommate, at the kitchen table eating a bowl of Cap'n Crunch cereal.

"You look like hell, Meyer," he said. "You been crying over your little flop of a strike?"

"Fuck you," I said half-heartedly.

I went to the sink to get a glass of tap water. I was in no condition to debate the success or lack of success of the strike.

"What a bunch of wimps over there," Jonathan continued. "Worrying about their fucking grades when the country's about to come down around their ears."

"I suppose you and your cohorts are the ones going to make that happen, huh?"

"Damn straight! It's in the works. Just wait and see."

"I won't hold my breath."

"You won't have to."

He stood up. "I'm going to change my clothes. Then I'm out of here again."

He started out of the room, leaving his bowl and the cereal box on the table. I should have demanded he clean up after himself, but I didn't want to waste what little energy I had, especially since I knew the demand would have no effect on him. All I'd get was a lecture on "petty bourgeois concerns" and the bowl and cereal box would stay where they were.

I went into the living room and plopped down on the couch. I was too tired to do anything, so I just sat. Jonathan came down the stairs in the same jeans he'd worn for weeks, but with a fresh t-shirt. It was bright red and had a picture of Karl Marx printed on it. He paused outside the entrance to the living room, looking smug.

"Think of me when you hear the news, later, okay?"

I hadn't the faintest idea what he was talking about.

"I'll be staying elsewhere for a while. It's best you don't know where. See ya'."

I gleaned from this, despite my fuzzy mind, that Jonathan and his communist buddies were up to something big. I had wondered when we'd be hearing from them.

After he left, I stretched out on the couch and fell asleep. Some time later, I got a rude awakening when Jonah threw himself on top of me.

"Wake up," he said. "John. Wake up."

I moved him off of my semi-nauseated stomach and onto the edge of the couch cushion beside me. "Is your mother awake?"

He looked around the room, as if she might be hiding behind a piece of furniture. "Mama? Where?"

"She must be sleeping."

"Sweeping."

"Want some breakfast, big guy?"

He leaped up and ran into the kitchen. He was too fast for me. I sat up slowly and stretched. Jonah came running back into the room and started tugging on my arm. "Cer'yl," he said.

I let him pull me up. He held onto my hand and led me into the kitchen, where he pointed to the Cap'n Crunch box on the table. "Cer'yl."

"Okay. Get into your high chair and I'll put some on the tray for you."

He did as he was asked. I snapped the tray into place and poured some cereal onto it. Then I found his covered cup with the teddy bear on the side, filled it with milk, and set it on the tray. He was munching away happily. I went out onto the porch, picked up the morning paper, and brought it into the kitchen. I sat in a chair beside Jonah and scanned the front page.

"What's happening in our screwed up world this morning, Jonah?" I said.

Seeing nothing of interest, I began paging through. On page four, a story caught my eye. It said that government officials expected demonstrations against the arms industry to happen, soon. They weren't certain of the nature of the protests, but had information that suggested stepped-up actions against various arms manufacturers would begin soon. It occurred to me that this was the sort of thing Jonathan might be involved in.

Tony appeared at the kitchen door.

"Daddy!" squealed Jonah.

"Hey, pal," said Tony. "Whatcha eatin' there?"

"Cer'yl."

"Cap'n Crunch first thing in the morning, huh? Yuck."

"Jonathan left it out," I said. "I didn't think to put it away before Jonah saw it."

"I don't give a shit," said Tony. "You're not responsible for him."

I retreated behind the newspaper. Tony poured a glass of orange juice and sat down directly across from me.

"Throw me some of that newspaper," he said.

I handed him the sections I wasn't looking at. We both sat reading.

"Paper," said Jonah.

"That's right, little guy," said Tony. "We're reading the newspaper. Look at this picture of a little boy just like you."

He turned the paper to show Jonah the photograph, which was of a boy playing with blocks at a day care center.

"Jonah?" said Jonah.

"No, that's another little boy," said Tony.

"Boy?"

"That's right."

A few minutes later, Claire came into the kitchen in a short nightie. I felt the tension level shoot up immediately. It suddenly felt as if the kitchen, big as it was, was too small to hold us.

"Mommy!" said Jonah.

"Good morning, sweetie," she said and kissed him on the top of the head. "I can't believe you guys haven't made coffee, yet," she said.

"I hardly ever drink it," I said. "You know that."

"Tony does."

Tony made no reply. He was concentrating on the paper as if he was trying to bore a hole through it with his eyes. Claire brushed against the paper as she went by him to the sink. He looked at her for the first time.

"Why don't you put some fucking clothes on," he said.

She stopped and turned to him. "What's your problem this morning?"

Tony looked back at the paper, as if he was going to continue reading, but it was clear he wasn't seeing what was in front of him.

"My problem is that I don't like you running around here like a fucking whore. If you bend over in that thing, people can see right up your ass."

I could see Claire struggling for self-control. "I know what's really on your mind, Tony. We can talk about that later. I want to talk about it."

"Gee, that makes me feel warm all over."

"John will watch Jonah and we can go off somewhere on our own."

"Good old John," he said, still looking at the paper. "What a saint. Always ready to lend a helping hand—or whatever part of his anatomy is required."

"Cut it out, Tony," said Claire. "This won't get us anywhere."

Tony slapped the newspaper shut and looked at Claire coldly. "We weren't exactly getting anywhere anyway, were we? Why start trying, now?"

"Don't be a prick, Tony."

"Fuck you, Claire."

"Fuck?" said Jonah.

"Great," said Claire, "now you've got Jonah swearing."

"I don't give a shit," said Tony. "He's my son, and I'll swear in front of him if I want to."

"That's real intelligent."

"You should talk about intelligence, Miss Pre-Med Failure."

"Go to hell!"

"Now who's swearing?"

"I'm going upstairs," said Claire. "If you decide you want to talk, instead of swearing at me, let me know. I'm ready."

"Yeah, you're ready for anybody who drops into your bedroom."

"Jesus, Tony. Grow up."

She started out of the room. For a split second, I thought Tony was going to grab her and escalate the fight, but he let her pass. I wanted to go after her, but I was too meek to leap right up. I was irrationally afraid of Tony's tongue. But he didn't turn it on me. He opened the paper again. I hid behind mine, too.

"Mommy?" said Jonah.

I saw he was done eating and took the opportunity to try to cover my escape. "Do you want to go up to your Mommy, Jonah?" I asked.

"Mommy."

I stood up.

"He's staying here with me," said Tony, not bothering to look up.

"But he's done, Tony. He wants to go up to Claire."

"He's staying here with me."

"Mommy?" said Jonah.

"Want some more cereal, Jonah?" I asked, hoping to distract him.

"Mommy?"

"Tony?" I said.

"Leave him the fuck alone," he said coldly, continuing to look at the newspaper. "I'll deal with him."

I took a deep breath. "Okay. But he's ready to go."

The newspaper came down fast.

"I know my own fucking kid, okay, Meyer. Now get the hell out of here and I'll deal with him."

I went up into my room and knocked on the door to Claire's room.

"Who is it?" she said.

"May I come in?" I asked.

"Not now."

"Why not?"

"I'm too upset."

"That's why I want to be with you."

"I want to be alone, John."

I hated it when she pulled away from me. The logical part of me understood why she did it, but every time felt like a rehearsal for the day when she would pull away for good.

"Can't I just sit with you?"

"I want to be alone."

"I wouldn't say anything."

"No."

"I'm worried about you."

"I'm not going to kill myself or anything, if that's what you're worried about."

"No, I just . . . want to be with you."

"Jesus, John, you're like Jonah at bedtime. Give me some space, will you. If it's not Tony badgering me, it's you."

I was offended at being lumped in with Tony. It only served to make me feel more insecure, as if she saw us as interchangeable.

"I'm not Tony, Claire."

"I know, I know. I'm sorry. But I need to be alone. I'll come and find you when I'm ready to be with you."

Reluctantly, I agreed. I sat down on my bed and picked up a book, which I read without comprehending. Minutes later, Tony came up the stairs with Jonah.

"Mommy?" I heard Jonah say.

My door was closed. I heard them knock together on Claire's door.

"Mommy?" said Jonah.

"It's open," said Claire.

I heard her door open.

"Jonah wants to be with you," said Tony. "I'm going upstairs."

"Wait, Tony. When can we talk?"

"Any fucking time you want, babe."

"How about now. We can go out for coffee."

"Fine."

"I'll get dressed and meet you downstairs in ten minutes."

"Fine."

I heard Tony go up to his room. It was quiet in Claire's room. Jonah must have found something to occupy himself. I was alternately pleased and terrified about Claire and Tony talking. What if they patched things up and got back together? Where would that leave me? I couldn't imagine being just friends with them again. Was I about to lose my lover and my home in one fell swoop? My nausea increased and my headache ratcheted up a notch. I considered telling them I wasn't up to watching Jonah, but that would only postpone their talk. If it had to happen, the sooner the better. I wanted to know where I stood.

A few minutes later, I heard Tony clomp down the stairs to the first floor. Then Claire knocked on the door between our rooms.

"John? Can you take Jonah, now?"

I really didn't feel up to it. "Yes," I said.

She opened the door. She wore jeans and a pink t-shirt. She looked beautiful. Jonah slipped into the room in front of her.

"John!"

He threw himself onto the bed—beside me, not on me, fortunately. I ruffled his hair.

"Hey, big guy! You going to stay with me for a while?"

"I think we'll go to the Downer Cafe," said Claire. "I don't know how long we'll be. You look a little pale. Are you sure you're up to this?"

"I'll be okay. You guys need to talk, so talk."

"Thanks," she said.

She leaned over the bed and kissed me. If there was anything that would cure what ailed me, it was that.

"Kiss!" cried Jonah.

"Here's one for you, too, buddy," she said, but Jonah squirmed away and slid onto the floor.

"No kiss!" he cried.

"Okay. I'll see you later, honey."

She started to leave the room. Jonah got up.

"Mommy? Go?"

"I have to, sweetheart. Daddy and I need to talk."

"Daddy? Go?"

"John will be here with you. See you later."

Jonah followed her out the door and started down the stairs after her. I got out of bed and followed him. Tony was in the living room reading a magazine. Claire was getting a jacket out of the closet, because the weather had turned cooler again during the night. Tony wore only his black t-shirt and jeans. Jonah went to Claire and attached himself to her leg.

"Let go, now, Jonah," said Claire. "Mommy and Daddy need to go. We'll see you later."

Jonah didn't say anything, he just clung to Claire like a baby koala holding onto its mother's fur.

"Okay, Tony," said Claire.

Tony closed his magazine and tossed onto the floor.

"Can you peel him off?" Claire asked me.

I managed to free her, but it wasn't easy. Jonah screamed and cried as Claire and Tony went out the door. I took him to the window to watch them go, though I wasn't certain it was the best strategy. It worked. He became so engrossed in watching them get into the car and back out and drive off that he seemed to forget what he was crying about. Then it was just Jonah and me, as it had been many times before, and he seemed comfortable with it.

I ate breakfast and cleaned up the kitchen, then took a bath with Jonah. The big tub gave us lots of room to play with boats and plastic figures and a big, floating bar of Ivory soap. The phone rang while we were in the tub, but I couldn't leave Jonah, so I just let it ring. The caller was obnoxiously persistent, but finally gave up. Just after we'd gotten out and I'd toweled Jonah dry, the phone started ringing again. I wrapped a towel around my middle and went down to get it. It was Tony's father, asking if Tony was there. When I told him he was out with Claire, he asked me—more like ordered me—to have him call the minute he got home. This was not like Mr. Russo, who was usually a laid-back kind of guy.

"Is everything all right, Mr. Russo?" I said. "Is there anything I can do?"

"No," he replied, his voice suddenly going dead, "there's nothing anybody can do. Just have him call me."

I wondered if something was wrong with Tony's mother.

Claire and Tony didn't return until after lunch. They didn't look happy exactly, but they looked a lot more peaceful than they had when they'd left. I told Tony about his Dad's call, so he called back right away. I started washing my lunch dishes while Claire looked in the refrigerator for something to eat.

"Hi, Dad," said Tony. "What's up? No, I'm not sitting down. What's wrong?"

Claire and I both turned to look at him. His face seemed to fall as he listened.

"Oh, shit. He's not going to die, is he?"

Claire and I looked at one another.

"How long do they think he'll be there?"

"How's Mom taking it?"

"You can't go over there. She'd freak out. I'll go."

"Fuck the union. This is my brother we're talking about."

So that was it. His brother Joe must have been wounded in Vietnam. Claire and I looked at one another again. This time there was guilt in our eyes.

Tony and his dad continued to talk for some time, trying to work out who would go to see Joe. After his dad had hung up, Tony stood there with the receiver to his ear, as if the dial tone that followed might give him more information. Claire finally went to him, took the receiver from his hand and hung it up. Jonah came into the room.

"Daddy?" he said.

Tony didn't hear him. Jonah seemed to pick up his father's state of mind immediately and said no more. He stood watching Tony.

Tony started to speak, but his throat was thick with emotion. He cleared it. "It's Joe. He's been wounded by shrapnel. He might lose his legs."

"Jesus," said Claire.

"They're taking him to an Army hospital in Guam, or maybe Hawaii. I'm going to go see him."

"What about—" Claire began, then caught herself.

I guessed she was about to ask about Tony's job, but then thought better of it. Tony didn't even hear her.

"When will you go?" she asked.

"Huh?" said Tony.

She repeated the question.

"As soon as I can. They're operating today."

Jonah went to Tony and put his arms around his leg. Tony reached down, half-consciously it seemed, and picked him up. Jonah nestled his head on his father's shoulder and started sucking his thumb.

"I'm going for a walk," said Tony. "I'll take Jonah along."

He left the kitchen and walked slowly down the hall and out the front door. Claire and I looked at one another. Neither of us seemed to know what to say.

"This is why I got involved in the strike," I finally said. "This shit has got to stop."

"I know," said Claire. "Poor Tony. Joe was like a god to him when he was growing up. Joe was always bigger and stronger and better at every sport. But he was a nice guy, too, most of the time. He didn't lord it over

Tony, the way a lot of big brothers would've. If Joe really loses his legs . . . I don't know what Tony will do."

"Maybe he'll get a chance to pay his brother back for being such a nice guy."

"I know he'll do that. I think he'd sooner divorce me than let Joe down."

"Claire!"

"Okay, okay, so I'm being cynical."

"I'm surprised. You two looked more peaceful than you've looked in a long time when you got back. I thought maybe you'd . . ."

"Kissed and made up? Hardly. We just clarified how far apart we are right now. I told him how I felt about you; he told me about Alicia—not that it was a surprise after I saw them together in the Union the other day."

"What did you tell him about me?"

"You know how I feel about you, John. Confused. That's what I told him."

"You didn't even mention that you might be in love with me?"

"Not in so many words. But he got the point. He knows how much I care for you. He's known that for a long time. It's just the sexual part that's new."

"So, what's going to happen?"

"Neither of us knows. We're going to go on just the way we've been, staying out of one another's business. Now it feels more like a real separation."

"Even though you're still in the same house."

"Even though we're still in the same house. Attitude has as much to do with it as anything. The break feels cleaner, now that everything is out in the open."

"Good. May I hold you, now?"

"I'd like that."

I went to her and took her in my arms. It seemed as if she held me less tentatively, but perhaps that was wishful thinking on my part. I was relieved we had no need to hide anything anymore. Not that we'd be making out in front of Tony, but at least we didn't have to pretend we weren't lovers. I felt guilty for being so happy, what with Tony's awful news, but I couldn't help it. I didn't know Tony's brother, but I knew Claire, and I knew I loved her. I kissed her and she kissed me back unhesitatingly. Perhaps it was the juxtaposition of near-death that made our bodies seem especially important at that moment. I pressed her against the wall with my whole body. She seemed to open to me. It would have been so easy to make love to her right then, right there. But she stopped us.

"We can't, John. I want to, but we can't. They could be back any second. Tony can't find us like this, now. I need to be there for him."

I felt helpless as jealousy overtook me. I wanted her and nothing else seemed important. I wanted Tony out of the way, so I could be with her. I fought back my selfish instincts and brought myself under control.

"I know," I said. "I love you, Claire."

"I love you, too," she said.

She kissed me deeply one more time, then gently but firmly pushed me away.

~12~

WITHIN A WEEK, TONY WAS on his way to Guam. His brother Joe had come through the surgery without losing his legs, but the doctors didn't know if he'd ever be able to walk again. A lot depended on how he healed and how hard he worked to rehabilitate himself. Tony was sure that, with encouragement, Joe, who'd been a star athlete in high school, would rally and get the use of his legs back.

Before Tony left, Claire had tried to get him to talk about what he was feeling, but he'd rejected her overtures. He claimed, as he so often did with emotional issues, that it was something he needed to deal with on his own. To my somewhat guilty pleasure, this pushed Claire into my arms. She was upset by what had happened to Joe, too, and needed someone to comfort her. We began sleeping together every night.

Tony was gone for two weeks, and I will always remember them as two of the happiest weeks of my life. Claire and I were able to live together as if we were husband and wife. I was able to pretend Jonah was my own child. It wasn't that we did anything special; it was just the fact that we could be together—eating, walking to the park, watching TV—without inhibition. With Tony gone and Jonathan apparently hiding out elsewhere, the house belonged to the three of us. It became our family home. Perhaps I should have felt guilty about play-acting with another man's family, but I didn't. I was too much in love with Claire and Jonah. I didn't want to spoil a moment of it by thinking too hard about the reality of the situation.

Tony never called or wrote, but we had occasional reports about Joe from Tony's father. He tried to sound upbeat whenever he talked to Claire, but she sensed all was not well. He was always positive about his son's physical progress, but he kept mentioning that Joe was "a little funny in the head" from the wound and the surgery. Reading between the lines, Claire took this to mean Joe was depressed and unable to cope with what had happened to him. Mr. Russo kept saying hopefully that Tony's presence would help Joe.

It turned out that no one and nothing could help Joe at that point. Tony returned bitter and depressed because of his inability to raise his brother's spirits. Instead, Joe had brought him down. Tony found himself angry about the war, angry about his job, angry about his relationship with Claire. The only good thing that happened was Joe had been transferred from Guam to Hawaii while Tony was visiting him, and Tony had fallen in love with the islands. He talked about getting away from Wisconsin, from the whole crazy mainland, to a place where the weather was nicer and the pace of life slower. Alternately, he talked about getting more politically involved, helping to bring down the government that had gotten his brother involved in a stupid, meaningless war. Visits from Kolvacik and Jonathan tipped the scales.

On Sunday morning, a week after Tony's return, we were all sitting at breakfast when we heard the front door open. We expected it to be Kolvacik, who'd been on vacation in Northern Wisconsin. But it was Jonathan. He stood in the kitchen doorway, no longer wearing his Karl Marx t-shirt, I noticed, just a plain, white one.

"I'm back," he said. "I'll be upstairs if anybody calls me."

"Wait," I protested. "Where the hell have you been? What happened to your little plot?"

He looked down at the floor, then around the table at each of us. He seemed more vulnerable than I'd ever seen him.

"The FBI planted a spy. He blew the whistle on the big shots, but the rest of us apparently didn't count. At least, they didn't haul us in this time."

"You done with trying to bring down the government, now?" asked Tony in a challenging tone I'd never heard from him before.

"No," said Jonathan. "I just need to lay low for a while. I won't do anybody any good in prison. I'm going to my room."

Not ten minutes after Jonathan went upstairs, Kolvacik appeared, but hardly in the state we expected. He banged on the front door glass so hard it sounded as if it was going to break. We all leapt up and went into the hall to see what was going on, leaving Jonah in his high chair. We saw Kolvacik's hairy face framed in the door window. He lifted his arm to reveal a bottle of Boone's Farm Apple Wine. But he didn't smile. In fact, he looked about as serious as I'd ever seen him. I went to the door and opened it.

"Hey, bro," he said. "The world sucks and everything's fucked. 'Scuse my shitty near rhyme. I'm drunk."

He wavered where he stood.

"Come on in," I said.

"Oooookay," he replied.

He took a few halting steps, managing to stay upright until he was in far enough for me to close the door behind him.

"What's up, Tim?" said Claire.

"Not me, that's for sure," he replied. "Tony! How is that brother of yours? Did they patch him up?"

"He'll be okay," said Tony. "How about you?"

"Me? Fine. It's my old buddy Mickey who's not so good. No, not so good. Dead is what he is. Fucking dead."

"Mickey?" said Tony. "Dead?"

"As the proverbial fucking doornail," said Kolvacik.

He took a long drink from the wine bottle, then dropped the arm that held it to his side and stood staring straight ahead, past Tony and Claire.

"I'm so sorry, Tim," said Claire.

"Mommy?" Jonah called from the kitchen. "Cer'yl?"

"Just a minute, honey," she called.

"Go ahead and feed him," said Kolvacik. "What was it old Jesus said? 'Let the dead bury the dead.' I'll be okay."

Reluctantly, Claire went to tend to Jonah.

"How did it happen?" I asked.

Kolvacik looked back at me as if he'd forgotten I was there and was surprised to hear a voice from that direction.

"Land mine. One stupid land mine. An American one at that. Ain't that a killer?"

Tony and I nodded gravely.

"Kablooeey!" Kolvacik cried out.

Tony and I both jumped.

"Hamburger. My best friend. Fuck it all. Fuck the whole goddamn war and the whole goddamn government."

Claire rejoined us. "Do you want to sit down, Tim," she said solicitously.

"Actually, I want to lie down. Lie down and die. I loved that bastard."

His voice caught as he spoke and his eyes filled with tears. Claire took him by the arm and led him to the couch. She sat him down beside her, took the bottle from his hand, and set it on the coffee table. He just sat there, catatonic. She put her arms around him and guided his head onto her shoulder. He took a deep breath and exhaled, as if he'd finally found peace, then he erupted in sobs that seemed to be wrenched from his chest. Tony and I stood there helplessly. Tony looked especially uncomfortable.

"I'll go take of Jonah," he said, and walked away down the hall.

I sat down in the overstuffed chair across from the couch. I knew there was nothing I could do, but I felt as if I should be there for Kolvacik. I studied Claire as she sat holding him. She was entirely present for him at that moment. This was the quality that had made me fall in love with her. There were no half-measures with her. If someone needed her, she was there one hundred percent. You could depend on her affection, her comfort, her willingness to listen. Even if she was feeling distracted, her thoughts elsewhere, she would bring herself back into the moment and be with you. And she was never bitter about having to do it. It seemed to come naturally to her. It was no surprise she worked with needy people and wanted to be a doctor.

Seeing her like that, love welled up inside of me. I wanted to be with her for the rest of my life. It would kill me to lose her, just as losing his best friend was killing Kolvacik. Did I want to continue trying to win her if it would cost me so much to lose her? It was a rhetorical question. I had no choice. But as I watched Kolvacik, I felt as if I was watching a preview of what I would suffer if Claire left my life.

Jonathan came down the stairs and, hearing Kolvacik's sobs, came into the living room to investigate. He looked at the tableau on the couch with a disdainful face. He'd never liked Kolvacik.

"What's his problem," he whispered to me.

"His best friend was blown up in Vietnam," I whispered back.

"Crying won't do any good," he said. "Instead of smoking his brains out all the time, he should've been thinking about his friend and taking action. If you're not part of the solution, you're part of the problem."

"Jonathan," I said, looking him square in the eye, "fuck off."

He raised his hands and eyebrows, demonstrating his innocence. "Hey, man, that's how I feel about it."

"Well, take your feelings elsewhere, okay? The guy's in pain."

"I'll be in the kitchen."

When Kolvacik stopped crying, he fell asleep in Claire's arms. She and I looked at one another over his sleeping head and shared an unspoken sympathy that felt deeper than anything we'd shared before. Perhaps it was because we were there together with Kolvacik, while Tony and Jonathan had retreated to the kitchen.

Eventually, Claire nodded toward the couch, indicating that she needed help laying Kolvacik down. I went to them and put my arms under Kolvacik as Claire tipped him back. We stretched him out on his back, lifted his legs onto the couch, and covered him with the afghan. We stood over him for a few moments, our shoulders touching, like parents watching over a sick child. Then we heard the clip-clop of little feet in the hall.

"Sweeping?" said Jonah. "Tim sweeping?"

"Yes, honey," said Claire, "Tim's sleeping. So you have to be very quiet."

Jonah put his index finger to his lips. "Ssssshhhhhh!" he hissed.

Claire and I looked at one another and smiled.

"I need a cigarette," she said. "Let's go into the kitchen."

Tony and Jonathan were deep in conversation when we entered, but stopped talking as soon as they saw us. All I caught was Jonathan saying, ". . . so we need some new people to commit to the project."

"How's he doing?" asked Tony.

"He fell asleep," said Claire.

"Poor bastard."

"He's going to need to talk to you about this, you know, Tony," said Claire.

"I know," he said resignedly.

"He shouldn't talk," said Jonathan. "He should do something about the situation."

"Can you give him a couple days to grieve before you try to recruit him?" I said.

"There's no time to waste," he answered, ignoring, or perhaps not catching, my sarcasm. "The longer we wait, the more innocent people get blown up. It's that simple."

"Nothing's that simple," I said.

"Jonathan's right," said Tony, looking very serious. "We've been pissing our time away back here while guys like Joe and Mickey are getting blown up over there. It's time to stop it."

"And how do you propose to do that?" said Claire, suddenly wary.

She had lit a cigarette and leaned back against the counter next to me, but she straightened up when she spoke. Tony looked at Jonathan, who knitted his brow and shook his head almost imperceptibly.

"There are ways," said Tony.

"Just don't go blowing up yourself or anybody else trying to save other people from getting blown up, okay? You've got a wife and child, you know."

Tony turned around in his chair and looked at her hard.

"Do I?" he said.

Claire didn't answer, she just stared back at him, looking, she later told me, for clues to how she'd lost the man she'd fallen in love with. She felt as if she didn't know the one who was sitting in front of her. Tony looked away and stood up.

"I'm going up to do some work on my room," he said. "I'll take Jonah up with me."

As he walked down the hall, he called to Jonah, who came running from the living room. I saw them start up the stairs, hand-in-hand. Jonathan excused himself next and went back up to his room. While Claire made another pot of coffee, I sat at the table, staring out the back window at the giant maple that overhung the garage. It had always looked protective to me, but suddenly its branches seemed to hover ominously. I didn't come out of my reverie until Claire set a mug of coffee down in front of me. I looked up at her sweet, pale face and nearly broke into tears.

"What is it?" she said.

"I don't know . . . I just feel vulnerable, all of a sudden. Afraid of losing people. Afraid of losing you."

She rested a hand on my shoulder, and leaned down to kiss my cheek, but she didn't linger. She picked up her own mug from the stove and sat down across the table from me, where she took a fresh cigarette from her pack on the table and lit it. I did the same. Then we stared at one another for a few minutes through the cloud of smoke.

"You know we'll always be friends, at least, don't you?" she said.

"I suppose," I replied. "But that won't be enough anymore. You know that."

"I know you believe that. I'd hate to think we could never be friends again because of all this."

"Are you trying to give me a hint?"

"No. I've told you before I don't know how things will work out."

"Meanwhile," I said, "I sit here with my heart hung out to dry. You can pluck it off the line any time you want, or you can leave it there. Very convenient for you."

"Does my life seem convenient to you? You're welcome to it, then. I'm not using you, John. You're my best friend. Maybe you'll be more, someday, but maybe not. I have a previous commitment to deal with. I'd be more than happy if we'd started with a clean slate, but we didn't, and I can't make that easy for any of us. If you can think of a way, let me know."

We smoked our cigarettes in silence. An absurd, panicky fantasy came into my head. I suddenly felt that, if we both finished our cigarettes while we were sitting there, our relationship would be over. I stubbed mine out and took another one before Claire could finish hers. I only took a few puffs, but it comforted me to have it burning in my hand.

"Do you love me?" I said, hating the whining sound of my voice.

She stubbed out her cigarette and reached across the table to take my free hand in both of hers. "I do love you, John. I'll always love you—no matter what happens. Even if I can't have you, because the price is too high. But I love Tony, too. I can't pretend you've taken his place. He and I have been through a lot together. Maybe we aren't meant to be together any more, but I'm not sure of that, yet. I can't rush into something new."

I looked deep into her mesmerizing green eyes—not mesmerizing because she was trying to make them so, but because I was so in love with them.

"I'll wait," I said. "It may kill me, but I'll wait. I couldn't give up if I wanted to."

Tony went back to work at the docks the next day. The union was so sympathetic to the fate of veterans they'd granted him a two-week leave-of-absence to be with his wounded brother. They'd knocked his number down a few notches, but he was still high enough on the list to get work most days. Within a few weeks, instead of enrolling for night courses, as Claire had expected him to, he started going off with Jonathan in the evenings. Jonathan had found it impossible to lay low for long and had begun meeting with some of his old comrades. He was too sure of the rightness of his cause to worry about the consequences, and Tony, radicalized by the visit with his brother, felt the same way.

He and Claire had one long, knock-down, drag-out fight over this—she accusing him of not caring about himself or her or Jonah, he accusing her of being selfish and apathetic—and then they'd stopped talking entirely. To his credit, Tony managed to see Jonah as much as he always had. He arrived home at 3:30 and never left with Jonathan until after Jonah was in bed, at 7:30. And since he and Claire weren't talking, he dedicated virtually all of this time to Jonah.

Only Kolvacik cut into Tony's time, as well as mine and Claire's. The death of his friend Mickey had sent him into a spiral of drinking and smoking dope that quickly cost him his job at the Harley plant and further estranged him from Mina. She kicked him out of the house most evenings, and he came to us. Mostly he sat in the living room, smoking dope or drinking or both, trying to reel in anyone who came by so he could retell his pitiful tale, like Coleridge's Ancient Mariner. Someone once said that there is a fine line between sympathy and disgust, and Kolvacik's self-pitying behavior pushed each of us over that line occasionally. Hardly a day went by when one of us—including Claire—didn't end up lecturing him about how his life was going down the drain. But that was exactly what he wanted; it fed his self-pity.

For a time, I did nothing political. Carl's plan for classes on the war had fallen through for lack of interest, and little else was going on politically, at least in public. After the national student strike failed to generate any palpable change in U.S. policy—except perhaps a slightly less aggressive stance by President Nixon, calculated to win him a few points from moderates, no doubt—most people, including me, returned to their normal life, unsure what to do next. It wasn't until things heated up over the curfew at Water Tower Park again, as they had the previous summer, that I felt drawn back in.

The curfew was a small thing, compared to the war, of course, but it seemed to symbolize for many of us the conservatives' desire to control things and take all the joy and spontaneity out of life. Besides, Claire and I had started going to the park together often that summer, alone when we could, or with Jonah, if he couldn't sleep, which started to happen more often that June. Perhaps it was the tension in the air between his mother and his father. Perhaps it was just a natural transition in his sleep pattern. Whatever the reason, he was often awake long after Tony tucked him into bed and went off with Jonathan.

So, Claire and I would put him in a stroller, or let him walk, if he wanted to, and stroll the few blocks to Water Tower Park to see the fountain. The sight and sound of the water always soothed Jonah—and us, for that matter, especially when it got dark and the fountain was lit up. And it was after dark the police always showed up to inform everyone they were no longer welcome there. Usually, we were ready to leave anyway, but it was the principle of the thing. There seemed no good reason to prevent people from congregating quietly—the loudest thing being an acoustic guitar—after dark in a public urban square.

It wasn't long before the alternative media began to call for protests against the curfew. The thing didn't take shape until July, but when it did, I was ready to be part of it. As I'd grown closer to Claire and Jonah, I'd begun to feel a new sense of purpose in political action. I wanted to help make a society for them that was less repressive, gentler, more open. Claiming that small piece of urban greenery called Water Tower Park for "the people" seemed a manageable step in that direction. Milwaukee had had a succession of socialist mayors in its history and the affects of their attention to the needs of the people was evident in the city, which had more public parks per square mile than any city in the nation and more public access to undeveloped waterfront than any city built on a large body of water that I knew of (except Chicago, which had its own socialist mayors). In light of that history, keeping Water Tower Park open to the public late in the evening seemed a small but noble cause.

I even tried to recruit Kolvacik, hoping an immediate cause might rouse him from his lethargy, but he'd been indifferent to the cause the previous summer, and in his current state he was hostile.

"Who gives a flying fuck about that little shit-ass park," he said, a drop of wine from the swig he'd just taken trickling down into his raggedy black beard. "If you wanna blow the fucking place up, I'll help, but don't bother me about curfews. Let the pigs wallow in the goddamn fountain. I don't give a shit."

"You don't give a shit about anything, do you, Kolvacik? I thought you might like to think about something besides yourself for one night, but I guess not. You're too busy wallowing in self-pity."

"I know," he said, suddenly self-abasing. "I'm a worthless piece of shit. I'm no good for anything."

He took another drink from the bottle.

"You go off and fight your battles," he continued. "You can do it better without me trailing along. I'd just fall on my ass."

Suddenly incensed, I leapt up and snatched the bottle from his hand.

"Put this shit away, Kolvacik. Do something. Stop feeling sorry for yourself. I know you lost a friend, but you're going to lose all your friends if you keep acting this way. Life goes on. You can suffer and still keep on living. People do it all the time. Some of them even take their pain and make something out of it. They start caring more for other people. You can't do anything with your pain as long as you keep submerging yourself in it. We can't see you anymore. You're under water. Come out here and join the living again."

He didn't answer me. He didn't even look at me while I spoke. He started searching slowly for something, first in his pants pockets, then in his shirt pocket, where he finally fount it—a joint.

"Wanna do this up with me?" he asked innocently, as if he hadn't heard a word I'd said.

The big confrontation at Water Tower Park took place spontaneously on a warm July night that felt uncannily like the night I'd met Tony, the previous summer. The whole scene was pervaded by a sense of *deja vu*. The police lined up in the same place, TV cameras were there, and the crowd chanted the same chants.

Claire had sent me off with a warning not to get my head bashed in, so I'd even planned to use the same escape route Tony and I had used the previous year, if necessary. The picture was completed when I looked across the crowd to see Tony on the other side, punching his fist in the air and chanting. At the same moment, he spied me, and in the few seconds our eyes were engaged, the whole year seemed to pass before me.

I saw him lying on the beach laughing with me, sitting beside me at the courthouse, cutting lumber to build the walls of his new room, heading off to the docks in the morning. I saw Claire in her short white dress beneath the standing lamp, sitting across the kitchen table from me, smoking and listening intently, lying beneath me on the front seat of her car. I saw Jonah on the couch, his young/ancient eyes looking deeply into mine. I saw Kolvacik grinning mischievously over his African drum, and I saw Mina perched on my lap. I saw the parties, the arguments, the demonstrations, the hugs and kisses, the comings and goings. It was all so rich, so full of life and passion. And Tony was the man who had led me into it all by taking me home with him that night, one long year before. Suddenly, the night seemed ominous.

When Tony broke eye contact, I noticed Jonathan was beside him. It seemed odd to me that the two of them, who seemed full of bigger plans, would participate in such a "petty-bourgeois" demonstration, but I didn't give it much thought. I didn't have time to. The crowd started surging forward suddenly, advancing steadily toward the police, who tightened their ranks.

There were a lot fewer police that evening than there had been at the big confrontation the previous summer and more demonstrators. There had been no indication the demonstration would be any larger that night. The police were caught unprepared. Even so, the small number who were there could probably have driven us back, if they'd chosen to, armed with shields and sticks as they were, but since we were moving away from the center of the park, their leaders chose to pull back and let us follow them out of the park. They backed across the street to the opposite sidewalk, and, when the crowd kept coming, they backed down North Avenue, which ran perpendicular to the park.

Police cars, their lights whirling, rushed to block off North Avenue at the next corner, where it met Prospect Avenue. I wanted to stop. I saw no point in leaving the park when our objective was to stay there. But the crowd had a life of its own, and I was carried along with it. Seeing the police retreat excited them. I saw Jonathan and Tony in the front rank, urging everyone on.

The pace of the action picked up slowly, until, as we approached the intersection, the crowd was almost trotting forward as the police backpedaled rapidly. I guessed the police would make a stand at the intersection, and they were apparently slowing down to do that when, suddenly, the crowd wheeled away from them and started streaming down Prospect Avenue, spreading out across the street in front of the Oriental Drugstore and the adjoining Oriental Theatre.

I got to the corner just in time to see Jonathan and Tony, a few hundred feet away, lift a large piece of broken pavement and throw it through a plate-glass window. I stopped dead in my tracks. Demonstrators streamed by me. The ones around Jonathan and Tony cheered. Dozens of them picked up small rocks and pieces of pavement and attacked adjacent storefronts. Others leapt up on traffic signs and bent them down to the sidewalk. I watched from the corner as most of the rest of the demonstrators joined in the destruction, as if it were a party game. Only a few others refused to join.

The police just looked on. I heard sirens in the distance and suspected they were waiting for reinforcements before following the mob. All at once, a group of demonstrators turned and threw rocks at them. I saw them look to their commander, who nodded grimly. Then they took off down the street after the rock-throwers. The crowd continued to surge down Prospect, stopping traffic and breaking virtually every store window they passed. The street glittered with broken glass. I could still see Tony in the lead with Jonathan, pausing to tear things up as he went, but I couldn't quite believe I was seeing it. Only then did I realize how angry and bitter he'd become.

I stood rooted to the spot as the mob continued down Prospect, harried by the police, but unstoppable. I watched until they disappeared over a little rise about half a mile away. Then I listened to the rise and fall of wailing sirens as the riot squads moved to outflank the mob, farther down Prospect. Finally, that ceased, too. Then it was quiet. The street looked like a London street I'd seen among pictures of the Blitz. It had not been hit directly, but the explosion had been near enough to blow out every window and had shaken the ground hard enough to topple street signs and light standards. I couldn't quite believe I was looking at the same thing on a familiar street in my own neighborhood.

Something crumbled inside me as I surveyed the scene. It suddenly seemed as if the whole "youth movement," the struggle that was supposedly

for freedom and political justice and against war was just a big, self-indul-
gent sham. First, the student strike had turned into a struggle for free passing grades. Now, this protest over use of a beautiful little urban park had
turned into an orgy of pointless destruction. Was anybody willing to give
up anything, to practice any sort of discipline, to achieve the noble goals
of the movement? It didn't look that way to me.

Feeling empty inside, I turned away from the scene of destruction and
walked back up the street. I entered the now-deserted park and sat on the
edge of the fountain and stared into it. I tried to let the sound of falling water
calm me, but adrenalin was flowing through my body, and my mind was racing. When somebody tapped me on the shoulder, I jumped. I looked up to
see Carl Lindstrom standing over me, looking as disturbed as I felt.

"I can tell by your face you saw what happened," he said. "How are
you taking it?"

I looked down into the water and ran a hand through it before I spoke.
"I feel as if something died inside me down there. It made me feel as if the
whole movement was stupid and pointless."

"Try not to judge the whole thing by the actions of a few."

"But the strike was the same way. People are such assholes."

Carl sat down beside me and sighed.

"I have to admit I'm feeling the same way. I was talking to myself as much
as to you when I said don't judge the movement by this. But this isn't the only
place it's happened. I wonder if we've all gone wrong somewhere."

"You know what I think at times like this," I said. "I think maybe my real
job is to go off and work on myself, get my own head together. Maybe that's
what all of us should be working on, instead of trying to change the world
out there."

"The civil rights movement would never have happened with that kind
of attitude."

"I know, I know. But this feels different, somehow. Maybe it's just me.
Maybe I need a break from political action. I just don't feel like there's anything worth being part of, right now."

"Well, you can always help people directly. That's one of the things I
love about my work at the Social Action Center. It lets me alternate between participating in political actions and participating in programs that

feed and clothe and house people. I may just focus on those programs my-self for a while."

"I'll keep helping out, too," I said. "I do get satisfaction from that. But I think I'm going to hang up the protest signs for a while. People get too crazy in big groups. They turn into selfish mobs."

"Not always. But the danger is always there. If you need to get away from it all, do it. But don't forget that you need to act on the outside as well as on the inside. We can change ourselves individually, but we can only change the world together."

I smiled at Carl.

"Didn't I read that on a poster somewhere?"

"No. But if you'd like to produce it, I'll take some for the Center."

"Speaking of which," he continued, standing up, "I'm going to head back there. But I think I'll avoid walking down Prospect. Keep in touch."

I said I would, and then watched him as he walked away toward the lakefront.

-13-

I SAT FOR A LONG TIME BY THE FOUNTAIN, letting the sound of the water slowly soothe me. By the time I got up to walk home, I was feeling calm and resigned. Something had changed inside me, but it would take some time to figure out what. When I walked into the house, Claire was standing in the kitchen doorway, talking on the phone. She seemed relieved to see me, and only then did it dawn on me she could have seen accounts of the riot on television and been wondering if I was okay.

"Look, Tony," I heard her say, "We don't have that kind of money. Everybody in this house put together doesn't have that kind of money. I'll call your dad. He'll—"

Tony apparently cut her off. She listened for a moment, then spoke again. "If you want to get out of jail tonight, it's the only choice we have. Okay?" She listened for second. "Yes, if your mom answers, I'll ask for your dad. I'll see you later."

She hung up, but kept her hand on the receiver and looked me over.

"What about you? Get your jollies breaking windows tonight, too?"

"I hung back when it started getting crazy. Give me credit for a little sense."

"I thought Tony had some sense, too, but apparently not. Now I've got to get him bailed out of jail. You can tell me what happened to you when I'm done here."

She lifted the receiver and started dialing. I went up to the bathroom to wash my face and neck, which felt grimy. As I was drying my face, Claire appeared in the doorway.

"Tony's dad is going to get him. He'll bring him back here. Tony's going to have a lot of explaining to do."

"I wouldn't count on any explanations."

"Why not?"

"He was there with Jonathan. My guess is this is part of some larger scheme. I doubt if he'll share the master plan with us."

"I think he's done with Jonathan. Jonathan got himself bailed out and didn't offer Tony any kind of help. Tony said Jonathan was as scared as a puppy in a pound. Once the crunch came, all he could think about was himself."

"I could have told him that would happen."

"Any of us could have."

"What's next?" I said.

"We'll see when he gets home."

"Meanwhile," she continued, moving in close to me and putting her arms around me, "you get a big kiss for being smart enough not to start breaking windows."

We kissed long and passionately. Dared I hope the tide was turning? Was she seeing in me the stability and willingness to be there for her that was lacking in Tony? I didn't want this to be a contest, but there didn't seem to be any other way for it. How else do you decide between two people you love, unless you compare? Then I remembered *Paint Your Wagon*. I'd never broached the subject of that relationship with either Claire or Tony, but it suddenly seemed the perfect way to avoid a contest for Claire's affections, to avoid the need for her to choose.

When we stopped kissing and stood holding one another, I asked her about it. I reminded her of what had happened in the movie and asked her if she thought such a relationship was possible.

"Do you think it's possible?" she asked.

"I don't know," I said, "but I'd be willing to try it, if it's the only way I can be with you for the rest of my life."

She melted in my arms and we started kissing passionately again. I backed her up through the hall and into her bedroom. We tumbled onto the bed, where we continued our passionate kissing and started caressing one another all over. I was desperate for her. I made love to her as if it were the last opportunity I would have.

We fell asleep with the bedroom door wide open. Luckily, I heard the car door slam outside when Tony arrived. I went to the window and saw him waving goodbye to his father. I closed the door and roused Claire. She had me toss her clothes into her closet while she climbed under the sheet. I gathered up my own clothes and, pausing to give her one short, intense kiss, went into my own room through the inside door. No sooner had I lain down on my bed when I heard Tony knock on Claire's door.

"Are you awake, Claire?" he said.

"Yes," she replied curtly.

"Can I come in?"

"I suppose."

The door opened and closed. I heard the click of a lamp switch.

"We need to talk," said Tony.

"I'll say," said Claire.

I heard her strike a match.

"I could use one of those, tonight, too," said Tony.

I heard another match being lit.

"What made you do such dumb thing?" asked Claire. "What would Jonah and I have done if you'd gotten yourself killed or maimed? Who would help support him? What will happen, now, if you have to go to jail and lose your job and can't get another one because you've got a criminal record? Did you think about any of that when you went on your little spree?"

"Look, I've been pissed off ever since I went to see Joe and let Jonathan talk me into doing some stupid things. This just happened to be the stupidest."

"What will happen when you go to trial?"

"I can't go to trial, Claire. That's what I need to talk to you about. I've got a juvenile record. That's not supposed to count, but I know it will. I can't do time. Not even in a minimum-security prison. I'd lose my mind."

"But if you run away and they catch you, you'll do more time, probably in a worse place."

"I'll take my chances. I've got to get out of here."

"Where will you go?"

"Hawaii. There are lots of places to hide out there. I don't think they'll come after me there for this, even if they do find out where I am."

He paused.

"I want you and Jonah to come along."

Listening on the other side of the door, my stomach seized up

"Hawaii? Now? The three of us?"

"Why not? You've always wanted to live someplace warm. We could start over."

There was a long, frightening silence. Could Claire really be taking seriously such an outrageous proposal? Then it occurred to me the proposal was coming from the man who was, as she herself had reminded me, her husband and the father of her child. Of course she was taking it seriously.

"When will you go?" she asked, not giving any hint if she was considering his proposal.

"Soon," he said.

Again silence.

"I can't just pick up and leave everything behind," she said, "and everyone."

I was finally able to let out a breath.

"Will you join me later, then?"

Again, there was a long silence. I could picture Claire searching Tony's eyes.

"I don't know, Tony. I want us all to be together, but I don't know if you and I . . . I just don't know. You're making it a whole lot harder by doing this. How can you leave Jonah?"

"I don't know what else to do, Claire. My life is totally fucked-up. I miss you. I miss . . . us."

It got quiet again, but then I made out the sound of Tony crying. Claire was probably crying, too, but silently.

"I love you, Claire," I finally heard him say.

"I love you, too, Tony," she replied.

Then more crying. Then it was quiet. Then I heard Tony snoring. Then I cried myself to sleep.

The next day, Tony made a reservation on a flight leaving within the week. The house was very tense over the next few days. Jonah cried a lot and had trouble sleeping. Claire spent a lot of time up in Tony's room talking to him, out of earshot from me. I didn't know if she was trying to talk him out of the move or exploring the possibility of going along. She wouldn't tell me. She often came down from these discussions and went into her room to cry on the bed.

Only Tony seemed relatively relaxed. I could tell he was excited to be going, though he tried to play it down. I don't think he really believed he'd be staying there for long on his own. I don't think he'd come to grips with what it would mean if he stayed in Hawaii, and Claire and Jonah didn't join him. I think it also helped that his brother was still there recuperating and he'd been there himself. I think it felt more like the start of a vacation to him than the start of a new life. I wondered if that was all it would end up being. I couldn't imagine how he could stay away from Jonah, even if he could live without Claire.

The day of his departure, Tony packed a big Army-surplus duffle bag and got money out of the bank. Claire and Jonah took him to the airport. I offered to drive them, but Claire said no. I was relieved not to have to see that goodbye.

Before they left, Tony and I shook hands and looked into one another's eyes. Then we hugged, surprising ourselves.

"It's been a long year, buddy," I said.

"That it has," he replied. "That it has. Take care of these two for me until . . . well, until whatever happens. Maybe you and I will see each other again, sometime."

"Of course we will."

I stood on the porch and waved goodbye as they drove off. I had a sinking feeling I wouldn't see Tony again, but that was a reflection of my fear of losing Claire and Jonah. The house seemed frighteningly cold and empty with all of them gone.

It did not warm up when Jonathan's father unexpectedly showed up at the door. He was a tall, imposing man with a perfect haircut and manicured nails. He was dressed in a gray suit and was all business. He had a box into which he was planning to put all of Jonathan's things—or all of Jonathan's things he deemed worth keeping, I surmised. He told me Jonathan would not be coming back, but they would, of course, pay the next month's rent to make up for his abrupt departure. He got Jonathan's things, wrote a check, and drove off in his black Mercedes, all in the space of fifteen minutes.

When Claire returned from the airport, she looked as depressed as I'd ever seen her. I took Jonah to a playground to give her time alone. As I pushed him on a swing, he kept saying, over and over again—almost singing—"Daddy fly. Daddy fly. Bye-bye, Daddy. Bye-bye."

When we got back, Claire was in her room with the door closed. We could hear her crying through the door.

"Mommy cry," said Jonah.

I opened the door just enough to let him in, then closed it and had turned to go back down the stairs. Claire called my name. I re-opened the door. She lay on her back on the bed, holding Jonah in her arms. Her face was wet and red, her eyes swollen. Jonah was sucking his thumb, an old habit that had resurfaced that week.

"I need you to hold me," she said.

I sat beside her and leaned against the wall. She shifted herself and Jonah so that she was leaning against me and he against her.

"You two are my bookends," she said, managing to laugh a little through her tears and sniffles.

She pulled a tissue from the box beside her, wiped her eyes, and blew her nose loudly.

"This is so hard," she said, tears streaming from her eyes again. "Tony and I were supposed to be together for the rest of our life. What happened?"

I took this as a rhetorical question—not that I would have been able to answer it if it hadn't been. I wanted to say, "Don't worry about Tony. I'll stay with you for the rest of your life," but I had a feeling it wouldn't matter. She was missing Tony, and no substitutes would do.

Eventually, both she and Jonah fell asleep. I was wide-awake, but my legs fell asleep. Finally, I had to move. I eased my body out from under Claire's, stood up slowly, and nearly crashed to the floor. I stood in one spot as the blood rushed through my legs, making them ache and tingle. When I felt able to walk, I left the room, closing the door quietly behind me.

Shortly after this, Kolvacik arrived, looking for Tony. I had been dreading this conversation, hoping Claire would deal with it.

"Tony's gone," I said as we stood in the entryway.

"Where?" said Kolvacik.

"Far away."

"Is he visiting someone?"

"He's going to live there."

"Yeah, sure. What's he really doing?"

"Do you want to sit down?"

"I suppose. What the hell's going on here?"

"Let's sit down,"

Kolvacik took his customary place on the sofa. I sat next to him.

"Tony was afraid of going to prison after he got arrested," I said. "He's gone to a place where he hopes he won't be found."

"Just like that?" said Kolvacik.

"Just like that. He didn't even tell his parents where he was going."

"Did he tell you?"

"Yes."

"Then you can tell me."

"No, I can't."

"Come on. You know I won't tell anybody."

"Not on purpose. But you drink and smoke a lot. It could slip out."

"You bastard. He was my friend a long time before he was yours. I can't believe the asshole left town without telling me. Where did he go?"

I didn't answer.

"Hawaii—that's it, isn't it? He's been dreaming of that place ever since he got back. So he found a way to get himself back there, huh?"

"I can't say."

"I can't believe he's just gone. Do you think he'll ever come back?"

"Hard to say. Not if it means he'll go to prison. He was pretty freaked out about that."

"No shit. The poor bastard. He should've stayed away from that prick Jonathan. Where's he?"

"His father bailed him out, I think. The old man showed up here in a black Mercedes this morning to get his stuff. A pretty scary guy. He looked like he could afford a good lawyer to get his kid off the hook. I imagine that's what will happen."

"Prick. The rich get richer and the poor go into hiding. I never did like that guy."

Kolvacik trained his eyes on me. "So, you've got a pretty cozy little setup here, now, huh? You and Claire and Jonah. You taking over Tony's family?"

I ignored his animosity. He was hurt by Tony's sudden departure and needed to strike out at someone.

"Tony asked them to join him in . . . to join him. Claire doesn't know what to do."

"I bet you're going to advise her, though, aren't you?"

"I'm just going to listen to her. She knows I'm here for her, if she wants me. But I'll be her friend, no matter what she decides."

He studied me. "You really do love her, don't you?"

I felt a large lump in my throat. "I told you that a long time ago. I'd do anything for her." Tears welled up in my eyes. I sniffed them back.

"You're going to be one sorry bastard, yourself, if she goes, aren't you?"

"That's putting it mildly."

"Well," he said, standing up abruptly, "I've got friends to visit. Things aren't very cheerful around here."

I walked him to the door, still fighting back tears. I was glad he was leaving. He went out onto the front porch and turned back to me.

"If she does leave you," he said, "come and see me. I could use a drinkin' and smokin' buddy. Misery loves company."

I felt oddly comforted by Kolvacik's offer. At least I wouldn't be entirely alone if the worst happened.

In the event, the worst happened sooner than I thought it would. It started with a notice from the landlord that arrived on July 15th. It indicated that our house, and several other beautiful old Victorian houses adjacent to it, had been sold to a contractor, who was going to tear them down and build an apartment building in their place. We had until August 15th to vacate the house. Claire seemed to go into shock when she read the letter. She loved that house and, with her marriage topsy-turvy, it had become a symbol of stability and continuity for her. She took comfort from living in a house that had been continuously occupied for almost a hundred years.

Two days later, the first letter arrived from Tony. Claire didn't let me read it right away, but eventually she had to. This is what it said:

Dear Claire,

Things are working out even better than I thought they would. After three days, I got a job working at the docks and a cheap room in clean little bed and breakfast. The pay is good. Things are more expensive here, but it's enough.

I've been to see Joe. He's not a heck of a lot better. He's still depressed. He won't talk to me about how he feels and won't co-operate with his physical therapist. I told him he was an asshole and he better get his shit together. You can imagine how much he appreciated that. But it might have done him some good. I had to say something because they're shipping him back to the main-land in a few days (just my luck), so I won't be seeing him for a while. Somebody had to tell him to get off his can and start reha-bilitating himself.

Seeing the way Joe is kind of freaked me out, to tell you the truth. I had this revelation lying in bed the other night. I realized that I can be just like Joe. I keep everything inside and push other people away, even when I need them. I know this isn't news to you, but I think I've finally learned it for myself. Being alone here has put a lot of things in perspective. I miss you and Jonah so much it's like an ache in my body. I can't believe how much I've taken the two of you for granted.

I don't want it to be that way any more, Claire. I see my mis-takes and I want to make up for them. I want to start all over again with you. I think we can do it. I hope you agree. There's nothing that would make me happier than to meet you and Jonah at the airport and hang a *lei* around your neck. It's beautiful here. It's the kind of place where we've always dreamed about living. I want to share it with you and Jonah. Join me.

Love,
Tony

As soon as Claire read the letter, I knew the jig was up. She became quiet and distant. For two days after that, she hardly spoke to me. She just kept saying she needed time to think.

On the evening of the second day, after Jonah had settled in, she an-nounced she was going to take a bubble bath and wanted me to meet her in her bed in half an hour. As always, I was excited by the prospect of making love with her, but something in the way she made the invitation left me wary.

I got into her bed before she was done in the bathroom. There were butterflies in my stomach. She emerged from the bathroom and appeared in the bedroom doorway in a long, sheer, white, silky nightgown that outlined every curve in her body. It made me think of the white dress I'd first seen her in, when she'd taken my breath away, but it was even more provocative than that. That memory underlined how much more I loved her than when I'd seen her in that dress. Lust was now a servant to love. I desired her body, but I craved her love.

Her lovemaking was uncharacteristically intense and aggressive that night. She seemed both desperate to please me and anxious to let me know she was in charge. It was almost as if she were another person. Afterward, I felt physically satisfied, but emotionally wrought.

"John," Claire finally said, and I knew instantly the rug was about to be pulled out from under me. "I've decided I have to go to Tony, that Jonah and I need to be with him."

I was so stricken by this declaration I couldn't reply. On the other hand, I was not surprised. It felt as if I'd just been waiting for the announcement I knew would be coming, sooner or later. I told her this.

"It should have been obvious to me, too," she said. "I couldn't live with myself if I just let Tony go off on his own and gave up on the relationship. He's—"

"Your husband and the father of you child. I know. You don't have to keep reminding me. So, his little ploy worked. He couldn't make you love him when he lived in the same house, but now that he's inaccessible, he's suddenly attractive. Why do women fall for that hard-to-get bit all the time?"

She pulled away from me, sat up and reached for her cigarettes.

"That's a shitty thing to say. I'm not falling for anything. I'm trying to get my marriage together. It deserves a chance."

"Yeah, especially when the chance is in Hawaii. You can send Tony to the docks and lay out in the sun and who gives a shit if it's a real marriage or not, huh? Maybe you'll find somebody else to fuck you while he's away."

She had lit her cigarette and taken a drag. She blew the smoke out fiercely.

"God, you can be a bastard when you're hurt."

"Most of us can," I said.

I flipped over onto my stomach, turning my face away from her. I was seething inside. Neither of us spoke. Claire finished her cigarette and crushed it out in the ashtray beside the bed.

"I think you'd better go," she finally said.

"Fuck you," I replied. "You make love to me, then dump me, and now you want to kick me out. I'm staying here."

"Fine."

She turned off the lamp. The window shades were up. Light from the streetlamps made the room glow eerily. Cars whooshed past on Downer. Occasionally, a motorcycle would roar by. I felt suspended in time. I didn't really believe I would be moving, that Claire would be leaving, that my whole life was being turned upside-down. Then I turned my head to look at Claire and found her asleep, angelically asleep, her beautiful face framed by a halo of blonde hair.

I felt a cold rage in my belly. How could she sleep at a time like that? Was she so little affected by her decision to leave me? Was I just one of the details she had to take care of before she ran off to Hawaii? I hated her so much at that moment I could have strangled her, if I'd let myself go. I've never come so close to feeling what a jealous murderer must feel. It scared the hell out of me.

I leapt out of the bed and went into my own room, but I was too agitated to lie down. I went back into Claire's room and took her cigarettes and matches from the bedside. I closed the door between our rooms, sat in my chair, and lit a cigarette. After taking several long drags, I held the glowing ash to my forearm, moving it closer and closer until the heat started to hurt my skin. I held it there for some time, debating whether to press it to my skin. When I pulled it away, I felt a tiny circle of pain the circumference of the cigarette tip. I couldn't see it in the dark, but I knew there was a red mark there, a memento of the night I lost Claire.

~14~

THE FIRST THING I DID THE NEXT MORNING was call Kolvacik. Mina answered, sounding brighter than she'd sounded for some time. She asked about Tony, and I said I couldn't tell her anything, that she'd have to ask Claire. I told her about Claire's decision to join Tony. She said she wasn't surprised. I said I didn't want to talk about it.

When Kolvacik got on, I told him what had happened and asked him to bring his dope over. He was reluctant. He and Mina had just had good sex—for the first time in a while, I gathered—and they wanted to loll around. She was thinking of calling in sick to work. He said he'd call later if she didn't. So much for misery and company.

Jonah slept late that morning, giving Claire a chance to do the same. When I finally heard them at the top of the stairs, about to come down, I had an anxiety attack that sent me scurrying out onto the porch. I felt as if I wouldn't be able to look at them without crying, and I was damned if I was going to let Claire know how vulnerable I was. I plopped down on the old, flowered couch Tony and Kolvacik had found on the street one day, early in the summer, and deposited on the porch. I was careful to keep my head away from the open window behind the couch, so Claire couldn't see me. I could hear her descending the steps with Jonah, asking him if wanted breakfast.

"Cer'yl," he said. Then, "Where John?"

"I don't know," said Claire. "Maybe he went for a walk."

"Walk?" said Jonah. "John walk?"

"He might have. Let's get your cereal."

213

Once they were in the kitchen, I could only hear the murmur of their voices. It felt as if they were far, far away. I tried to pretend they were, tried to get a sense of how I'd feel when I wasn't able to see them and could only talk to them on the telephone, but my mind refused to accept the reality of what I was imagining. It kept saying, *They're right in the kitchen. Go see them.* I was torn between wanting to see them, because shortly I wouldn't have that opportunity, and wanting to avoid them for the same reason.

Kolvacik rescued me. While I was sitting there, debating whether or not to go in, he arrived in a beat-up, old, red, two-seater Triumph convertible with the top rolled down. He pulled it up to the curb, revved the throaty engine, and waved me over.

"Want to go for a ride?" he called.

I walked out to him before replying. I didn't want to yell back and risk having Claire to hear me.

"Where the hell did you get this?" I asked.

"Bought it from a neighbor, last night. It's far out, isn't it? There're only a couple dozen of these in the whole country. He gave me a deal because of the rust. I couldn't pass it up. I'm going to fix it up and sell it someday."

Judging from what I knew about Kolvacik and his projects, "someday" was unlikely to arrive.

"What does Mina think about it?"

"Fuck her. We had a good day going until I told her about it. I thought she'd be a little more receptive after the good time we had in bed this morning, but she flew off the handle and started lecturing me about wasting money. I hate that shit. So I came over here. Still looking for something to distract you?"

"Absolutely."

"Then jump in. We'll smoke a few j's and take a ride in the country. Maybe we'll go skinny-dipping at this pond I know. It's too fine a day to spend worrying about women—unless we happen to meet a couple of choice ones at the pond, if you know what I mean."

He winked at me in his impish way, and I smiled back at him.

"Beats sitting around the house feeling depressed," I said. "And I don't have to work until this afternoon."

"Fuck work. You'll call in sick. Hop in."

I stepped right over the little door and slid down into the black bucket seat, which was already getting hot from the sun. Kolvacik revved the engine.

"Doesn't this baby sound great?" he cried over the noise. "I can't wait to get it out onto a country road. It's going to be like Le Mans."

He shifted into first and, just before we shot away from the curb, I glanced toward the house and saw Claire watching us through the front door glass.

We followed Lake Drive up through the northern suburbs and continued on until we were out of the city. The Triumph alternately purred and whined beneath us. The wind created by our motion swept over us, keeping us cool. The first thing Kolvacik did when we left the city behind was to reach into the pocket of his t-shirt and pull out a lighter and a joint about the size of a cigarette.

"Set this thing on fire, will you? It's party time!"

I held the joint in my lips and leaned forward to light it, trying to keep the flame out of the wind. It lit unevenly, but neither of us cared. We started toking away on the joint, watching it burn down one side. Ashes flew all over, but in a few minutes we were sailing so far above the car that it could have burst into flames and we would hardly have noticed. It was blessed escape for me. I forgot all about Claire and Jonah as I lay my head back and watched tree branches fly overhead.

"Oooo-eee, that's good dope!" cried Kolvacik.

I just nodded. We were roaring down a deserted country road that twisted back and forth and up and down, through woods and marshes, past lakes, across farmland. I felt as if my entire body was expanding to take it all in: Wisconsin, my homeland. It was as if the geography of the countryside and the geography of my body were one-in-the-same. One moment, I was in the car, racing across the land. The next moment, I was the land and the car was racing over me, tickling my skin. Kolvacik was a fast driver, but a good one. I felt safe with him at the wheel. God knows, I couldn't have driven in that state of mind!

"How about a swim?" he called over the whine of the engine as he downshifted for a curve. "That pond is up here a little ways."

"Why not?" I replied.

Kolvacik took us around a few more curves, then slowed as we passed a field of high grass on the right, at the edge of a woods. We came to a break in the grass, which revealed a road, or, more accurately, a track, two parallel ruts where car tires had created a road. Kolvacik turned onto the track, and we tilted to one side as the tires on my side rested in the rut while the ones on his side rode the grassy hump between the ruts. The track ended at the edge of a woods. Half-a-dozen cars were parked there, flattening the tall grass.

Kolvacik pulled in beside the first one and turned off the engine. The silence and heat hit me like a wind. The only sound that broke it was the twitter of birds.

"Gotta walk from here," he said. "Let's finish up this joint on the way."

We got out and started down the narrow path that led through the woods. It was dark and a bit cooler beneath the trees. I felt as if I was in somebody's house—Mother Nature's house, I thought. Kolvacik paused to re-light the joint, took a hit himself, then handed it to me. We walked in silence, passing the joint back and forth as the path led gradually downward through the woods. My head was buzzing from the dope, but it felt like natural energy, like the energy I sensed buzzing through the trees and the birds and the little animals scurrying through the brush. I didn't feel like a stranger in the woods, as I had so many other times in my life.

After a quarter mile or so, the path flattened out, and a hundred yards later, the trees parted, revealing the wide, grassy bank of a small brown pond. And on the bank were naked people of all different body types, some lying on their back in the grass, soaking up sun, others sitting up or lying on their side, talking. There was a tall, lanky, man with a dark scraggly beard, straight hair halfway down his back, and a string of beads around his neck. He sat cross-legged talking to a short, fat woman whose white body made her look like a mushroom sprouted from the earth overnight. A beautiful blonde lay in the grass, her tanned body nestled back against the body of slim black man with a wide Afro. A few teenage boys sat brazenly on towels at the water's edge, their knees cocked, their eyes taking in the scene. A few people were in the brown water, paddling about aimlessly.

I followed Kolvacik to a spot near the bank, where he immediately began to shed his clothing. I felt shy for a moment, then thought "What the hell" and started stripping.

The sun felt wonderful on my naked body. Spontaneously, I turned to face it, closed my eyes, opened my arms, and spread my legs. I felt as if I were an ancient sun worshipper offering my body to God.

"Far out," said the bearded man, who was sitting near us. "Makes you wonder if the pagans didn't have something going for them, doesn't it?"

"It does," I said, keeping my eyes closed. "It surely does."

"I'm hot," said Kolvacik. "Let's hit the water."

I opened my eyes to see Kolvacik take three quick steps and launch his body into the air over the pond. In my stoned condition, it looked to me as if he hung in the air for several seconds before plunging feet first into the water, which, it turned out, was only waist deep. Ripples from his impact spread out across the pond in concentric circles. I watched the ripples, mesmerized.

"Hey, you stoned freak," called Kolvacik, "what are staring at? Get your ass in here."

Not feeling inclined to plunge, I waded in, walking toward Kolvacik. The pond was spring-fed, so the water was cool enough to be refreshing. The bottom was squishy mud and leaves.

"What a pussy," he said. "I'm not waiting for you."

He turned and plunged underwater toward the middle of the pond. I kept advancing, watching the brown water rise over my thighs and genitals. The color was strange—so unlike the greenish-clear water of lakes I was used to—that I wasn't entirely comfortable in it. It seemed dirty. Yet it didn't feel dirty on my body.

Kolvacik came up in the middle and turned back to me, treading water. He saw me staring down at the water.

"Don't get freaked out by it," he said. "The color comes from the tannin in dead leaves. Get out here."

Finally, I took the plunge, diving underwater. It was like swimming through miso soup. I swam in the general direction of Kolvacik, but I didn't see his white body until I was almost upon him. I pulled up short and lifted my head out of the water, inches from his face.

"Whoa, there, Moby Dick," he said. "Don't ram the good ship *Lollipop*—if you know what I mean."

"You can't see shit under there," I said.

"That's funny," he replied. "It looked exactly like shit to me."

"Gee, thanks. I really needed you to introduce that image into my head. Now it feels like we're swimming in a cesspool."

"Nah, it's clean. Just nature's way of spreading things around. Your skin will feel nice and soft when you get out. I came here with this chick once and we fucked on the bank afterward. She kept saying how soft my skin was. Her skin was so soft I was speechless."

"Don't get any ideas about doing that to me," I said, smiling.

"You wish! But I'd take that blonde over there, huh?"

The blonde in question had just cocked her knee and her randy boyfriend was running his hand up between her legs. It didn't seem to bother either of them that they were in public.

"I'm glad we're underwater," said Kolvacik, "or she'd know I was interested in her, too."

"Maybe we should join them," I said.

"In your dreams," said Kolvacik. "Besides, I couldn't go through with it, could you?"

I looked over at the two of them going at it and felt my blood heating up.

"I do believe I could," I said.

"Then we'd better get you out of here. I didn't come out here to watch you have an orgy. Let's go get something to eat. I'm starved."

"We just got here! Let me swim around awhile. The water feels great."

We swam back and forth across the pond for a while, then got out. Luckily, the blonde and her boyfriend had gone off into the woods, fondling one another as they walked. Apparently they'd decided they needed privacy for the consummation, if nothing else. We pulled on our jeans, sans underwear, and left our shirts and shoes off. The path through out the woods felt cool beneath our bare feet. Kolvacik pulled a slightly bent joint out of his t-shirt pocket as we walked, handed it to me, and lit it for me. In the fresh country air, the marijuana tasted especially sweet. I felt happy—happier than I really was inside. The dope did a good job of masking my internal state, which was exactly what I wanted it to do. When I thought of Claire at all, it was as if she were already thousands of miles away.

We went to a small-town diner near the pond. We ate huge burgers smothered in fried onions, big steak fries with the skin still on them, and tall chocolate malts. Afterward, I felt as if I was going to explode. Kolvacik lit up a roach as we sat in the car—" To settle our stomachs," he said. And, to my surprise, it did settle my stomach as we drove toward Holy Hill, our next destination.

Holy Hill was the highest hill for a long way north of Milwaukee and had a huge Catholic Church on top of it, from whose towers one could see fifty miles back to downtown Milwaukee. We climbed the hundreds of steps to the top of the tower with much less effort than I thought it would take. With the dope in my lungs and all the calories from lunch to burn, I felt as if I was being lifted up them. The view from the top was breathtaking, miles and miles of rich Wisconsin farmland bearing its fruit, acres and acres of forest, the edge of Lake Michigan visible to the east. I felt as if I could launch myself from the tower and fly. But, fortunately, I didn't try. One poor, stoned freak had tried it, the summer before, and had found out very quickly it was an illusion.

We blew the rest of the day cruising up and down the shore of Lake Michigan, getting out to run on the beach, eating supper at Kopp's Drive-In, where I used to hang out in high school, having a beer at a tiny East Side bar that had classical music on the juke box. I got back to the house well after dark. I was relieved to see all the lights were out. I was exhausted, and all I wanted to do was crawl into bed. Kolvacik had made me share one more small roach with him—" It'll help you get to sleep," he said, then he took off for home.

When I walked in the front door, the silence of the house revealed the rushing in my ears from the dope and the constant noise of the Triumph. As I walked past the archway that led into the living room, I saw a figure on the sofa out of the corner of my eye before I realized it was speaking. It was Claire. I turned to her. She was wearing a long t-shirt.

"What?" I said. "My ears are ringing."

"You didn't go to work, did you?" she said.

"Oh, shit! I forgot to call in!"

"Well, you won't have to go in tomorrow, either. They fired you."

It took a long moment for this information to seep into my stoned consciousness. And, when it did, I have to admit that I felt relieved, instead of upset.

"It wasn't much of a job, anyway," I said.

"Where are you going to live when we have to leave here?" asked Claire.

"What do you care?"

Claire looked right into my eyes. I turned away.

"I still care for you, John. You're still important to me."

Grief welled up in me, but my addled brain refused to deal with it. I felt a headache developing.

"Yeah, well . . ." I muttered, "don't bother. You'll have enough on your mind dealing with flying cockroaches."

Claire shivered, then smiled

"Don't remind me of those," she said.

I smiled back. Suddenly, she looked good enough to eat.

"Let's make love," I said. "For old times sake."

Her face turned serious again. "I can't, John. I want to, but I can't."

"That's bullshit."

"I've decided to try with Tony again. I can't just pretend I haven't made that decision."

I went to the couch and sat down beside her, drawn to her like an insect to a light bulb. She had apparently taken a bubble bath. The sweet, clean smell of her body aroused me instantly.

"You'll be with Tony in Hawaii. There's no reason you can't be with me until then."

"Except that I don't want to be."

Anger welled up in me. I took her face in my hands and kissed her hard. She pulled away and slapped me on the side of the head, catching my ear as well as my cheek. My ear started ringing and the sound seemed to reverberate through my head. By the time I recovered, she was standing in the archway, across the room from me.

"You just made it a whole lot easier for me to leave," she said.

"Fuck you!" I replied. "You used to like it when I was spontaneous."

"That wasn't spontaneous. That was selfish. Besides, I just told you things have changed. Don't pretend you didn't know what I meant."

"Oh, fuck all of you. Fuck you, fuck Tony, fuck Jonah. Fuck your cozy little nuclear family. It's nuclear all right—it's a fucking nuclear bomb. Go blow yourselves up in Hawaii. I don't give a flying fuck."

Claire turned on her heels and went upstairs. "Good riddance" was all I could think. I wanted a joint. I wondered if Tony had left any dope behind. Fat chance. I waited for Claire to get into her room and close the door, then I went up to the attic to check out his room. It seemed like a very long walk. My body was exhausted from the dope and food and constant motion I'd indulged in all day.

There wasn't much left in Tony's room. It had never been anything but wallboard and a couple pieces of furniture, anyway, so I wasn't too surprised. There wasn't even a dresser to look into. I got down on my knees and looked under his rollaway bed. There was small, green, glass ashtray beside one of the legs and—bingo!—it contained half-a-dozen roaches of various sizes and a box of small wooden matches.

I pulled the ashtray out, sat down, leaned back against the bed, and lit up one of the roaches. It tasted sweet and good. As I sat smoking, I felt an affinity for Tony in his exile to that room. I wondered what he'd thought about everything going on down below him. Had he thought about it much or felt detached from it, the way I did sitting there smoking his dope? The room felt far away from everything and everyone. I decided on the spot I would stay there for the duration of my life in that house. It felt like a way station on the road out. After smoking a couple of roaches, I managed to pull myself up off the hard floor and onto Tony's bed. I fell into sleep like a rock falling down a well.

Without work to interfere, and with little sense of what I wanted to do with myself, I fell back into the habit of hanging out with Kolvacik. We got stoned every morning and stayed stoned until we went to bed. Half the time I woke up stoned. Sometimes we were out all day, enjoying the sun, going on excursions in the Triumph. Other times, we just sat around the house—his or mine—smoking dope, talking, reading aloud to one another, watching B movies on television. It was an aimless and painless existence. I became so detached from Claire and Jonah that the day of their leaving came upon me totally unprepared.

It was the first day of August, and I woke up half stoned. I trudged down the stairs in my cut-offs to go to the bathroom and heard Claire moving around her room in some kind of purposeful pattern that roused my curiosity. I went to her door and saw two suitcases open on the bed and a trunk open at the foot of the bed.

"Going on a trip?" I asked.

She turned to looked at me, a wad of underpants in her hand, unsure, I could tell, if I was being a smart-ass or if I was so far gone that I'd forgotten she and Jonah were leaving that day. Apparently, my face made it clear that it was the latter.

"I told you over and over again we were leaving today," she said, "but it never got through that haze of marijuana smoke you live in, did it? Jonah asked me the other day if you were gone. I told him, no, of course not, you weren't gone, that we still saw you around here, sometimes. He looked at me as if I didn't understand the question and said, 'I know.' Then he repeated, 'Is John gone?' He knows you're not here, John—even when you are here."

"You mean, this is it? Today? You and Jonah are leaving?"

"Yes," she replied.

Then she seemed to soften.

"I'm sorry," she added.

I had no idea what to say. I didn't even know what I felt. My nerve endings were anesthetized. I felt as if I were standing in front of a giant wall of rock, something so high and wide I had no idea how to get around it. I didn't have the strength to climb it.

"Can I ask you a favor?" said Claire.

I nodded.

"Will you go with us to the airport? Katie's driving us, but I'd like you to come along."

I said I would.

"And one more thing. Will you not smoke any dope before then? I want to say goodbye to the man I was in love with, not to some zombie I don't know anymore."

That stung. But it helped me to say yes. I wasn't sure I could make it through the goodbye not being stoned, but now I'd have to, if I wanted to say goodbye at all. It scared me but also relieved me. I was sick of being stoned.

"What time are we leaving?" I said.

Claire smiled, understanding I had agreed to her terms.

"One o'clock. Come here and hug me, now."

She opened her arms to me. I went to her and let her wrap them around me. She nestled her face in my neck.

"You'll be okay," she whispered. "We'll both be okay."

I wasn't so sure. I felt as if I should explode with grief in her arms, but all that happened was that my eyes filled with tears. I felt Claire's tears on my neck and shivered, but she held on tight.

"Am I crazy to do this?" she asked.

"You're asking the wrong man," I said, sniffing, "but let me put it this way: if I could have you committed to keep you from going through with it, I'd do it."

We stood holding one another for a long time.

"You're never coming back," I said, suddenly knowing in the pit of my heart that it was true.

"I don't know about that."

"I do."

With his usual impeccable sense of timing, Jonah walked into the room.

"Mommy John hug?" he said.

"Yes, sweetheart," said Claire, "Mommy John hug. And now we're going to kiss."

She turned her face up to mine. I slid my arms around her and pulled her tight against me. God, how I loved that body! We looked deep into one another's eyes, then kissed for a long time. Then Jonah was tugging at my pants leg.

"Mommy go airplane," he insisted. "Jonah go airplane. John stay home."

Reluctantly, Claire and I let go of one another. As she pulled her body away from mine, I felt as if the places where she had pressed against me— my lips, my chest, my pelvis—were indelibly imprinted with impressions of her body. I wanted to feel those impressions forever. But within moments they were gone.

Katie arrived at eleven-thirty. I loaded the suitcases and the trunk into her car. By noon, we were on our way. I sat in front with Claire, but instead of taking the last opportunity to be close, both of us sat primly beside one another, treating the inch of air space between us on the seat as if it were a glass wall. The airport seemed unreal, as airports often did to me. The idea that people were going to step onto giant metal contraptions and fly away—in some cases, very far away—was never quite believable. I said goodbye to Claire and Jonah almost perfunctorily, as if I would be seeing them the next morning. Perhaps, at some level, I was hoping that pretending it was so would make it so.

Katie and I hardly spoke on the way back to the East Side. Her children were unusually subdued, too. When she dropped me off, she asked if I wanted to come over to her house for supper, but I could tell she didn't want me take her up on it. She was just trying to say that she understood how I felt and wished she could help me out.

But she couldn't. Nobody could. Kolvacik showed up with a fistful of joints, just sure I'd be ready to smoke my brains out, but I wasn't interested. Not that day. He left, disgusted, and I went up to bed in broad daylight. I chose Claire's bed, which still had her bedclothes on it. I stripped and lay down across it naked, smelling her on the sheets and on the pillow. I held her pillow and tried to pretend it was her, but it was a pitiful substitute. I crushed the pillow to me and started crying. I cried myself to sleep.

I moped around for most of the next day, too, feeling sorry for myself. But by the evening I felt lonely and wanted desperately to escape my thoughts about Claire. I called Kolvacik, who did a hurt dance about the day before for a few minutes before agreeing to come over. I reminded him to bring his dope—not that he would have gone anywhere without it.

We got stoned that night and pretty much stayed stoned for the next week and a half. Kolvacik lived at the house. It was easier than going home to face Mina, I guess. He ended up sleeping in Tony's room, while I continued to torture myself by sleeping in Claire's bed. Some nights, as I lay there stoned, I could imagine her beside me so clearly that I could smell her.

I got more and more depressed as the days passed—with agonizing slowness, it seemed. I should have been doing other things—such as deciding where I wanted to live when the lease was up and how I was going to get the furniture into storage, as I'd promised Claire I would—not to mention how I was going to make a living. But all I did was smoke dope and listen to music and eat. Kolvacik had told me I could stay with him until I found a place, and I could always round up a bunch of friends to help move furniture.

Three days before I was supposed to vacate the house, I fell asleep in my underpants on the bed with the windows wide open. I awoke just before dawn. A car whooshed by in the dark. The air had turned unseasonably cool. I shivered and pulled up the sheet. I longed for the warmth of Claire's body, for the comfort of her love, for Jonah's matter-of-fact affection. Lacking that, I suddenly yearned for my own family, for the house I grew up in, for the only other place I'd ever felt unconditionally loved. I coughed from the chill I'd caught. Then, my brain still tranquilized by dope, I quickly fell back to sleep.

~15~

THE COUGH AND CHILL I FELT DURING THE NIGHT turned out to be harbingers of much worse. I awoke the next morning with a mild fever, which I welcomed as an excuse to stay in bed and do nothing. I got out only long enough to put on some light pajamas, eat a piece of dry toast, and drink some orange juice. When Kolvacik got up and saw I was sick, he went off to find someone else to play with.

I slept all day and into the night, and woke feeling even hotter. There was no thermometer, so I couldn't put my theory to the test, but I guessed my fever was over a hundred. I went to the bathroom, where I drank a lot of water, but food held no appeal. Besides, I had no desire to walk all the way downstairs to the kitchen and back up again. It seemed miles away.

By the next morning, the morning of the day I was supposed to vacate the house, I wasn't sure I would be able to make it to the kitchen, even if I wanted to. This, time, when I got up and went to the bathroom, no more than twenty-five feet away, and returned to my bed, I felt as if I'd run around the block. It seemed impossible that so little physical exertion could lead to exhaustion, but I fell back into bed like someone who hadn't slept for days. I knew I was in trouble, then. What if I really couldn't get down the stairs to the phone and call somebody? Would I have to lie there like a deserted old man and cry out for someone on the street to come and help me? Would anyone come if I did, or would they dismiss me as a ranting lunatic?

Later that day, my throat began to hurt, and when I instinctively reached up to feel it, I encountered glands that had swollen to the size of robin's eggs. I remembered friends describing the symptoms of mononu-

226

cleosis and suspected that was what I had. If so, I was going to need help soon. I'd need to get penicillin and have total bed rest, neither of which I could accomplish on my own. It was with some relief that I realized I was going to have to go home to my family.

I gathered my strength, sat up, stepped out of bed, and slowly made my way down the steps and into the kitchen to the phone. I was sweating from the exertion. I dialed my parents' number and collapsed onto a kitchen chair. As I waited for someone to answer, I looked around the kitchen and thought about all of the things needing to be packed and moved, supposedly that day. I hadn't done a thing about arranging it all. Clearly I wouldn't be able to play any part in it. I was vaguely wondering what I would do, when my mother picked up the phone. I said hello.

"What's wrong with your voice?" she said. "You sound terrible!"

I told her how I was feeling and how long I'd felt that way.

"Then you'd better come right home, young man. Good heavens! Living in that big house all by yourself. You could have died and we wouldn't have known about it. I'll be right down to pick you up."

Good old Mom. Always prepared for a crisis. She was at her best when her children were sick.

I managed to make it to the foot of the steps, but realized I'd never make it up them. I went into the living room and lay on the sofa, which was where my mother found me, twenty minutes later.

"You kids! Your front door is wide open! Don't you know someone could waltz right in here and rob you?"

"They could come in the window, too, at this time of year, Mom," I croaked.

She was in no mood to be argued with, especially by a sick son.

"You just be quiet, young man."

She rummaged around in her purse and came up with a blue plastic tube, from which she removed a thermometer. She shook down the mercury and put the thermometer under my tongue.

"I'm going to go up to your room to get you some clothes."

I didn't particularly want her poking around in my things, but I was in no position to argue. In a few minutes, she came back down with a pile of clothes in her arms.

"It looks like a cyclone struck up there," she said. "I thought I'd taught you kids to clean up after yourselves. I couldn't find a suitcase. I'll just take these out to the car and come back in to get you."

She went out the front door with her load and returned a few minutes later. She took the thermometer from my mouth and went over to the window to see it better in the light.

"Aren't you supposed to be moving out of here today? Who's going to move all this furniture for you?"

"I haven't made any arrangements, yet."

She looked at me incredulously, the thermometer suspended in front of her face.

"You haven't made any arrangements? What have you been doing?"

I could hardly tell her that I'd been depressed because my married lover had left town and, consequently, I'd been stoned for the last week and a half.

"I've been sick," I said.

"I don't care how sick you've been, you could have asked somebody to help you out. I don't know how you kids can be so irresponsible."

She looked over the living room and dining room, assessing the amount of work that needed to be done.

"I suppose your father and I and your brothers and sisters could move it for you. But we won't be able to do it today. We'll have to call your landlord and ask for more time. Do you have a place to put it all?"

"No. But Claire and Tony gave me money to pay for storage, so we just have to call one of those places."

"Just call them up, the day before you want to store all this, huh? What if they don't have room? What if they need more notice? You didn't think about any of that, did you? You're darn lucky you've got a family to take care of you. That's all I have to say."

She looked back at the thermometer.

"My goodness, you've got a hundred and three fever. Let's get you home to bed. Your father and I will deal with the rest of this."

She got me home, and they did deal with the rest of it, quite efficiently, as a matter of fact. My father talked to the landlord, who gave him several extra days, because the demolition of the house wasn't scheduled for another week. My mother found the least expensive storage company in town and paid the first month's fee. The next night, my dad borrowed a public works truck through one of his old cronies and went over to the house with my mother, my brother George and a couple of his friends, and my sister Marion. They cleared out the furniture and took it to the storage bin, bringing home only leftover food and my clothing and personal effects.

I was just as happy not to be a part of it all. It was a relief to have virtually every reminder of my life with Claire in storage. The illness, and the drug I was given for the pain of my mono-induced strep throat, helped me feel as if I'd put my feelings for Claire in storage, too. When I thought of her, it was as if I was looking down on her from high up in the sky, almost as if from outer space. I sensed that I had feelings for her, but they were distant feelings, like the pain in my throat, from which I felt utterly detached. It was as if they were someone else's feelings and I was looking in on them, an interested but uninvolved observer.

My family treated me with great tenderness. Dad never reprimanded me for the shoddy way I'd handled closing down the house. Mom always made sure I was comfortable and continually produced good food soft enough to be easy on my throat. George let me stay in my old bed, despite the fact that this kept him out of his own private room, which he'd inherited from me. This was extraordinarily generous of him, considering how long he'd had to wait to get a room of his own. He slept in the next bedroom with my little brother, Steven, who was thrilled to have me home.

Steven was sensitive enough to my condition not to run into my room and throw himself on me every morning, the way he always had when I lived there, but he had a hard time staying away. Since he was starting to read more on his own, I often asked him to read to me, which made him very proud. Marion and Ruth came by often, too, and chatted with me or read to me from something a little closer to my tastes than the Dr. Seuss books Steven favored.

After two weeks, I went off my painkillers. The physical pain had subsided, but the emotional pain came roaring back, filling the artificial void the drug had created in my psyche. I felt deeply loved by my family, but it suddenly came home to me full force that my old life was finished. I was going to have to start all over again, and I had no idea where to begin. Still feeling very weak, I couldn't imagine exerting the energy it would take to accomplish a new start. I fell into a depression deeper than the one I'd experienced before my illness. I started pushing my brothers and sisters away from me as I sunk deeper and deeper into self-pity.

It was George who made me realize I had to snap out of it. He had a way of making me see things in a different light. One day, he marched into my room as I lay on top of his bed, staring out the window, and dropped what looked like a cheap newsprint magazine on the bedspread beside me.

"This is the fall class schedule for UWM. It just came in the mail. It's time for you to sit up and figure out what you're going to take this fall. And, by the way, you can start sleeping in Steven's room tonight. You're feeling better, now, and I want my room back."

He turned on his heels and walked out, closing the door behind him.

"Go to hell," I said under my breath.

But, after a while, I started leafing through the catalogue aimlessly. When I came upon the theater section, my mind perked up. I'd always thought about taking a theater class, but had never done it. I read the description of a class called Theater Games:

> An excellent introduction to acting for the beginner. Various improvisational theater games are used to explore movement, motivation, intention, perception, action, and interaction on stage. No prerequisites.

This stirred my imagination. I could see myself doing something like that, something creative and entirely new, something that had nothing to do with the life I'd been living for the past year, something that challenged me and brought new things out in me. Though I still felt very weak, I could envision the dim outline of the new life whose prospect had frightened me so much until then.

I sat up and continued looking through the catalogue. I found a beginning dance class that sounded equally intriguing and would complement the theater work. Suddenly, I could envision an entire semester of exploring new subjects, a semester that would stretch my imagination. I found an introductory class on Astronomy and another on Existentialist philosophy. Before I knew it, I had found a pencil and was filling out the registration form. I felt like a man who had been lost at sea for weeks and had suddenly spied land. I asked George to mail the registration form that day, because I didn't want to take a chance on not getting into the classes. He was happy to do it and proud of himself for getting me out of my self-involved stupor.

Over the next two weeks, I got stronger, and by Labor Day, I was well enough to participate in a family reunion at a park overlooking Lake Michigan, near our house. My cousin Jerry was up from Chicago, the one who did transcendental meditation, and when he heard about my recent troubles, he asked me if I wanted to go for a walk and talk about it.

I hadn't realized how hungry I was for an ear until I started telling him about the past year, about my involvement with Claire, about the frustration of my political activity, about my overindulgence in marijuana—all the things I didn't feel comfortable talking to family about. It seemed as if nothing I'd done over the year had given me lasting satisfaction. As all of this poured out of me, I realized how empty I felt at the core. At various points, tears welled up in my eyes, but I was too self-conscious to let them go.

Jerry listened calmly and attentively. Just his presence seemed to make me feel better. When I was finished, he told me in more detail than he ever had before about how transcendental meditation had changed his life. He'd been an engineering graduate student and all he'd thought about was grades. He was determined to be first in his class and get job offers from the best engineering firms in the country. He had a girlfriend, but he gave the relationship as little attention as he could get away with as he single-mindedly pursued straight A's. It wasn't until she left him that he realized what a stabilizing influence she'd been. He fell apart, physically and emotionally, his grades plummeted, and he was forced to reassess his whole life.

It was then that a friend took him to a TM lecture. He was impressed by the calm demeanor of the teacher and by the fact that TM didn't demand membership in a social cult of any sort. He decided he had nothing to lose and took the initial training. Immediately, his consciousness opened up. He found depths of creativity within himself that he never knew existed. He gave up engineering for architecture, excelled at that without having to obsess and, ironically, ended up first in his class, with offers to join the best architecture firms in the country. He chose a Chicago firm and, while working with a client during the first year, met his wife.

It was exactly the kind of story I needed to hear at that point, a story of hope for the future. I decided on the spot that I would attend the first TM lecture I could get to at school, when the new semester started.

For most people who attend school into early adulthood, fall is a time of fresh starts—especially in September, when summer is still in the air and the sight of falling leaves has not yet introduced bittersweet thoughts of dying light and cold weather. Having just returned to full health, the sense of a fresh start was palpable for me in the fall of 1970. Health alone was a great gift. The theater and dance classes made me more aware than ever of my body and helped distract my mind from thoughts of what I'd lost.

Though not entirely. Claire wrote to me, but I couldn't bring myself to write back. She sounded too happy in her own new world, though she said little about how she and Tony were getting along. Jonah was thriving in the sun and clamored daily to be taken to the beach. She was more than happy to take him. She hadn't found a job, yet, but it was hard to worry about that in such a beautiful place. She kept promising to send pictures, but she never did. I was just as happy she didn't. I wasn't sure I could bear to see her, tanned and glowing in a bathing suit, with Jonah at her side. I still loved her and I wondered if she loved me.

I was initiated into transcendental meditation on a crisp, sunny morning in early October, the day I turned twenty-one years old. I met my teacher at a suburban house in Shorewood, just north of the university, which was owned by a dedicated meditator. Like my cousin Jerry, I had found the simplicity of TM attractive and was ready to accept any kind of help that might straighten out my confused life.

My teacher met me at the door and led me up the stairs to a second floor study, where she had set up a simple shrine on a small table. It had a photograph of the Maharishi Mahesh Yogi, smiling blissfully through his graying beard, backed by vases of flowers. As instructed, I had brought a flower and piece of fruit, which the teacher took from me and presented to the image of the Maharishi in a simple ceremony before the shrine.

Then we sat down in comfortable, straight chairs, facing one another, and closed our eyes. After a brief time, the teacher taught me my mantra, a few syllables developed over the centuries that have the effect of taking the mind to deeper levels of consciousness. I said the mantra out loud to myself a few times, then, as instructed, began to repeat it in my mind, which is how I was to do it ever after. For a brief time during this first session, I lost normal consciousness. It was not sleep. I know that. We all know what it feels like to doze off. But my mind went somewhere, someplace outside of where it usually functioned. And when it returned I felt utterly refreshed, as if my mind had been running nonstop since the day I was born and had finally had a chance to stop running momentarily. I felt lighter, happier, more centered.

When the session was over, I thanked my teacher and she escorted me down the stairs to the front door, where I said goodbye to her. Then I opened the door and stepped outside. Sunlight hit me full in the face and bathed my body in warmth. It felt as if the light actually entered my body, my being, my core, and lit it up from inside. It was like some magical gold liquid that filled me up.

I stood there with eyes closed, tears filling them. For the first time in months, perhaps years, I felt a true sense of hope. It wasn't as if all my problems has been solved—I was still alone, still estranged from my family politically and spiritually, still without a job, still unclear about what I wanted to do with my life. But, for the first time in a long time, I believed that my life *could* get better, that it was possible to find love and purpose and meaning. I couldn't remember having felt so happy to be alive for a long time. I could have stood in that spot for hours, until the sun fell behind the trees.

But I didn't want to. I wanted to move on. I wanted to engage life. I wanted to walk down the block and turn the corner, just to see what was around it. Instead of seeing life as a static state of uncertainty and anxiety, I had a glimpse of it as a great adventure that was unfolding before me and would continue to unfold in new and interesting ways as the years went by. I moved off the porch and onto the sidewalk and stepped into the future, whatever it might bring.

About the Author

Photo by Joseph A. Cohen

Lawrence Kessenich is a fiction writer, poet, playwright, essayist, reviewer, and editor. He has published a number of short stories and won the 2010 Strokestown International Poetry Prize. He has three books of poetry: *Strange News*, *Before Whose Glory*, and *Age of Wonders*, and he has had three poems featured on Garrison Keillor's *Writer's Almanac*. He has also published essays, one of which was featured on NPR's *This I Believe*, and appears in the anthology *This I Believe: On Love*. His short plays have been produced in New York, Boston, and Colorado, where he won the People's Choice Award in a national drama competition. Kessenich is the co-managing editor of *Ibbbetson Street* literary magazine. *Cinnamon Girl* is his first novel.